Grace Restored Series, Book 3:

Spring Shadows

By

C.J. Peterson

Texas Sisters Press, LLC

C.J. Peterson

ISBN 978-1-952041-07-5

Published by Texas Sisters Press, LLC. Lufkin, TX U.S.A.

Texas Sisters Press, LLC.
2020

Second Edition

This book is dedicated to my loving husband and dear family who love and support me.

You all mean more to me than you will ever know. Thank you! I love you!

A special Thank You goes out to Lori and Darrel Cook, and Andy DeLobel who've helped me by sharing their time and stories from their work as Police Officers.

Thank you to all those who serve in the Police Force and Federal Agencies around the country and the world. Your time and service is appreciated!

A portion of the proceeds will be donated to Hope's Door, whose mission is to offer intervention and prevention services to individuals and families affected by domestic violence and to provide education programs that enhance the community's capacity to respond. To learn more about them, check out their web page: http://www.hopesdoorinc.org/

To learn more about C.J. Peterson, visit:

http://cjpetersonwrites.com/

'While the stories are fiction, the journey is real!'

<u>Summary</u>

Spring Shadows, the third book in the *Grace Restored Series*, follows the life of Katie MacKenna. With the Rossi Family dismantled, the only thing left for Katie to do is to graduate and hopefully move on to the police force before going to Quantico and a career in the FBI. But, had she tied up all her lose ends? A new boss is in town – one who has a score to settle with Katie. With threats against her on all sides, Katie doesn't know who to trust.

Song of Solomon 2:11-12

For behold, the winter is past; the rain is over and gone. The flowers appear on the earth, the time of singing has come, and the voice of the turtledove is heard in our land.

Proverbs 3:5-6

Trust in the Lord with all thine heart; and lean not unto thine own understanding. In all thy ways acknowledge Him, and He shall direct thy paths.

Table of Contents

Preface

Scenes from Book 2 of the Grace Restored Series:

WINTER'S VERDICT

"They found her," Lucca Rossi confirmed over the phone approximately three hours after they changed the direction of their investigation toward the Cook brothers. Cheers echoed throughout the house. "They're taking her to University Hospital."

"If you don't mind, I would like to go with Nick to the hospital?" Giovanni asked his dad.

"Of course, son. Keep in contact. I will handle the issue downstairs."

"Leave him for now. Let him sweat for a bit," Giovanni said, doing his best to follow what Nick said about not doing anything he would have to arrest him for. "I'll take care of it later."

"If you could drop me at the café, Seb and I will meet you guys at the hospital?" Ethan asked.

"Sure. C'mon," Nick agreed.

After they dropped Ethan off, Giovanni turned to Nick and said, "I know you want to get to Katie, so do I, but I don't want anything else to happen and chance me chickening out on this."

"On what?"

"You want my dad and the police and FBI moles? I can give them to you. How are you going to help me?"

"We will protect you until you can testify at their trials. Then afterward, we'll give you a new start, a fresh start. You can do anything you want."

"I want to follow my dream."

"That's all Katie wants for you, too."

"Then, let's do this."

*   *   *

"How is she?" Nick asked one of the two agents guarding the door when he finally arrived at the hospital several hours later. He had to get all of the information from Giovanni and get him settled in a safe house before he could go to her.

"When they brought her in, she was reciting some verse. They gave her a tranquilizer and got her body temperature under control. She's in shock, man. I don't know what she'll be like when she wakes up. You should have seen that basement." He shook his head. "It was twisted. There were photos of her all over, along with a wedding dress. They also found the scarf with Aaron's bloody handprint and the earrings. I can't imagine what all she went through."

"Any good news?" Nick huffed.

"The doctor said outside of that and the mental trauma, he didn't rape her. He did try to strangle her, though."

"I see," he said, glancing at her through the door. "Thank you."

*   *   *

Katie woke up in the hospital a couple days after she was rescued. Reaching over, she ran her fingers through his blond hair while he was asleep with his head on the bed.

"Katie?" he asked. She nodded. "I would really like to hear your voice. You haven't said a word for over two days. Please talk to me?" he asked. He had been trying to get her to talk for a couple days without any success.

She took a deep breath before she asked, "Dominic?"

He frowned. "We don't know where he is."

Looking toward the ceiling to stop herself from crying, she shook her head and said, "He said the Bahamas."

"We'll keep an eye out for him, but that's not a lot to go on. Pretty sure he wouldn't tell you exactly where he was going, but we'll look into it."

"I'm scared."

"I know. Look, what you did in the last month is something we have not been able to do in years. You helped not only shut the Rossi family down, but you also gave Giovanni his freedom. He'll be safe and be free now for the rest of his life thanks to you."

"What about Lucca and Joey?"

"Lucca's in jail, and won't be getting out for quite some time. Trust me, Director Shaw is pushing the DA hard on this one. And, Joey didn't do anything against the law, so he's free."

"You know Jillian and Aaron were killed and those girls were raped because of me?"

"What? No. That wasn't because of you."

"He wanted me." She sighed. "I wish he would have taken me from the beginning, because then both Aaron and Jillian would still be here…and be together."

"Don't say that. You can't control what he did. One thing you will learn while working at the FBI is that there are some twisted people. It's our job to catch them. We not only have to catch them, but also need to do it with enough evidence that they won't get back out."

"I understand that," she took a deep breath to control her emotions, "but in this case, he even admitted Jillian and Aaron's death were accidents. He said he thought Jillian was me. If I would have went to the dorm first, Jillian would still be alive. He also said Aaron's death was in self-defense. He said he thought Aaron was me, and once Dom realized he wasn't, Aaron was too angry. He said if he didn't kill Aaron, he would have killed him."

*   *   *

As they continued to talk, Katie admitted to Nick, "When I was in that basement, I made a decision. Even though I was scared out of my mind, I wanted to know that whatever happened, I would be with God in the end."

"Are you saying what I think you're saying?"

"Remember the challenge I gave to God at the beginning of break?"

"Yes," his heart rate picked up speed in excitement, "do you have a verdict yet?"

"Yes."

"And?"

"I was guilty, and He forgave my sins."

*   *   *

A little over three hours after he left Katie, Dominic pulled up to the Canada border via the Rainbow Bridge in New York State. Guilt filled him to the point that he thought for sure blood still stained his hands, no matter how hard he'd tried to scrub them clean.

Choking Katie to the point that she went unconscious was something he never intended. He wanted her to love him. He saw the way she treated her friends and those she held close to her. The only thing he ever wanted was love and acceptance, but now he messed it up.

"Documents please," the border officer asked as Dominic pulled up for his turn.

He scanned the passport, stamped it to Dominic's relief, and handed it back to him. "Enjoy your stay, Mr. Cook."

"Thank you," Dominic said, tucking his documents into the bag on the passenger's seat.

As he passed into Ontario, Canada, he knew this would be a new beginning. He got through into Canada before they flagged his passport. He knew it would set something off as soon as they notified the borders to be on the lookout for him. He would have to use his new identity.

Would he be able to forget Katie, though? Would he be able to move on? She was all he thought about. He grabbed a couple of her photos before he left. They would have to be enough until he could see her again.

Chapter 1

Spring Forward

Katie's rapid heartbeat was all she heard pounding in her ears while she scanned the area. Shadows danced around her, playing tricks with her eyes as a few strategically placed fluorescent bulbs lit what they could of the warehouse. Crates of various sizes were strewn about in uneven stacks, making navigation difficult. The musty warehouse smell, along with the scent of the wooden crates, overpowered Katie's senses while she continuously reminded herself to breathe with each step she took. *A warehouse? How original.* She shook her head.

The scuff of a shoe to her left made her jump. Silently, she crept around the wooden crate with her gun aimed and placed it on the back of the young man's head. "Police. Place your hands on your head. Otherwise don't move."

"Officer MacKenna, it's me, Damian. You know, Nick's friend?"

Katie let out a breath of relief. "Damian! What in Sam Hill are you doing here? You scared me to death!"

"I live here. Scary people work here, though, so I'm hiding."

Katie knelt beside him and asked, "Do you think you could get out of here safely? Is there a back way out?"

"I can get out the front unseen. What are you going to do, though? You can't stay in here. I've seen some nasty stuff over the last few months. These people will kill you on sight!"

"I'm not in here alone. There are three other officers in here with me."

"They have someone tied to a chair. I already called Nick. He's on his way."

"Where?"

"That way, on the other side of the warehouse," he said, pointing to his left. "He's got some vest on him with what looks like gray clay bars."

"Got it. I need you to get out there and tell Nick what's going on. Look," she placed her hands on his shoulders, crouching down to look at him at eye level, "I don't want anything to happen to you. You're only, what, eighteen years old?"

"I'm nineteen," he corrected.

"You have your whole life ahead of you. You're straightening out your life. Your GED should be in the mail any day. I want you to continue to chase after your dream."

"You're not all that old either. You shouldn't be in here."

Glancing around the warehouse, she explained, "I'm here because they're after me. I want to end this."

"You can't do it alone."

"I'm not alone. If I'm not done with what God has planned for me, He'll protect me."

"I hope you're right."

"I know I'm right," she said, confidently. "Now, go," she said, and then shoved him in the direction of the front of the warehouse.

Running outside, almost blinded by the amount of flashing lights from the federal, along with the police and rescue vehicles, Damian spotted Nick in the distance, talking with several people. Practically running to him, Damian hugged Nick, relief evident on his body.

"Wha...?" Nick was stunned for a moment before he saw the dirty face and grungy clothes of the young man he had been taking care of for several years. "Damian, what are you doing here?"

"She's here," he said, slightly panicked.

"Who?"

"Officer MacKenna! Katie! She's here. She's in the warehouse."

Looking toward the building Nick's stomach lurched. "Are you sure it was her?"

"Yes, I talked to her. She said – " A loud 'BOOM!' cut him off.

To Nick, everything suddenly began to move in slow motion. Damian's body slammed into his before Damian flew overhead, landing like a rag doll several feet away. Seeing his other friends and co-workers near him soar through the air, along with the debris from the warehouse, Nick curled into a ball under the car next to where he landed in order to prevent further damage. Covering his ears when glass shattered, metal twisted and turned, and screams and shouting joined the mix, creating a cannonade of thunderous disharmony. A deafening crash of vehicle that flipped and landed within feet of him sent a shockwave through his body that took his breath away. The ringing in his ears irritated him while he struggled to recover from the daze of surviving the devastation created around him. Looking toward the warehouse, he gulped when he remembered Katie was now encased in the mountainous remains. Adrenaline coursed through his body as he pushed to stand before staggering toward the warehouse – to Katie.

Seth grabbed him. "No, man, you can't go."

Dakota and Todd leapt in front of him to push him back as a secondary explosion went off toward the back of the warehouse. Hoping nothing else would explode, it took all three of them to hold Nick down.

"You can't go in there!" Seth shouted over the chaos.

"I have to get her! I can't leave her! I'm not losing her! Katie!" he shouted, struggling to get off the ground and get to the rubble that the warehouse had become. "KATIE! KATIE! NO!"

*   *   *

Katie gasped as she sat straight up in her bed. Breathing heavily, she looked around the room. "No. Nothing. Just another nightmare," she said aloud, as her heart raced out of control and the echo of the explosion pounded in her head.

Body shaking, she got out of bed and paced the room to release the anxious energy. "It was a nightmare. It's not true. It's not real. God's going to keep me safe. I graduate on Friday. Nick kept his promise, and I will make it to graduation. God won't let me down."

Flipping on the light from her desk, she picked up the approved apartment lease and scanned it again. A couple weeks prior, Nick told her that Crystal was moving out, which meant the apartment across the hall from his would be open. The security of the building brought comfort to Katie, so she applied for the apartment. She then contacted Jim Anderson to let him know her intentions, since she would need money for a security deposit and the first and last month's rent. Without a credit history, the apartment manager wasn't taking any chances on her. Truth be told, the only reason she got it was due to Nick's recommendation.

Living across the hall from Nick would make it easier for them to continue to work together. Nick was Katie's mentor in her journey toward being an agent, and he took that seriously. Over the last year, he taught Katie many self-defense techniques to the point that the moves become instinct. He also taught her how to fire a gun with extreme accuracy up to twenty-five yards and good accuracy at fifty. Working on defensive driving and tactical training were the bigger challenges, but they survived. In doing the training, it would give Katie a leg-up in the police academy, as well as Quantico.

It took her four long years, but her goals were slowly coming to fruition. Her graduation was on Friday, and she was to move into her apartment on Memorial Day weekend. The interviews, along with written and physical fitness tests were completed and she was set to begin the police academy the first week of June. On top of all that, her twenty-second birthday was quickly approaching on July 3rd.

While her last several years were dramatically eventful, and at times terrifying, she wouldn't change any of it. All of those events made and shaped her into who she was, and ultimately landed her in the position she was currently in on that day.

"'For I know the plans I have for you," declares the Lord, "plans to prosper you and not to harm you, plans to give you hope and a future,'" she said, quoting Jeremiah 29:11. She looked toward heaven and said, "I know Your plans are perfect, and that You have everything under control. Thank You for looking out for me. As things continue to progress, please continue to protect me. Thank you also for all of my friends. Please keep them safe as they move forward in life and go out each day. I have a crazy couple of weeks coming up, so if You could keep things on schedule, I would appreciate it. And, please, no surprises. In Jesus' name I pray…Amen."

Glancing at the clock, she cringed. She had four more hours until she had her first appointment, but she didn't want to go back to sleep and chance falling back into the nightmare. Choosing to scan her social media page, she flipped down the postings half-heartedly. With everything that went on over the last two years and her graduation this year, Katie's friends from Oklahoma, as well as from college, convinced her to get on social media so they could stay connected easier. Seb jumped at the chance to spend time with her, taking over an hour to educate her on the ins and outs of her page, along with a couple other social media sites she wasn't aware of. While she knew it took longer than necessary, she didn't mind the company, and they ended up going out to eat afterward.

Glancing over to see who was online, she noticed Seb was on. "Speak of the devil," she said aloud. Clicking on his name, she typed, *'You awake?'*

'Yep. Question is why are you?'

'Bad dream.'

'Want me to call?'

'Yeah,' she typed, and got off her computer as the phone rang in her room. "Hello?" she answered the phone, jumping in the bed under the covers.

"Morning, Katie. What was your nightmare about?" Seb asked as he snuggled under his own covers. His dad had the air conditioner cranked a little too high for his liking, even for May. He was looking forward to moving into his own house in few weeks down near the café.

Just after Dominic created the mess for Cook's Corner Café, Riccardo asked Seb to be a partner. It was an intelligent move by Riccardo. The restaurant almost had to shut down with all of the bad press, but when Seb became part owner, it gave new life to the café. It took them a bit, but things had turned around in the last six months, and Seb felt comfortable in purchasing a house of his own.

"I don't want to talk about it. Can you distract me instead?" Katie asked, bringing him back to the conversation.

"Sure. We graduate on Friday, right?"

"Yep. I also get my apartment in two weeks, just before I head to the police academy."

"Ugh. Please don't remind me."

"What do you mean?"

"The idea that you're going to be a cop here in Cleveland terrifies me. It gives *me* nightmares."

"I'll be fine."

"I've lived here for the last five years. I know what kind of riffraff lurks around here. This world is not a safe place, especially for a young lady with as sweet a heart as you have. I'm afraid your heart will become jaded…or worse, that you'll get killed. I don't think I could handle it if something happened to you."

"God will protect me."

He sighed. "I know. You keep telling me that. I just wish I could be as confident as you."

"I trust God. He hasn't let me down yet."

"Okay. I think we need to move onto a different subject."

"What would that be?"

"Well, we're graduating on Friday."

Katie giggled. "We've been through that."

"Would you go out with me now that we're graduating?"

Katie abruptly sat upright in bed again for the second time that night. "What did you ask?"

"Katie, it's no secret that I'm in love with you. Would you please do me the honor of going out with me? I've waited four long years to take you out."

"Are you serious?"

"Very. If you would, I was thinking we could go to Sandusky and take the ferry across Lake Erie to Kelley's Island for the day.

There are a lot of little shops that I know you'll like, and we can get lunch and dinner on the island before we come back. How does that sound?"

Katie felt her heart drop into her stomach. *Could she really date one of her best friends?*

"Well?" he asked after a long minute of silence. It was almost more than he could handle.

"Actually." She inhaled a deep breath. She'd made a promise to Aaron two Christmases ago that she had yet to keep. "Yes," she said, releasing a sigh of relief to have finally fulfilled that promise. "When?"

"Would Saturday work?"

"Yes," she said, almost proud of herself. "I would love to go out with you."

"Sweet!" he shouted. Then he quickly changed the volume of his words. "I mean, sweet! I hope I didn't just wake…Hi, Dad." He cringed as his dad walked into his room.

"Oh no! I didn't want to get you into trouble," Katie said, slightly panicked.

"What are you yelling about? It's four in the morning," his dad pointed out.

"I, uh, Katie finally said she would go out with me," he explained, weakly.

"Really?" His voice sounded pleasantly surprised, which eased Seb's anxiety. "That's great! Way to go!" He gave Seb a high-five. Before he left, he mentioned, "Just keep it down, okay?

While I have to be up in a half-hour, the rest of the house still has about three hours until they have to be up."

"Yes, sir," he said with a grin. When the door closed, Seb added, "I love my dad."

"He seems cool," Katie agreed. "I would have gotten in big trouble had I been home."

"Have to admit I was a bit nervous, but he knows how long I have wanted to go out with you."

"I know. I'm sorry. I'm looking forward to going out with you."

"Me too! I'm too excited to sleep. Want to go to breakfast?"

"Now?" she asked, stunned. "It's four in the morning. I should actually go back to sleep. I have some things to take care of in the morning and my first appointment is at eight."

"All right," he relented. "Sweet dreams and I'll see you and Stacey for lunch at the café?"

"Yep. Oh!" A thought struck her. "I have to get my bridesmaid dress for Stacey's wedding today." Getting out of bed, she went over to her desk and scribbled the new listing on her 'to do' list. "Speaking of which, what are you doing next weekend?"

"By the direction of the conversation, can I assume I'm going to a wedding in Pine Crest?"

"If you would?"

"I already was, but of course I'll go with you." He grinned. "Kelley's Island this Saturday, wedding the next Saturday, and helping you move the Saturday after that. Good grief! My schedule just got incredibly full."

"Imagine my schedule. It's all of that, along with unpacking an apartment, and getting ready to start the police academy right after that. That's not including the graduation trip to Oklahoma either."

He took a deep breath. "Going to support you. Not happy about the police thing, but I know it's important to you."

"Thank you," Katie said, relieved.

"In the meantime, my schedule will be happily full."

"Good. Now, go get some sleep."

"Too excited and thrilled to sleep. I'll see you at lunch."

"See you at lunch," she said, and hung up.

Knowing she would hear it from Ethan, she justified it by reminding herself that Seb asked first. She knew that wouldn't pacify him, and that it could potentially decimate their friendship, but with college over she was moving on. It would be up to Ethan if he wanted to end their friendship or continue.

*   *   *

"Heard a rumor this morning," Ethan said as they met on the staircase of their dorm.

"Did you?" Katie cringed. *The rumor mill worked faster than even she gave it credit for.*

"Yep. But, I said it couldn't be true, because I was sure you would tell me yourself."

"Unless I didn't have time before you heard it. How did you hear it by the way?"

His face reflected the shock and hurt that ripped through his heart. "It's true?"

"Yes. Seb asked me out this morning around four, and I agreed."

"But…I can't…." He shook his head, beside himself, as he leaned against the wall with his arms crossed.

"I told you both I wasn't dating until graduation. We graduate on Friday, and he asked me for Saturday."

"Wow. He works fast."

"You had the same opportunity. Look, can't you just be happy for us?"

"Ah-ah-ahhh," he shook his finger in front of her, "you haven't gone out yet. Who says it will work out?"

She crossed her arms in a huff. "That's encouraging."

"A guy can always hope." He shrugged. "Besides, if it doesn't, then it may be *me* taking you to Stacey's wedding next week."

"Who says I'll go out with you?" Katie snapped, irritated by his presumptuous attitude.

"You will."

"How do you figure?"

"You like me."

Anger flashed through her eyes as they turned a steel green. "How *dare* you!"

"Look," he put his arm over her shoulder, but she shoved it off and crossed her arms. "Katie, we're destined to be together."

"Oh really?"

"You know it."

"I really hope you're joking."

"Nope. I'm being realistic. Seb's too overprotective. I understand you. I get why you want to be a cop and want to move on to the FBI. I know you're fixated on that goal and nothing is going to stop you. I respect and admire that about you."

Katie sighed, shaking her head.

"Let's change the subject. When are your friends and dad coming in?"

"They should be here on Wednesday."

"Who all is coming?"

"My dad, Cami, Ryan, Abby, Steve, Eden, Emily, and Ty. Then, next week I go to Oklahoma for their graduation on Thursday night. I'm also going to clean out my storage shed on Thursday morning and head back right after their graduation to get here in time for Stacey's wedding rehearsal dinner on Friday night."

"Good grief! You're going to be exhausted!"

"That's not including the move into my apartment on Sunday before the academy. I'll need to go to the police academy just to get a break from the crazy schedule."

"Are you going to stay with your dad while you're in Oklahoma?"

She nervously tucked her hair behind her ear as she admitted, "I don't know."

"Okay. Well, you'll have to do an immediate turn-around after being up all day emptying your storage and then graduation in order to get back for Stacey's wedding rehearsal on Friday, right?"

"Yep."

"Want some company on the drive? That's a long haul, with not a lot of time in between."

"I don't think that's a good idea."

"Tell ya what," he said, thinking how to make his proposition appealing to her. "What if Cierra, Seb, and I go with you? He and I can share a hotel room, and you and Cierra can share one. I can drive my truck, too, so you won't have to rent a trailer."

"I don't know." She shook her head. "If I'm going to go, I would rather go on my own."

"What happens if you break down?"

"Call for help. That's what the auto club is for."

"Some days you can be so stubborn."

"Look, I haven't been home since I left to come here. I think I need to face this myself. I need to be a big girl."

"You don't have to do it alone, though."

"Yes, I do."

"Stubborn," he said under his breath as he shook his head.

"I have a crazy schedule over the next several weeks. I need to keep on track. If you want to support me, the best thing you can do is not be so pessimistic about my date with Seb, and support my decision to go to Oklahoma on my own. The last thing I need this week is stress."

Ethan cringed as jealousy ripped his heart out regarding Seb.

"I gotta go. I love you like a brother. Please be supportive?"

"Oh!" Ethan grabbed his middle and slammed against the wall as if he were shot. "The 'b' word! Oh! That's torture!"

A smile finally crossed Katie's face as she giggled. "Yes, a brother."

"Well, at least you admitted that you love me. I'll take what I can get."

"Please, and thank you."

He gave her a hug, and then watched her bolt back up the stairs for her backpack. He couldn't believe Seb beat him to asking Katie out. Seb knew how Ethan felt about her. He wasn't sure which was more hurtful…the fact that Seb asked her out or that she accepted. Walking outside into the spring air, he hoped with every bone in his body that it wouldn't last. He was still hoping to get his chance to go out with her before she headed to Quantico. If he could, he knew it would be a strong possibility that he may be able to talk her out of going into the FBI. He hoped to protect her and keep her from the dangers that came with that career choice. His only hope was that she would listen.

Chapter 2

Spring Cold Snap

"Wow! You look gorgeous in that! Looks like I picked the perfect color for you," Stacey gushed as Katie tried on her mint green dress for Stacey in Katie's dorm room.

"I've never been a part of a wedding before," she admitted. "I think the idea of a rainbow wedding will be pretty."

"I hope so. I used pastel colors in hopes of toning it down a bit, but Scott loved the idea and so did the other girls."

"Who all is in it?"

"Well," Stacey said, thinking aloud, "I have to go down the rainbow to remember the order. Even though Becky is my step-mom, she's also Scott's sister, so she starts the rainbow. As the matron-of-honor, she's wearing rose. Then Harmony Taylor is wearing peach. She'll be closely followed by her twin, Melody Dalton, in pale yellow. Then there's you in light green. After you, Marissa James follows in light blue. Then last, but not least, my other friend from college, Larissa, will be in lavender."

"That's really cool! I'm excited!"

"You and me both. Scott was very patient in waiting until I finished college, so I did my best to respect that in planning the wedding close to graduation. Oh! And I thought of you when we figured out the male counterparts. They'll be in black tuxes, with their ties and cummerbunds the colors of their female counterparts."

"And the men are?"

"Well, for best man, Scott picked his partner from the station. Dad doesn't mind, though, because he's known him about as long as we've known Scott, and he can't be in it because he has to give me away. Then, Harmony and Melody are partnered with their husbands, Randy and Brian. Marissa's paired with another close friend of ours, Alex Crestwood. And Larissa's partner is her boyfriend, Pete."

"What about me?"

Stacey giggled with a mischievous grin on her face.

Katie crossed her arms with a smirk. "What did you do?"

"Well, I know you have been shy about dates, but I'm pretty sure your counterpart will be appealing to you."

"What did you do?"

Stacey laughed again as she admitted, "Scott and I got together and we decided to ask another firefighter friend of Scott's, Lance Montgomery. He's cute, sweet, and turns twenty-three on May thirty-first."

"You know I'm going out with Seb on Saturday, right?"

"Who says it will work out? Just exposing you to some fresh blood."

"You're a brat!"

She shrugged with a grin. "I have my moments. Anyway, it's just for the wedding, and seating for the reception. You'll be able to be with Seb during the reception when we're not at the head table."

Katie sat down on her bed and asked, "Can I admit something to you and have it not go anywhere?"

"You have to ask?"

"No. I know you won't tell. I have to be honest. I'm nervous about going out with Seb. He's the first guy I've gone out with since Jax."

"You've known him for four years," Stacey pointed out.

"Right, but this will be on a new level. Can I think of him as something other than a friend?"

"Guess you'll find out on Saturday."

*　　*　　*

"Katie bug!" Katie's dad greeted her with a hug when she walked into the hotel dining room.

Katie casually gave him a hug in return. "Where's Cami?"

"I was, uh, hoping to tell you at a later date," Brent admitted.

"Tell me what?"

"Cami chose to not stay married to me. Our divorce was final about a month ago."

"Really? I'm so sorry, Dad," she said, and gave him another hug. "I was hoping it would work out."

"Thank you, but it won't work out when both parties are not willing to work on it. It takes two. Anyway, on to something happy. I have some good news for you."

"What's that?"

"Jim Anderson sent this with me for you. Since you graduate on Saturday, this closes out your trust," he said, handing her an envelope, that she promptly tucked into her front pocket. "It's a deposit slip. It shows that the remainder of your trust has been deposited into your account."

"Great. Thanks!"

"Hey, Katie," Ryan hugged her, as she went around giving everyone else a hug as well. "You're looking great!"

Katie blushed. "Thanks."

"I know your schedule is busy, but I would love to take you out while we're here for dinner one night…you know, to catch up," he offered.

"Sure. I think that would be great! I know an awesome diner near the college that you would like. A guy I'm dating is part owner of it."

"You're…you're dating? Why didn't you mention that in any emails or calls?"

"It just recently happened."

"I see. Well, how about when we go out, I pick the restaurant? My treat. Emily, Eden, and Ty can come along as well."

"What about Cook's Café? They serve great food. The guy I'm dating, Seb, not only works there, but he's also part owner."

"I kinda just want us as a group. We haven't gotten to see you in almost four years. Can't we just enjoy you for a bit?"

"If you insist."

"What if we order pizza and have it delivered to the room?" Ty suggested. "We could do a movie night. You graduate tomorrow. Let's spend tonight together as a group in celebration?"

"Which room?" Emily asked.

"Ours will work," Eden volunteered. He was rooming with Ryan and Ty.

"Wouldn't miss it," Katie said, with a feeling of foreboding churning in her stomach. *Would dating Seb cause more issues than it's worth?*

*   *   *

Seeing her friends from back home brought back some good memories, as well as some hurtful ones. When the group got together, instead of watching a movie, they talked all night into the early morning about Jax and Anna. They also talked about growing up in West Springs. After that, she was actually looking forward to going home the next week instead of dreading it.

*   *   *

Graduation was great for Katie. She not only had her friends and family from Oklahoma, but also her friends from college, along with Nick, Seth, Emma, Dakota, and Todd in attendance. Her FBI friends told her that morning they were going to come and that wild horses couldn't keep them away.

After graduation, they all headed over to Cook's for a graduation party. Since Katie didn't schedule a venue, Seb volunteered Cook's Café. Of course Riccardo didn't mind, that would make it a full house, and with that came good money.

Halfway through the night, Ty wheeled up to Katie. "Hey, there." He smiled. "Shouldn't you be happy?"

"I am…sort of," she said, sitting at a booth in the corner, watching everyone at her party having a great time dancing, talking, and eating.

He propped his elbows on the table. "Wanna clear that up?"

"Well, my life is chaotic at the moment. I mean, I know it's officially starting, and with that comes a little chaos. I'm excited about all of the changes, but a little nervous as well."

"Yeah, still not following."

"Hey, Katie! Come dance with me?" Seb asked, sliding into the booth beside her, propping his arm over her shoulders.

"If you don't mind, I'd actually like to talk to Ty for a bit. They're leaving early in the morning."

"Totally understand. Come find me when you're ready," he agreed. He kissed her cheek before he left the booth, and the crowd quickly swallowed him up.

Suddenly, Nick was standing by the table. "Katie, we gotta go. Got something we need to act on. Congratulations on your graduation. See you on Sunday afternoon for our standard?"

"Definitely," she agreed. She hugged him before he bolted from the diner with his counterparts.

"Okay, and *who* is *that*?" Ty asked, surprised.

"He's an FBI agent. His name is Nick. He's been my mentor and trainer since the December Jillian and Aaron were killed."

"He's a tank!"

"That he is."

"Katie, you're confusing me. You feel shut down, like you're in auto mode or something, when this should be a happy day for you."

"I am. There's a ton of stuff going on over the next few weeks and I'm not sure how everything is going to fit."

"Spell it out for me."

"Well, graduation was a biggie. Then there's tomorrow with Seb."

"The guy who was just here a minute ago?"

"Right. He asked me out and I agreed."

"I see. What else is there?"

"Next Tuesday I'm fixin' to hop a plane to Oklahoma for y'all's graduation. While I'm down there, I have to rent a small moving truck to hold all of my belongings for my new apartment. I have to load it Thursday morning, y'all's graduation is Thursday night, and then I take off that night after graduation to get back up here. I have to keep everything in the truck until after the wedding, because I move in that Sunday. *So*, I have Stacey's wedding rehearsal dinner Friday night and her wedding Saturday night. After that, I move in on Sunday into my new apartment, only to start the police academy the following Monday."

"Hmm, nothing like cramming it all into two weeks."

"I know, right? I have one day to move in before starting the academy. My apartment has to be somewhat settled, because it's my understanding that the police academy is like opening your mouth and them firing a fire hose of information into it."

"That much information?"

"Yep. They want to make sure we're safe on the streets when we graduate."

"I know I would appreciate it. I *was* worried about you heading to Quantico after that, but seeing who your trainer is, I'm satisfied he'll keep you safe."

"Oh, he will, but I have to get there first. I have to survive two years as an officer before heading to Quantico."

"I'm sure you'll do fine. You've got this uncanny ability to stay focused on what you want. Gotta ask, though?"

"Yeah?"

"Well, in staying focused, you've refrained from dating. Is now a really good time to date? Don't you have enough on your plate?"

"I don't think that's any of your business," Seb snapped as he walked by the table with refreshments.

"Seb, we were talking," Katie chastised him.

"And, he seems to be talking you out of dating me."

"Really?" Anger flashed through her eyes. "I don't appreciate you eavesdropping on my conversation. That's rude! And, since when do I let people tell me what to do?"

"You don't."

"Now, apologize to my friend and carry on. You do something like that again, and I'll have to rethink tomorrow," she warned.

"I'm sorry, man." He rested his free hand on Ty's shoulder. "You have to understand how long I have waited to date her."

"You have no idea, brother," Ty said. "I've waited since seventh grade."

As soon as he said that, Katie gasped as she looked at him wide-eyed.

Ty dropped his head into his hands. "Not quite how I wanted to tell you. It just slipped out."

"Sorry, brother, but you'll have to wait in line," Seb got his last cut in before he disappeared into the crowd once again.

"Good heavens! What is this? Open season on Katie?" Katie sighed, dropping her head into her hands. "I swear I'm about to become a nun and commit myself to a convent!"

Ty rested his hand on her arm. "Oh, please don't do that. You're too nice and sweet for that. You'll find the right guy. I'm just not sure if that's your buddy Seb. He seems quite possessive and angry. You really need to pick someone who understands you and isn't trying to possess you."

"Meaning?"

"Not to speak ill of the dead, but Jax was a bit controlling when it came to your time as well. This Seb guy seems to be the jealous type too. That's not you. You need someone who will look out for you, but give you the breathing space you need."

"Like you?" she asked.

"I would give you the space you need, but I think you would find better alternatives up here. Besides, I'm broken." He gestured toward his wheelchair.

"You're not broken. Your legs don't dictate your heart."

"See, that's what I'm talking about. You need to be with someone who has a heart like yours. Because you're strong-willed, he needs to be strong, yet soft at the heart level. I may be in love with you, but I'm not who you need. You've changed more than you know over the last four years. You've become stronger, but you've also become harder. You are open in some areas, but those are few and far between. Realistically, I don't know if you're even ready for a relationship yet."

"What about Ryan? He's hinted that he wants to date me as well."

"Oh, no way!" Ty laughed aloud. "You and Ryan? No." He shook his head. "Absolutely not. He is *so* not your type anymore. Had you stayed in Oklahoma, I would say that would be a possibility, but not now. I'm telling you that you've changed…and in some ways not for the better."

"I'm not sure if that's a compliment or not."

"You grew up too fast. You're also more of a city girl now. You've become a bit jaded. Things have changed back home, but you have no idea how much."

"Such as?"

"Did you know your dad's a Christian?"

"What?" Katie asked, stunned.

"Haven't you noticed that his heart is softer?"

"No, I guess I haven't."

"That's because yours has become harder. I started going to church several months after I was mobile. I saw something on the day of the accident that changed me."

"What was that?"

"I can't talk about it yet, but I may tell you some day. Anyway, I started going to church, right?"

"Right."

"A year or so later, your dad shows up, and he and Eric had it out for several weeks. Long story short, he accepted the Lord as his Savior within six months and has been working with Eric ever since. You haven't talked to him all that much, so you wouldn't notice his shift in disposition or heart."

"No. He still unnerves me a bit."

"That's understandable, but for your peace of mind and heart, it might not be a bad idea to get to know your dad again. He may surprise you."

"I don't know about that."

"Is there room in your heart and mind for forgiveness?"

"I would hope so!" she said, surprised by the question. "I haven't changed *that* much…have I?"

"You tell me."

"It's a lot to think about."

"You know he's been going to Alcoholics Anonymous, right?"

"He mentioned that," she said hesitantly, knowing there was more.

"He's to the point of making amends to those he's hurt through his alcoholism. He's cleared most of his list, with the exception of you. He's even spoken to Cami and gotten her forgiveness."

"How do you know this?"

He pulled out a coin and set it on the table between them.

"What is this?" she asked, picking it up. It was marked with 'three years sobriety' on it. "Whose is this?"

"It's mine."

"What?" She shook her head. "I don't understand."

"I went into a deep depression after the accident. I wanted nothing to do with a world where I couldn't even walk. I was mean to everyone and shut everyone out. Much to my parents delight and my chagrin, Eric hounded me and stayed on my back until I gave in and went to AA. To be honest, I went with him just to shut him up. I also made him go with me. I figured if he was going to torture me by making me go, he would have to go through it with me. I found people there who understood me. I found people whose difficult life situations paled in comparison to mine, and who had been at it a lot longer too. Even though Eric made me go, it was the best thing he could have done for me. Since I wasn't an alcoholic for too long, while it had a hold on me, I could still battle it. With the help of God and my sponsor, I have continued to stay on top of it for three years as of last week."

"Are you serious?" she asked, appalled. "How did I not know?"

"I didn't want you to know. It's not like it's something I'm proud of and want to make sure everyone knows. Anyway, after your dad found the Lord, Eric and I worked on him. He's done an amazing job and has flown through the twelve steps. The divorce was almost a relief to him, but hit him hard at the same time."

"I'll bet," she said, still focused on the coin in her hands, baffled that she missed something so dramatic in Ty's life. She even felt a twinge of guilt.

Ty reached over and rested his hand on Katie's. "Katie, I'm Brent's sobriety co-sponsor, with the help of another man at AA. You are his biggest and most difficult hurdle. He drank to take away the pain of losing Meg. When he did, it caused him to become angry, and he took it out on you. In turn, he felt guilty, and the guilt ate him up, causing him to drink more. It was a downward spiral he never knew he could remotely recover from. He needs your help."

"You make it sound as if I should just forgive him so he can move on."

"Well…" he nodded, unsure of what else to say.

"So, you're taking his side?"

"Absolutely not! I'm doing my best to find a way for one of my best friends, along with her father, to finally find peace about this."

"Peace?" She sighed in frustration. "Whenever I reach a point of starting to find peace, something else pops up and crushes it. Look," she pleaded, "you have to understand that God and I have gone many rounds about what all I've gone through."

"That brings me to another concern. Do you think it's wise to become a police officer after everything you've already been through? It's not an easy job. I'm afraid it may push you over the edge."

"I appreciate your concern, but it's not your decision."

"I understand that, but as your friend –"

"One of my best friends," she cut him off.

"Okay, then as one of your *best* friends, I would hope that I've earned enough respect for you to consider my opinion."

She could see on his face that he was upset. She knew she had to choose her words carefully. "I do appreciate your concern, but it's what I need to do to reach my goal."

"I don't know why you're so dead-set on this FBI thing. Before you answer that," Ty held his hand up, stopping her objections, "Know that I respect you and your choices. That's not my reason for talking to you. I wanted to let you know about your dad, so when he came to talk to you, you would have a basic understanding of what he's trying to do. I love you and want you to achieve your dreams. You deserve it. If you want to be a police officer and then an agent, I'll support you. I had to let you know my opinion, though."

"Thank you," she said, relief evident on her face.

"Katie," he rested his hand over hers, "I only want the best for you."

"Same for you."

"Then know that there is something about Seb that concerns me. I'm not sure what it is, but it concerns me."

"I'll remember that and keep an eye out. You have a way of recognizing things in people that I don't always catch right off the bat. I have to tell you that he's been a great friend for almost four years, though."

"You're better at seeing the inside of a person than you know. However, you need to keep in mind that friend and boyfriend are two different things. One doesn't give you the control that the other does."

"No one controls me."

"Be careful. That could be a challenge to some guys," he warned.

*　*　*

Katie struggled through the rest of the night with Seb continuously doing his best to consume her time, even though she wanted to spend it with her friends from Oklahoma. She was glad she turned Ethan's offer down to go to Oklahoma with her. After that night, she was looking forward to the time she would have by herself in travelling the next week.

*　*　*

Seb picked Katie up around nine the next morning for their day on Kelley's Island. For the most part, he was a gentleman, until they sat down for dinner that night before catching the ferry back to Sandusky.

"Katie, there's something I need to tell you, but I didn't want to ruin our date," Seb said, after they ordered and the waiter had dropped off their drinks.

"What?"

"Well, in working your graduation party, there were many times that I could float around unnoticed, and I heard what people were saying."

"Such as?" Katie asked, feeling disturbed by his tone of voice.

"Well," he took a deep breath, "I didn't want to tell you, but I feel if it were me, I would want to know."

"Want to know *what*?" Katie asked, impatiently.

"Well, there were a few upsetting conversations. One was in regards to that guy Ethan calls a corn fed toe-head."

"Ryan?"

"Yeah, that's his name. Ryan was talking to the guy in the wheelchair –"

"Ty?" she asked, the frustration evident in her voice.

"Yeah. They were talking, saying how you've changed and that they don't like the changes."

"What do you mean?"

"They said you weren't the same, and they didn't like the new you."

Katie was taken aback by his words. "I don't – I don't know what to say."

"I'm just telling you because, like I said, if it were me I would want to know. They said they wished you had stayed in Oklahoma, and that they didn't like the whole police officer/FBI agent goals you seem to have either."

What he was saying didn't make sense. Ty told her something along those lines, but he also added that he would support her decision.

Seb took Katie's hand into his. "I want you to know that while it doesn't thrill me, I'll support what you want to do. I know that God of yours will keep you safe."

Her body stiffened at his words. They didn't match what she had been hearing from him since he found out what she wanted to do.

"I've done a lot of thinking over the last week," he admitted. "I love you and want to support you and your choices. I want to be there for you and give you the freedom you need to make the choices you want in life."

Katie shook her head in confusion. What he was saying didn't mesh with what she had seen and heard herself at the party.

"There was also another conversation I'm hesitant to tell you about."

"Whose?" Katie demanded.

"Well, that big guy, Nick?"

"From the FBI?"

"Yeah. He was talking to that Seth guy. They were talking about your training. Nick said it was a pain, but if Seth wanted him to do it, he would."

"Nick doesn't mind the training we're doing."

"Not to your face. You'd be amazed at what I hear, though."

"I'm not all that thrilled right now and I don't know what to think."

"I think you may need to rethink who your friends are. Let me rephrase that to, 'you may want to rethink who you call a friend.'"

"I'm not hungry anymore. I want to go home."

"We just ordered," Seb objected. "Look, have a seat and we'll talk things out."

"I don't *want* to talk. I *want* to go home."

"You know you're being selfish right now," Seb pointed out.

"What do you mean?" she asked, cross.

"I don't get that much time off, and I took the day off to be with you. You don't seem to be appreciative of it right now."

"I appreciate it."

"You don't seem to be. I respected your choice of not wanting to date until you graduated and this is the thanks I get? Good grief!" He threw his napkin. "If I would have known it would be cut short, I wouldn't have waited for you."

Anger and shame were both evident on her face. As the anger won, the steel green flashed in her hazel eyes. "No one asked you too!" she snapped.

"You did."

"I most certainly did not!"

"Yes, you did. Every time I mentioned it, you pointed out that you wanted to wait until you graduated." He shook his head as he crossed his arms. "Unbelievable! What a shame. We could have been great together."

Katie shook her head in confusion again. He was all over the place with emotions. It was making her dizzy. "What are you saying?"

"That I'm sorry I took you out."

"Really?" she raised an eyebrow in surprise.

He sighed before he flagged the waiter. "We'll take it to go. This date is finished."

Katie gave the waiter an apologetic look before the waiter left to bag their food. "That was rude," she pointed out when the waiter was out of earshot.

"You're being rude too."

"No, I'm not."

"Yes, you are."

"Well then, you don't have to put up with my rudeness any longer," she said, standing. She threw her napkin on the table and left the restaurant for the dock, praying the ferry would leave before Seb could get on the boat.

Several minutes after she took her seat, with only a minute or two until the ferry pulled away from the dock, Seb got on the boat.

"Great," she sighed, shaking her head. She turned toward the water, hoping he would leave her alone.

"We need to talk."

"No. We don't," she said, not even looking at him.

As he walked away, Katie let out a sigh of relief. She didn't want to deal with him at that moment, she was too angry.

*   *   *

During the entire forty-five minute ride back to the dock in Sandusky from Kelley's Island, Katie was fuming. She was so angry, she couldn't think straight. Once it docked, Katie got off the boat and a realization suddenly hit her. It was six o'clock on Saturday night in Sandusky, and she was over an hour from home. *How was she going to get home if Seb left her?*

Seb walked up behind her and roughly grabbed the back of her upper arm. She could feel it pulsating under his grip. Her past experience told her his grip would generate bruising. "I'll take you home."

"No, you won't," she said, jerking her arm back.

"How else are you going to get home? Look, my dad would have my head if I didn't at least make sure you got home."

"I don't know that I can make this any clearer…leave-me-alone."

He threw the food into the garbage can and grabbed both of her arms, forcing her to face him. "I'm sorry, Katie. I really didn't mean for things to turn out this way."

Katie shook her head, confused. "What are you on?"

"Nothing. Why?"

"Maybe you should be. Are you bi-polar or something?"

"No. Why?"

"Because your mood swings are giving me whiplash. This is not worth it. I'll find my own way home, thank you."

"I can't let you do that."

"Yes. You can and you will."

"I can't leave you. I just wasted money by throwing away our food. At least let me take you home? I don't want to have to waste more money on a cab for you too."

"No. And I'm not asking you to pay for a cab."

"Fine. Suit yourself," he growled, and left her standing at the docks.

Once he drove away, Katie took a deep breath and slowly let it out. She had never seen that side of him, and she didn't want to ever again.

One of the boat workers, who looked like he just got off work, waved to her right after Seb stormed off. "Saw the two of ya. You okay?"

Katie walked over to him. "I am for now. Do you have a phone I could borrow to make a call?"

"For a beauty like you. Most definitely. When you're done, you can add your number to the call list," he said with a wink as he passed her his phone.

Shuddering as she turned away from him, she dialed the only number she had memorized.

"Agent Locke," Nick answered.

"Nick," Katie said, relieved. "You answered."

"Katie?" he asked, confused. She could almost feel him checking the number again. "Where are you?"

"Are you busy?"

"I'm always busy. What's up?"

She took a deep breath before she admitted, "My date with Seb was horrific. He offered to take me home, but to be honest I was too scared."

"Scared?"

"His moods shifted so fast it made my head spin. What he was saying didn't make sense. It was like I wasn't talking to my friend at all."

"Where are you?"

"I'm at the Jet Express Ferry dock in Sandusky."

"That's over an hour away!" he said in shock. "He left you over an hour from home without a ride or a phone on a Saturday night? Speaking of which, where did you get the phone? I'm going to have to get you a pay-by-use if you continue to refuse to get one."

"I borrowed a dock worker's phone."

"Katie," he asked, cautiously, "is there a restaurant near you that you can get to? I don't feel comfortable leaving you in the hands of a dock worker."

"Yeah, he's a bit creepy. He told me to add my number to the phone directory when I was done."

"Yeahhhh, head to the closest restaurant when we hang up. What's up there?"

"The Walter Street Bar and Grill is right here."

"Sounds good. When we hang up, go there, and I'll meet you over there," he said, jotting down the name of the restaurant.

"I have to admit that I'm scared."

"Don't be. Just go over there and I'll be there in," he glanced at his watch, "I'll be there in about an hour and a half. Because of traffic, I don't want to promise any sooner."

"Thank you."

"My pleasure. I'm bringing a friend with me," he said, glancing at Damian, who was sitting with him in the park.

"Okay. Thank you," she said, and hung up.

"Wanna go on an errand with me? Dinner is included," Nick asked Damian.

"Nice!" Damian grinned. "Yeah, I'll come."

"Here." He handed him a bag. "Change in the bathroom first. I got you some new clothes for the summer. Wouldn't want Katie's first impression of you to have you in clothes a couple sizes too small for you. Speaking of which, we need to get you a couple more pair of jeans if they fit well."

"Sweet! Thanks!" Damian grinned before running over to the bathroom in the park.

While he was gone, Nick thought about what Seb did to Katie. In reality, he was bringing Damian for two reasons. The first was to give Katie her first snitch. Damian could provide her with a lot of information and teach her a thing or two about the streets of Cleveland. The other is because he was sure if Seb was there, he may get arrested for assault if he saw him, and he knew Damian wouldn't let him.

Chapter 3

Spring to Action

"What's a nice girl like you doing in a place like this?" Nick asked Katie as he and Damian walked over to the table.

Damian looked at the young lady at the table. She was gorgeous! He couldn't believe Nick knew her. What really boggled his mind, was what had possessed this Seb guy to do what he did to her? Nick filled him in on the way as to where they were going and why.

"Nick," she breathed out, and her body instantly relaxed as soon as she saw him. "Thank you so much for coming for me." She gave him a hug.

"In a heartbeat. Katie, this is Damian. He's one of my resources. I think he could be a great resource for you for when you start in the police department."

"You're going to be a cop?" Damian asked, stunned, as he shook her hand. "Why?"

"Because I want to help people."

"Oh, wait! I know you! I've seen your face. You were the girl that…" his voice trailed off.

"Yes. I was kidnapped two years ago," Katie confirmed.

"By that dude who raped girls and killed people on your campus, right?"

"Yes."

"Okay," Nick sat down, "we need to eat. We were getting ready to go to dinner when you called."

"Oh! I'm sorry!" Katie said, mortified. "I didn't mean to ruin —"

"Nonsense." Nick waved her off. "We can eat anywhere. Right, Damian?"

"Hey, as long as I'm not paying, I'll eat anywhere you take me."

Nick chuckled as he scanned the menu. "You provide payment in a different form. You're information is more valuable than you know. So, Katie, what are you having?"

"I'm not hungry," she said, feeling like she wanted to throw up.

After they ordered their meal, which Nick insisted that she eat something, Katie explained what happened toward the end of her date. She also explained the conversation between her and Ty so he could understand her confusion.

"Well, have to tell you that Seb is full of it," Nick finally said after she was finished. "Those words never exited my mouth. I *did* say that I felt you were more than ready for the police academy *and* Quantico, but if Seth wanted me to continue training you, that I would. Seems Mr. Creswell has a way of twisting what he hears."

"More like he's telling you a story close enough to the truth that it sounds like the truth, but it puts him in a better position. It also sounds like he's isolating you," Damian pointed out. "I've been on the receiving end of manipulation, and this sounds like a clear cut case of it."

"You think?" Katie asked, stunned that Seb would attempt to manipulate her.

Damian nodded. "I *know*. Been there, done that. I'd stay away from him. He doesn't sound stable."

"I agree," Nick said. "However," he held his hand up to stop her objections, "I know you well enough to not tell you what to do, but to let you know that he sounds like bad news. I trust your instincts."

"Thank you," Katie said, feeling her stress slowly melting away. She propped her head on her hand and asked, "Why do I attract guys who want to control me?"

"You don't. There are plenty of guys out there who only want to love you for who you are, just the way you are."

"Where?"

Nick sighed, shaking his head. "They're right in front of you," he said, referring to himself. Of course he would never admit it, but he had been in love with her for quite some time. "May I make a suggestion?"

"Go for it."

"Why don't you wait until you're done with the police academy before you commit to someone? Dating just to go out, I would think, would be a good idea. That will give you a chance to get to know different people and experience dating, but I wouldn't commit if I were you. I don't think your mind or heart is in it at the moment. You have quite a bit going on."

"You're not the first one to suggest that. Ty said the same thing."

"He seems like a nice guy. And, I know he knows you very well."

"So do you," she pointed out.

"This is true."

She sighed again. "I guess time will tell. In the meantime, I'm just going to take things one day at a time."

"Sounds like a plan."

*   *   *

After Nick dropped Katie off at the dorm, she went up to her room. The dorm had been eerily quiet since graduation the day before. She didn't blame anyone for the mass exodus. If her apartment was ready, she wouldn't be there either. Thankfully, the school allowed her to stay in the dorm for the extra week until her apartment opened up. Of course, she had to pay extra to do it, but it was worth it to her to only move her belongings once.

She sighed for what seemed like the umpteenth time that night as she took her shoes off and rested her feet on the coffee table. "So glad this day is finished," she said, resting her head on the back of the couch with her eyes closed for several minutes before there was a knock on her door around nine. She slowly got off the couch and looked through the peephole to see Seb standing there. "No way," she whispered, shaking her head. "Not tonight. I'm done."

As she walked away, Seb kicked the door in. Katie gasped as she spun on her heels, turning to run to her room. She almost got away before Seb grabbed her arm. "What are you doing?" she demanded.

"I thought something happened to you." Cupping her face in his hands, he said, "I was so worried, and when you didn't respond, I had to force my way in to make sure you were okay."

"You're paying for that!" Katie shouted, visibly angry, upset, and on edge.

She tried to pull away from him, but he held her tighter. "I don't care about the door. I care about *you*."

Grabbing his hands that were literally hurting her cheeks by that point, she hoped to be released, but he held firm. "You need to leave," she hissed.

"No. We need to talk."

"No, we don't!"

He kissed her with such force, that she couldn't take it anymore and shoved him away with all her might. With pain in his eyes, he pleaded, "Why won't you just let me love you?"

Bolting for her room again, she shouted, "You're insane! I'm going to call security!"

As she dialed the phone, he grabbed her arm, throwing her across the room away from the phone. Jerking the phone from the wall, she had to duck as it whizzed past her head, crashing against the wall in the hall.

Katie looked at him in wide-eyed horror. She wasn't sure what to do. He took her lifeline to safety. Scrambling from the floor, she bolted for the door. She almost made it, when two hands yanked her from behind and slammed her into a chair in the kitchen. Holding her down by her shoulders, he demanded, "We need to talk."

"You need to leave this place, or I will press charges," Katie snapped, crossing her arms in defiance.

Seb crouched down in front of her. Seeing the vibrant green that signified trouble in her eyes, he asked, "Why are you so obstinate?"

She took the moment and kicked him between his legs. When he grabbed himself and rolled on the floor in pain, she kicked him in the back before running from the apartment. Knowing one of her dorm mates was there for summer school, she prayed he was in his apartment on the first floor. When she didn't get an answer, she ran to the storage room down the hall. It was unlocked, so she closed the door and locked it from the inside.

Plastering her ear to the door, she strained to hear any sound. *How would she know if Seb came down the stairs? Would she have to stay there all night?*

After several minutes, she found a spot on the floor and sat down, wrapping her arms around her legs as she rested her chin on her knees. *What was she going to do? How would she get out of this one? In a city full of thousands, she felt cut off and alone.*

Resting her head on her knees, she prayed to God for safety and guidance. She decided right there to get a cell phone the next morning. If she had one, she knew who it was she would call for help.

*   *   *

Staying in the storage room for what felt like hours, she finally stood and stretched. Her back cracked from being in a cramped position for so long.

Slowly opening the door, she listened for any noise that would give her a hint that someone was near…mainly Seb. She couldn't believe she was so wrong about him. To be rid of him, she decided to pay for the door. That was the least of her worries at that point.

Seeing the lobby desk across the room, she could see the phone resting atop of it. *Did she dare make a run for it?*

Silently, she moved through the lobby, staying in the shadows as much as possible, while her heart raced out of control. When she neared the desk, she ducked under it to stay out of sight. Grabbing the receiver, she dialed "0", which took the line to the security gatehouse before she ducked back under the desk out of sight.

"Security," the guy answered who was on shift.

Katie quietly said, "I need help."

"Who is this? According to my phone, this is the lobby phone in Euclid Commons."

"Yes. This is Katie MacKenna. I need help. Please send someone here."

"What happened? Do I need to call the police?"

Suddenly the line went dead. Peeking over the desk she saw Seb with his finger on the base of the phone, disconnecting the line. "I *told* you that we need to talk."

Katie gulped, her nerves running rampant. *Would the security officer take her call seriously?*

She didn't have to wait too long for an answer. As she slowly stood, she could see the flashing lights of security pull up to the door of the dorm. She backed against the wall, hoping to stay out of Seb's reach while keeping an eye on him and the security guard.

The security officer yelled something into his radio as he ran to the door. He had it open in seconds. "Miss MacKenna, are you okay?"

"No," she shook her head while Seb narrowed his eyes at her with his back to the security officer.

"I've already called the police," the security officer said loud enough for Seb to hear. "They're on their way."

"There's no reason for them. I only wanted to talk to her," Seb explained.

"No. He kicked my door in. He pulled the phone from the wall so I couldn't call you. He jerked me back into the apartment and was going to *make* me talk to him."

"Did he hurt you?" the security officer asked.

Katie just stared at Seb as she backed further into the wall.

"No. She's having flashbacks," Seb dismissed her. He turned and explained to the security officer, "We had an argument tonight on our first date. She made me leave her in Sandusky. So, of course I wanted to check on her. Now, keeping in mind that two years ago she was kidnapped from this very dorm, when she didn't answer her door, of course I became concerned, so I kicked the door in to see if she was in there."

"Why didn't you just call us?"

"I didn't think about that," he lied. "I just felt the pressing need to get to her. Anyway, when I kicked the door in, I guess it threw her back to her childhood, where her father abused her. Look at her. She looks like a scared cat. Do you see any bruises on her?"

"No," he admitted.

"She's having flashbacks."

"No," Katie finally got out, finding her voice. "No! He's lying!"

"Look, this is going to be a he said-she said," Seb walked over to the security officer. "Why don't I just pay for the door, and we'll call it good?" he asked, taking out his wallet.

"No!" Katie shouted, with the fear written all over her body. "He's lying! Don't let him leave!"

Just then, the police car pulled up to the dorm.

"I've already called. I'm afraid a police report needs to be filed," the security officer explained.

Seb waved him off as he walked toward the door. "I'll just explain the situation."

"Hold it right there, son," an older, heavy-set police officer said with his hand out to stop Seb from taking another step. As he walked with his female partner to the dorm, he stated, "You're not going anywhere until this is sorted." Walking back into the dorm with Seb and his partner, the older officer asked, "Who called?"

The security officer raised his hand. "I did."

The African American female officer finally saw Katie plastered against the wall, pale and shaking. "What's wrong, honey?"

"He-he kicked my door in. He threw my phone on the floor after pulling the cord from the wall. He was going to make me talk to him whether I wanted to or not."

"Look, she kicked me between the legs and kicked my back. I *could* file assault charges against her, but I'm willing to walk away. I'm even willing to pay for the door I kicked in," Seb said in a calm voice. "This is bigger than it needs to be."

"Why did you kick her door in?" the older police officer asked. In his time as an officer, he had seen this scenario on many occasions and instantly recognized the reality of the situation. His goal was to get to the truth. He would get his side, while his partner would get hers, and the truth would be somewhere in the middle. He was confident they could sort it out. "Why does she look so scared?"

"Why don't you talk to him, and I'll talk to the lady?" the female officer offered. "We may be able to make more sense of things when we get both sides."

"I don't want to make this a big deal," Seb pleaded. "Let's just say it is a he said-she said thing and get on with our evenings. I'm sure you have better things to do then to be here sorting this out."

Katie looked at him in wide-eyed terror. *Was he really going to get away with it?*

"You want me to call someone for you, honey?" the female officer asked as she cautiously approached Katie. With as scared as Katie looked, she knew something happened and she didn't want to spook her.

Katie nodded, not taking her eyes off Seb.

"Do you want to use my phone?" the officer offered.

Katie accepted the phone. Her hands shaking, she dialed the number.

"Agent Locke," Nick answered his phone.

"I–I…It's Katie," she stammered, unable to get anymore out.

"Here, honey, I got it," the officer put her hand out for the phone. When she gave it to her, the officer said, "Hello, this is Officer James of the Cleveland Police Department."

"I'm sorry, *who*?" Nick sat up in his bed in shock. He had gone to bed after dropping Katie and Damian off. It was a long day and he knew it would be another long day tomorrow. "Did you say you're Police?"

"Yes."

"I'm Agent Nick Locke with the FBI. That sounded like Katie MacKenna. Is she okay?"

"We're not really sure. We just got here and are doing our best to determine that ourselves. When I asked if there was someone she could call, she dialed your number."

"Is someone else there?"

"Yes. There's a young man here as well."

"Is his name Seb?"

"Seb?" Officer James called to him. When Seb looked up, giving away his name, the officer said, "Yes, he answered to Seb."

"Don't let him leave. He left her in Sandusky earlier tonight. Get as much information as you can and I'll be there in less than ten minutes."

"Yes, sir," she said, and hung up the phone. She leaned on the desk as she said, "He'll be here in about ten minutes. So, you know a fed?"

"Yes, ma'am."

"I see." She turned to her partner and explained, "Don't let him leave. There's a fed on the way."

The other officer looked up, stunned. "A *what*?"

Seb crossed his arms, agitated. "Why is Locke coming?"

"Because I called him," Katie squeaked out.

"Of course." Seb rolled his eyes. "The big bad agent to the rescue."

"Just mind your business," Officer James snapped at Seb, beginning to understand what was going on. "Get his statement, but don't let him leave."

"Got it," the other officer agreed.

When Officer James turned back to Katie, she asked, "Can you tell me what happened?"

By the time Katie finished her side of the story, Nick pulled up to the dorm. He yanked the door open to see Seb standing to the side talking to one officer, while Katie was sitting in a chair talking to another officer behind the lobby desk, with the security officer between them, standing closer to Katie. "G'day, I'm Nick Locke," Nick shook Officer James' hand before he showed her his badge.

"Evening, Agent Locke," the officer greeted him. "I was the one you spoke with on the phone."

"What happened?"

After the officer filled him in on Katie's side of the story, Nick asked the other officer for Seb's side before he headed upstairs to look at Katie's apartment with Officer James, while the security officer stayed with Katie.

"In hearing both sides of the story, the evidence is leaning more toward Katie's side," Nick pointed out as they stood in her room with the phone shattered on the ground just outside her bedroom door. It clearly looked as if it was thrown into the hall, and the main door to the apartment was mostly intact, except that the sides were splintered with parts of the door still attached to the doorframe.

"I agree, but we have to take both sides into account. Now, I'm sure I can talk Mr. Creswell into not pressing charges for assault when I point out that she can press charges for breaking and entering, *and* assault. Having said that, off the record, I don't like him. I don't believe him."

"I like your style, Officer James," Nick said with a chuckle. "And, for the record, I don't believe him either. I've already been a victim of his twisting of words. It's so close, you almost start to doubt your own memory of the situation."

"Is there somewhere she can stay until she moves into her apartment? I don't think it's a good thing for her to stay here. She seems too vulnerable."

"I'm sure I can find somewhere. In the meantime, if you can have her pack a bag, I need to go have a conversation with Seb."

"Ya know, I don't like many Feds, but I like you," she smiled. "I have a feeling you could do some damage to him if he pushed you."

"Let's just say he should count himself lucky you guys are here."

*   *   *

Reports written and Katie packed for a few days, Nick led her to his SUV next to the police car. Officer James told Nick they would hold Seb there for several minutes in order to give Nick a head start in getting Katie away.

"Where are we going?" Katie asked, slumped in her seat, exhausted from the evening events.

"You're going to sleep in my bed, while I sleep on the sofa-bed in the living room. Tomorrow morning we can go to church for the eleven a.m. service if you're up to it. Then on Monday, I'll let Seth know I'll be in late, and we'll talk to the manager and see if your apartment is ready early. If it is, then I'll take the day off and we'll get you moved in on Monday."

She looked over at him in surprise. "Don't you have to work?"

"I have several cases on the burners, but nothing is cooking at the moment. Since the Rossi case finally closed a couple of weeks ago, and Giovanni is settled in his new life, things have massively slowed down. There is a power play going on, though, as the other families scoop up Rossi's territory and men. It's like a bunch of ants descending on a peanut butter sandwich." He chuckled at his analogy. "The frenzy is interesting to see. We're keeping an eye on it, seeing where the chips land."

"I see. And, am I staying on Sunday night, too?"

"Yes."

"You're comfortable with that?"

"I'm comfortable for a couple of nights. Besides, I would rather you were with me so I can keep an eye on you. I have way too much invested in you to let anything happen."

"I'm an investment?" Katie asked. Her face was still pale, and she wasn't wearing the stress well. She looked like she had been through a battle.

"You're more than that and you know it. I wouldn't be here if you were just an investment."

"Thank you, by the way."

He glanced at her for a moment at the red light before it flipped to green. "Do you want to go to the hospital or something? The most I have at home is aspirin."

"No." She rested her head on the headrest, watching the scenery of the night pass by while they drove. "I'll be fine."

To Nick, she sounded hollow…not herself. "Get some rest while I make a call."

"Fine," she sighed, closing her eyes, while Nick dialed his phone.

"Simmons," a sleepy Seth answered his phone.

"Hey, Seth, it's Nick."

"What time is it? What's going on?"

"Sorry to call so late, but I've been down at the college collecting Katie. Seems Sebastian Creswell is not who he seemed to be."

"I don't understand."

"Let me see if I can make a long story short…" Nick said, and explained what all had happened through the evening. By the time he got to the end, he pulled into the parking deck of his apartment building.

"Wow," Seth said, stunned. "Didn't see that one coming. He's good."

"I know, right? Anyway, I know Sandy is a doctor, and I wondered…" his voice trailed off as he put the Explorer in park. He glanced toward Katie, who was asleep, but not resting comfortably. Seeing her contorted face, he could only imagine the nightmares plaguing what little rest she was getting.

"Yeah. Let me give her a call. I'll have her call you after I explain it all to her."

"We just pulled into the parking deck, so the sooner the better. Poor girl needs a decent amount of rest. She's been through the wringer tonight."

"I'm surprised she has gotten any rest at all since she was kidnapped…for most of her life for that matter. Poor thing just needs to be cut a break somewhere."

Nick sighed. "From your lips to God's ears."

"Get her upstairs and settled. Maybe put a movie on – comedy preferably. I'll have Sandy call you as soon as she can."

"Thanks, Seth."

"Give me a call tomorrow after church and let me know how she's doing."

"Thanks. I will."

As he hung up his phone, Katie moaned in her sleep. "Hey, Katie." He gently jostled her. "We need to go upstairs. Can you wake up for a few minutes?"

She gasped, sitting upright as she grabbed the door and his arm. Breathing heavily, she looked around, panicked.

"It's okay. You're safe," Nick said, loosening her fingers from around his arm. "We're at the apartment building. I'm sorry. I needed to wake you to get you upstairs."

"I-I know. I'm sorry," she said, breathless. Panic was still in her eyes as she looked around to get her bearings. "I know this place. You're right," she said, calming down. "I know I'm safe with you."

Nick smiled to himself as he got out of the SUV. After rescuing her bag from the backseat, he went around and opened her door. "Seth is going to call his sister to see if she can get you something to help you relax."

"I'm fine. I'll be fine," she insisted, trying to convince herself more than Nick.

"Nooooo, you look like a scared child. C'mon," he rested his hand on the small of her back as he escorted her to the elevator.

By the time he got her upstairs and in the bathroom for a shower, he barely had time to change the sheets on his bed before his phone rang. "Locke," he answered. Glancing toward the bathroom, he noted the shower was still going.

"Nick, it's Sandy," Seth's sister said on the other end of the phone. "I hear you've had your hands full tonight."

"She's a mess. She's jumping from her own shadow at the moment and I don't blame her. It threw her back to the kidnapping, I think. She said she was locked in a storage room for about an hour or so, too scared to come out."

"That would do it. I'm on my way over right now from the hospital. I'll be there in about five minutes. I'm bringing Diazepam. They are ten-milligram pills. I want her to take one at night for ten days. That should help keep her sedated enough to get through the next several days."

"Um," he glanced toward the bathroom to make sure the shower was still running. He didn't want her to hear what he was going to ask. "She's supposed to be getting on a plane on Tuesday to go down to Oklahoma. Her friends are graduating and she has to get her stuff from a storage room. Is that something she can do on this stuff?"

"Not a smart idea. Can you go with her?"

Sighing, he shook his head as he dropped it onto his hand, his mind working overtime. "I'll have to clear it with Seth."

"I'll handle Seth. You take care of her. If she's headed to the police academy the following week, you'd also better get a hold of that psychology friend of hers to talk her through this."

"Yeah. Stacey's good. She's getting ready for her wedding, though."

"Explain what happened. I guarantee she'll help. She doesn't need much. You can even do part of it with her. Stacey can show you how to get her centered enough to get through the next week."

"You don't understand. She's going back to Oklahoma. Her father will be there. She's going to have to face things she's avoided for four years."

Sandy swore. "Isn't there a way you can talk her into postponing that?"

"I may be able to postpone getting her stuff here, but I highly doubt I can talk her into not go to her friend's graduation. I'm sorry, but that's not happening. She'll regret it and I don't want her to regret anything."

"Fine. Go with her for that, and fly back with her. Get her to not get her stuff or face the loss of her friends from there just yet. She's got a truckload of stuff she's going to have to face when she goes through the academy. Her belongings have been in storage for four years, what're a couple more months?"

"Police Academy is twenty weeks," he corrected.

"Fine," Sandy said, exasperated. "Just make it work! That's an order! I'm here, by the way."

"I'll call down to the garage to get you in," he said and hung up. He went over to the phone on the wall that went to the security building and called Sandy in. She was right in everything she said. The trick would be getting Katie to agree.

As Katie shut off the water, Sandy knocked on the door. "Nice timing," he answered the door, but she put her finger up to halt him as she was in an intense conversation.

"I don't care how you do it. You guys want her to get through this, Locke has to go down to Oklahoma with her. If you want her to get through the academy, and then head to Quantico, we're going to have to work together here." She paused, listening to Seth. "Good. Thank you. I'll let him know he's cleared until a week from Monday," she confirmed.

Nick did a fist pump, unable to control his relief. Sandy had a way about her that allowed her to convince her twin to do things that no one else could. Seth could not combat her logical line of thinking. Born only a few minutes apart, Seth and Sandy looked quite a bit alike. There were times Nick would shake his head as he saw the uncanny resemblance between the two, with the exception that her features were obviously smoother and more feminine. Seth was older, but Sandy learned early how to work with what she commonly referred to as the 'male species.' Having four brothers allowed her the rare opportunity to study and learn how they thought and functioned. Somehow, she was still able to come through with her femininity intact.

"You're cleared through until a week from Monday," she said, hanging up her phone. "Now, where's Katie?"

"She's in the bathroom."

"Still?" she asked, stunned.

He shrugged. "Yeah. She took a long one, I guess."

"Oh, for crying out loud! You know nothing about women," she said, tossing her jacket and purse onto the couch. "She was probably crying in the shower."

She went over to the door and knocked lightly. "I'll be out in a minute," Katie said through the door.

"Katie, it's Sandy Simmons," she responded.

Katie unlocked the door, letting her in. "C'mon in."

When Sandy walked in, she saw the puffiness around Katie's eyes, confirming Sandy's thoughts. "Aww, honey, it's okay. You're safe here," she said, giving her a hug as she stood there in her sweatpants and a tank top, and Sandy was still in her scrubs.

"I know. It's just," Katie sniffed, wiping her eyes, "I don't know what I do to these guys to make them want to hurt or control me."

"It's not you. It's them," she said softly.

Katie sat down on the toilet lid, while Sandy crouched in front of her, wiping her stringy, wet hair out of her face. Sandy tucked it behind her ear as Katie admitted, "I called Nick because I knew he would come and help me."

Sandy cleared her throat nervously and asked, "What does that mean?"

Seeing the hopeful look in Katie's eyes, Sandy understood more at that moment what Katie's feelings were for Nick. "Nick's more than a friend to me," Katie explained. "I don't know if he feels the same or if he even thinks of me like that. I'm such a mess at this point, I don't know anyone who would want me."

"You're not a mess. Well, in this moment you are, but normally you're a strong, independent young lady that any guy in his right mind would be happy to have and would cherish. I'm not sure about Nick, though. He's quite a bit older than you, isn't he?"

"He is, but we kissed once."

"You did?" she asked, taken aback.

She nodded. "It was on a case. I don't even know if he remembers." She took a deep breath. "Then, if we did, we wouldn't even be able to be on the same unit. That's a clear rule."

"I see. Can I ask why you went out with Seb if you're interested in Nick?"

"Because he asked…Nick hasn't."

Sandy nodded in understanding. "Do you like Seb that way?"

"I don't know. Well, I know *now*," she corrected herself. "He's a manipulative jerk."

"At least you found out early."

"But now I'm scared. How can I trust my instincts when I totally missed that?"

"You weren't the only one. Seth and Nick missed it too, and they're FBI agents."

"He was good."

While Katie took a moment to get her emotions under control, Sandy explained, "Here's what we're going to do. You're going to take this pill," she said, taking the pill bottle from her pocket. Filling the cup next to the sink with water, Sandy gave it to her. Watching Katie obediently take the pill before handing the cup back, Sandy explained, "Okay, that's going to relax you. You're going to take one of these each night for the next ten days to help you sleep. I'm going to give them to Nick to hold onto for you. You're going to be with him for the next several days, so he can keep an eye on you."

"What? No. He has to work."

"No. It took some finagling, but my brother finally saw things my way," Sandy said with a twinkle in her eyes. "You see, when you go to Oklahoma, Nick's going with you. He has been given instructions to not let you go to your friend's graves *or* to get your stuff from the storage shed. You are going to fly down, be there for a few days to enjoy your friends and celebrate their graduation before flying back to celebrate Stacey's wedding on Friday."

"But, when will I get my stuff?"

"After you are finished with the police academy," she explained. "It may take you more money to get it shipped up here, but I think it will save you major stress. Also, Nick is going with you to the wedding. If Seb shows up, I want Nick there to look out for you. This will get you through until the next Monday, when you start the academy."

"How am I going to do this? Am I cut out for this?"

"Don't doubt your dream now! You're so close. You've worked so hard. You're feeling beat up at the moment thanks to Seb...the cretin," she added. "You have been focused all these years with noble goals and pure intentions. Not even Dominic deterred you from this dream. Don't let Seb do it. Nick will help you stay focused."

"Okay," she agreed.

"Good. Now, are you ready for bed?"

She nodded in response.

Sandy quickly ran a brush through Katie's hair and braided it so it wouldn't be a mess when she woke the next morning before she ushered her into Nick's bedroom. "Nice," Sandy commented, looking around the room.

The dark wood furniture allowed the burgundy and tan comforter to stand out in the room. Everything had its place and was clean and cleared off.

"A bit O.C.D., but at least it's clean," Sandy joked as she pulled the covers up on Katie. "There, do you feel better."

"I feel safer," she countered.

"Are you tired yet?"

"Starting to feel it, but it's a strange room."

"Okay, just a second," she said and left the room. Nick looked up from the chair he was sitting on when Sandy came out to the living room. "Do you have a sound machine? You know, something to create white noise?"

"Actually, I do. I use it when I go to hotels." He disappeared into the bathroom for only a moment, when he returned with the tiny machine. He gave her instructions before returning to his seat.

He was worried about Katie. He only had a brother, so he had no idea how to handle a girl. He had girlfriends in his past, but he felt nothing like he felt when he was around Katie. Remembering the conversation he and Todd had on the day of the snowball fight, he realized that Katie did, in fact, fit his 'list' of what he wanted in a wife. *Was their age difference holding him back? When Seb did what he did to her, he wanted to rip his throat out. Why? Was it because of all of the time he invested in her, or was it more?*

"She's asleep," Sandy said, coming into the living room ten minutes later. "Not sure how long she'll stay that way, but she's asleep for now. Here are her pills," she said, handing them to him. "She's a mess."

"What did she say? I feel so stupid not checking on her. I didn't think twice about it."

"Her head is all over the place. She's struggling with whether or not she can handle being a cop."

"Really? She's been so focused."

"What he did tonight threw her. What ticks me off is that he more than likely knew what he was doing. I'm sure he was less than supportive of her wanting to be a cop."

"That's putting it mildly. He never made that a secret."

"So, if he manipulated her enough, he could get her to doubt herself," Sandy pointed out. "That's how it starts. The normal pattern includes isolating her from those who matter the most to her."

"Yeah, he already started that as well."

"Wow! He works fast."

"His timeline was short. He had to. Fortunately for us, he did. This allowed us to see it quickly and save her from potentially years of being under his thumb."

"Oh, I don't think it would be years." Sandy shook her head. "I don't think it's Seb she's destined to be with."

"Really? Are you an oracle or something?" Nick teased.

"No," she laughed. "I just know people."

"And, do you know who she will be with?"

"I have an idea."

"Who?"

"Can't tell you. You'll just have to wait and see."

"You're a brat! You know that?"

"And you, Agent Locke, are dense," she said, putting her coat on. As she picked up her purse, she added, "Call me tomorrow to let me know how she is. It will take her a few days to come out of the fog she's in. Great job springing into action to save her. She thinks highly of you."

"Thanks," he blushed. "I really didn't think about it. I just did it."

She rested her hand on his shoulder and said, "That's what makes you a great guy. Never lost your heart."

Chapter 4

Spring Thaw

Over the next few days, Katie continuously woke up through the night sweating profusely, while screaming. Nick would patiently come in to calm her down, get her settled, and back to sleep. The lack of sleep was wearing on both of them, and they ended up taking naps through the day as well.

On Monday morning, the manager approved Katie moving in early to her apartment since it was ready. Even though she was going in a week early, due to the extenuating circumstances the manager said he wouldn't charge her.

Only stopping for a short nap in the mid-day, Nick and Katie got her room in the dorm cleared, and her belongings into the apartment. They also went furniture shopping for her, to be delivered while she was gone. The manager said he wouldn't mind signing for it and letting them drop it off in the apartment. Nick assured him there would be no ramifications and he told Katie they would set it up when they got back from Oklahoma.

Finally, on Tuesday morning when they were settled on the plane and in the air heading for Oklahoma City, Katie said to Nick, "Thank you so much for everything you've done for me over the last few days. I know I wouldn't have made it without you."

"No worries," he squeezed her hand, "I know you would do it for me."

"In a heartbeat. Um, what do you want to do when we get to West Springs? Do you want to stay in a hotel or at my dad's house?"

"That's up to you. Would staying in the house bring up bad memories? Sandy told me to do what I could to make this as stress-free as possible. She wants you to be strong for the wedding and starting the police academy. Besides, when we get back we're going to have some home supplies we'll have to go shopping for in regards to your apartment, so you need to be well rested."

"Right. Then, I think we'll stay in the hotel. I'm sure we can get connecting rooms if you want?" she offered.

"With your nightmares, I think that would be a good idea. Are you comfortable with leaving the doors open between the rooms?"

She shrugged. "It won't be any different than how we have been operating over the last couple of days."

"True. I just don't want to do anything you're not comfortable with."

"Thank you. I appreciate it," she said and turned toward the window. After several minutes deep in thought, she asked, "Can I know what happened to Giovanni?"

Nick looked around the cabin of the airplane and gestured for her to come closer. When she did, he whispered in her ear, "He's staying with my grandparents in Jordan, Montana, working on their ranch while he saves money to go to college for Veterinary Medicine."

"Nice!" Katie smiled for the first time in days. Then she furrowed her brow, confused, and whispered back, "I thought you told Lucca that your grandparents lived in Wyoming?"

"I'm not going to tell him the truth." He rolled his eyes. "That's insane."

"So, are you saying that lying will have to be added to my résumé?"

"If you want to keep your friends and family safe, yes."

She sighed. "I'm not a good liar."

"You did well when we were lying about our relationship."

She cringed.

"What?" he asked, sitting back in his seat. "What's wrong?"

She shook her head. "Nothing."

"This is going to be a long flight if you're going to shut me out. We need to continue to be open with each other if we are going to work well together."

"Do you want to work together on the same unit?" she asked.

"That's a given. Seth has made that clear from the start. Why?"

She turned back to the window again.

"Katie, you're going to have to stay open with me. We've worked hard to thaw that Ice Queen heart you had when we first met, to get us to where we are today. Please don't shut me out now."

She looked into his eyes as she asked, "Where are we?"

"What do you mean?"

"You said that 'we've worked to thaw that Ice Queen heart you had to get us to where we are today.' Where are we?"

"I don't understand the question."

Katie grunted in frustration.

"Okay. Take a deep breath and ask the question a different way."

"I don't know if I want to," she admitted, looking down as she nervously tucked a piece of her hair behind her ear.

He lifted her chin so she would stay focused on him. "What are you asking?"

"Where are we?"

He had an idea of what she was asking, but he didn't know how to answer it. "I don't know," he finally admitted.

"Where do you want us to be?"

"That's a good question."

"Do you have a good answer?"

"Unfortunately, not at the moment."

"Care to explain?"

"Well, I know what I want, but I also know the rules. I know where my heart is, but I don't know where yours is."

"Yes, you do."

Surprise and delight both spread across his face. "But, what about the rules? I don't want you on another unit."

"Maybe we need to let God sort that out," she offered.

"Sandy and Seth will kill me. I'm not supposed to stress you out. Besides, with what happened, maybe we need to give it more time."

"Do you really need more time?" she challenged. Seeing the stress on his face, she asked, "What did you think when you found out that Seb asked me out and I agreed?"

"Honestly?"

"I would expect no less."

"Two things, really. I thought first of all that you lost your mind," he said and she giggled. "And secondly, I was upset. To be honest, I was glad you called me. My concern though is that I don't want to start anything until your mind is clear."

"Then, what if we just date, like you said? You know, go out with no commitment. That way no one can say we're actually dating."

"You mean, go out as friends?"

"Yeah. Just going out, enjoying each other's company. No stress, no commitment, no deep relationship. We can find out if we're meant to be together."

"Without really going out," Nick clarified. "I mean, I don't want to lose your friendship over a relationship."

"You won't. We were friends first."

"That didn't work out so well with you and Seb," he pointed out.

"Okay, first off, you and Seb are entirely different guys. Secondly, the only thing Seb's good for is shark bait."

Nick chuckled. "Okay. We'll just keep it laid back. Personally, I'm not going out with any other women anyway."

"And, I really don't want to date any other guys."

"Then, it's a deal," Nick said as they shook hands. "We have officially agreed to continue our friendship."

Katie laughed. "At least we got somewhere."

"Ahhh," Nick sighed, "Been a while since I've seen your smile. I've missed it."

"Me too."

*   *   *

Katie thoroughly enjoyed her time in Oklahoma, and it did wonders for her as far as Nick was concerned. It was uneventful, yet allowed Katie to spend time with her friends. Her dad tried a couple of times to separate her from Nick, but she refused, much to Nick's relief. He didn't want to have to face Sandy when he got back if he let something happen in Oklahoma. With four brothers, she was a force to be reckoned with, and he knew that all too well.

After her friends graduated, Nick and Katie were able to get a good night's sleep before boarding the plane on Friday morning. According to Nick's timeline, the plane would land in plenty of time for them to get a little decorating done before they had to head to Stacey's rehearsal dinner.

When they returned home to her apartment, they had some time to straighten out the furniture and decorate a bit. After Nick left to get ready for the rehearsal dinner, she closed the door and sighed. It felt awkward to be alone after spending almost the entire week with him, but she knew it wouldn't last.

Knowing she didn't have a lot of time to dawdle, she jumped into the shower to get ready for Stacey's rehearsal dinner. She was glad Nick was going with her. It eased her anxiety about the possibility of seeing Seb the next day at the wedding. Even though Seb wouldn't be at the wedding as her date, Stacey and Scott had already invited him, and she knew he was planning on going.

While Nick was getting ready in his apartment, he got a call from Seth that he was needed in the field for a break in a case. Ready to head out, he stopped by Katie's apartment first. "I'm sorry, but Seth called me in. There's a break in a case."

"No problem. I understand."

"You look great, though!" he said, reminding himself to smack Seth upside the head for making him miss going with Katie.

"Thank you!" Katie's grin lit her face. "And, don't worry about me. I'll be fine."

"You've got your license, are you going to carry your gun with you tonight? I would feel better."

"I can," she agreed. "I'll put it in a leg holster."

"Good. I know you got it several months ago, but haven't carried it with you."

"I haven't felt the need…until now."

"If you're going to be a cop, and then an agent, you'd better make that thing a part of you getting dressed in the morning. Actually, I'm going to add that to your 'to do' list as your trainer. When you get dressed to leave the house, put it on…no exceptions."

"Yes, sir." She saluted. Then with a mischievous grin, she asked, "What about when I wear a swim suit? Pretty sure I can't hide a gun on me then."

Fighting the picture that popped into his head, he responded, "You are way too cute for your own good." He sighed as he admitted, "I'm afraid to take that next step. I don't want to lose your friendship. It means too much to me."

"Then we won't." She shrugged. "Until we're both comfortable, we'll keep it where we have it."

"Which is?"

"Best friends who go out a lot.

"Sounds like a plan," he agreed.

"Be safe out there, eh? I don't want to get a call from Seth telling me you've been shot, therefore deserting me for the wedding tomorrow."

"Not a chance," he said before his phone rang. "Duty calls!" he shouted, running down the hall. As he pushed the staircase door open, he answered his phone, "Locke."

Katie sighed as she watched him take the stairs, not wanting to wait for the elevator. While she admired and adored him, she didn't want to push him. They weren't ready.

*　　*　　*

Stacey practically ran into Katie when she walked into the church. Shoving her out the doors of the sanctuary, she ushered her out of the view of the others in the sanctuary. "Okay, what happened? I've been on the phone with Seth all week. He's worried sick."

"Don't be. Nick and I have been working on it."

"Great." She pouted. "Now that I'm officially a counselor with a degree and everything, I can't help you."

"Not at the moment. You need to enjoy your well-deserved wedding and honeymoon. Y'all have waited long enough for each other."

She blushed. "I know."

"You're not supposed to be the blushing bride until tomorrow. Ohhh," she sighed, admiring her friend, "you're going to make a beautiful bride."

"Thank you! Your partner is in there and waiting. Now, I have to ask, it's the counselor in me. How are you really doing?"

"I'll admit I was a mess at first. Sandy put me on Diazepam, and that's helped me to get some semblance of sleep over the last several days. It has been broken up by nightmares, but I got some."

"Well, you look strangely happy. Care to share?"

She crossed her arms, not sure how to answer the question.

"Katie?" Stacey asked, as a grin spread across her face. "Is there something I need to know about?"

"Not really. Nick and I talked and…well…we've agreed to be close friends."

"Huh? I thought you were already there."

"Basically, we admitted that we like each other, but we're not ready to take that jump yet."

Stacey bobbed her head in thought for a moment. "Well, I guess that'll work. All right, you look pretty good to me. Ready to meet everyone?"

Katie took a deep breath to calm her nerves. "I don't like walking into situations where I don't know people."

"You know me and Scott. Come on, do it for me?"

"I'm here for you. I wouldn't abandon you. Besides, I want to see the church."

Stacey looped her arm through Katie's as they walked arm-in-arm into the sanctuary. There were bows on the pews and the candelabras. Before Katie could ask, Stacey explained, "The florist will be here in the morning to put fresh flowers all over the sanctuary. I have different colors of lilies, along with orchids, freesia that will be accented by aster, baby's breath, star of Bethlehem, and peonies. The flowers will be the various colors of the dresses, continuing the 'rainbow' effect."

When they got to the front, Stacey introduced Katie to everyone. When she got to Katie's partner to walk down the aisle, she said, "Katie, this is your partner for tomorrow, Lance Montgomery. Lance, this is Katie MacKenna. Be nice or you're dealing with me," she warned.

"I wouldn't dream of being mean to her. Scott already threatened me within an inch of my life if I even remotely stepped out of line," he said with a smile as he kissed Stacey's hand. He then kissed Katie's as well. "Would you be so kind as to be my partner tomorrow?" he asked Katie.

"I will, only because Stacey's making me," Katie said with a smirk. When he looked at her in surprise, she quickly added, "I'm only teasing. I don't mind being your partner."

"I kind of liked the feisty answer." He smirked. "I like a girl with spunk."

"You may regret that," Stacey warned. "She's been known to humble some rather large FBI agents."

"Oh really?"

"Yep. She also heads into the police academy on Monday. Know she can hold her own," she cautioned, and then left the two of them to get to know each other.

Leaving an awkward feeling between them, Katie broke the silence, "So, been to many weddings?"

"Always a groomsman, never a groom," he sighed dreamily.

Katie burst out in laughter. "Cute."

He grinned. "I try. So, looks like we're just waiting for the pastor. I hope he hasn't decided to leave them at the altar."

"You're funny."

"Thanks!"

"So, are you from here?"

"Actually, nope. I hate to admit this up here, because they give me a hard time, but I was born and raised in Texas."

"Really?" Katie grinned. "What are you doing here?"

"It's where the job took me. Where are you from?"

"Oklahoma."

"Really?" he asked, pleasantly surprised. "What area?"

"Near Oklahoma City. You?"

"Deep in the heart of East Texas. Pretty much the middle of nowhere, but the best place in the world to grow up. Wouldn't have it any other way. My parents have a ranch, so I grew up on horses, with cows, chickens, and pigs about. Gardening was a must, but I enjoyed the rodeos the most."

"You rode in a rodeo? What did you do?"

"I was a team roper, along with a bull rider."

"Seriously? Doesn't that cause major broken bones?"

"Ha! That's what makes me a great paramedic. I know what it feels like to break pretty much every bone in my body. I can also set most of them on myself at this point."

"Do you still ride?"

"Riding's few and far between up here, but when I go home I do."

"Nice! There are times where I miss the south," Katie admitted.

"Do you ride?"

"Actually, no. Never been on a horse before."

"Really? An Oklahoma girl who can't ride a horse? Please tell me you at least know how to shoot?"

"Oh yeah," she smiled, relieved that Nick took the time to teach her.

"Whew! So, what did you do down in Oklahoma if you didn't ride? You're not a mall rat, are you?" He crinkled his nose.

"No. Oh, heavens no! Can't stand the mall! I avoid it unless it's unavoidable. Even then, I go in with a list."

"Good. So, what did you do in your spare time? You look fit. Did you play sports?"

Katie laughed. "No. Not hardly. I'm an artist."

"An artist? Why are you being a cop if you're an artist?"

Katie debated in her head for a moment on how to answer before she explained, "I want to help people who are not in a position to help themselves. And, the police officer position is a stepping stone to FBI agent."

"You're going to be an FBI agent?" he asked, stunned. "Wow! That's awesome! I like her!" he yelled to Scott. "She's cool! Great choice!"

Scott and Stacey laughed before turning their attention back to the pastor, who arrived only few moments before he called to them.

"So, big question of the night, do you have a boyfriend?"

Katie was taken by surprise. "I…no."

"Why the hesitation?"

"That question came from out of nowhere."

"Well, I wanted to know if I would have full custody of you tomorrow or if I would have to share."

"Well, you'll have to share me. I'm bringing my best friend with me tomorrow. He's – "

"Your best friend is a he?" he asked, cutting her off.

"Yep."

"And, he hasn't asked you out?"

"We're not there yet."

"How long have you been friends?"

"About two and a half years."

"And, he hasn't asked you out yet?"

"No."

"Wow. Sounds like he and I need to have a conversation."

"What? Why?"

"Well, if he hasn't asked you out yet, I need to ask him if he's lost his mind." He chuckled. "You seem like the perfect girl."

"Oh no." She shook her head. "I need to clear that one up. I *am not* the perfect girl…far from it. There's a lot I can't do. I'm not all that. I promise you."

"Aw, you're shattering my image of you."

"We're ready to begin," the pastor announced.

They went through the ceremony before breaking off into groups to head to the restaurant for the rehearsal dinner. Katie wasn't originally looking forward to the wedding, but over the course of the evening, with all of the laughter and joking around, she was a lot more at ease. She was still grateful Nick would be with her the next day, though, she didn't want to encourage Lance in the wrong direction. He was a nice guy. Stacey picked a good one. He was well built, due to his firefighter position, loved horses, had these amazing blue eyes, and this dark, almost black hair that made his blue eyes stand out. Katie sighed. She had to keep her mind clear. She couldn't afford to make another mistake as she did with Seb. Nick was correct, she wasn't ready.

*   *   *

Getting home around midnight that night, she was thankful she lived in a secure building. Knowing she could safely go from her car to the apartment, and that her apartment was secure as well, gave her a sense of comfort. While the gun strapped to her leg gave her a little more added security, she was still relieved to know she was walking into *her* apartment and not the dorm. It made her feel more grown up when she walked down the hall to her door. She laughed at her silliness as she unlocked it.

"Nice!" she exclaimed, glancing around the apartment. She knew what she had in the storage shed, and decorated around it. Most of her belongings in the shed were for her bedroom, along with what was left of her mother's dishes (Cami and Brent had bought new dishes for them and packed Meg's up for Katie), along with some of her mother's belongings that her dad didn't mind parting with. This left the remainder of the apartment still left to decorate, which she and Nick did when they got home earlier in the day. "Homey, yet comfy," she said satisfied, and headed to bed for the early start in the morning, not seeing the answering machine flashing that she had a message.

*   *   *

Katie met the girls at the salon near Stacey's house around ten the next morning. Stacey's house was an hour south of Cleveland, so between the late night and the early morning, Katie grabbed breakfast on the road in her rush to get there on time. She and Nick had already agreed as to where and when they would meet while they worked on her apartment the day before, so she didn't worry about not hearing or seeing him that morning.

"Just so you know, this is my treat," Stacey said to all the girls as they waited for their appointment. When the objections flew, Stacey explained, "I've waited too long, and want everything right. I have us set for hair and nails today. Your nail polish will be a glitter/iridescent of your dress color. If you don't like it, you can take it off in the morning."

"I think that'll be perfect!" Melody said, excited.

"I'm just glad we all got colors that make us look good," Harmony added.

"I took everyone into consideration in the planning of this," Stacey explained. "Speaking of which, Katie, you and Lance seemed to hit it off last night," she hinted.

Katie's face immediately flushed in embarrassment as the girls pressed for more information. "No, no," she put her hands up in surrender. "No, I don't know him well enough for anything. He's a nice guy."

"A southern gentleman," Stacey corrected.

"Yes." Katie jokingly narrowed her eyes at Stacey as she crossed her arms. "A little detail you neglected to tell me."

She shrugged. "Well, I figured it would come out in conversation soon enough."

"Um, I heard you and Seb Creswell went out last Saturday. How'd that go?" Larissa, Stacey's friend from college, asked.

"Not good." Katie shook her head. "It's not a repeat. I wouldn't recommend him either."

"Really? He seems like he's got it all together. He already owns half a business, has a business degree, and I heard he's moving into his first house here in a couple of weeks."

"That may be, but that doesn't attest to who he is at his heart."

"I see," Larissa said, shocked by Katie's cool response.

"It wasn't good," Stacey said, bailing her out of the conversation. "Besides, I'm sure Nick will be coming with you tonight as well, right?"

"You're bad!" Katie laughed, shaking her head. "Nick and I are just friends."

"*Best* friends," Stacey corrected. "And, who knows what will happen in the coming weeks. Maybe his eyes will become opened."

"Who's Nick?" Marissa asked.

"He's my trainer," Katie explained.

"Trainer? For what?"

"For the police academy and FBI."

Marissa smiled. "Whoa! That's cool!"

"So sorry I'm late," Becky, Stacey's step-mom, ran into the salon. "Have you guys been called back yet?"

"No, ma'am," the salon owner greeted the group, with seven other girls behind her. "Ladies, these are your appointments for the next few hours. My instructions were hair, manicure and nails, and pedicure and nails."

"Nice!" Harmony cheered. "I haven't been spoiled like that since Randy and I got married."

"Well, you will be today." Stacey grinned, pulling out her dad's credit card. "It's on Dad."

They laughed as each stylist claimed a young lady and took them back. Katie had *never* had a full manicure or pedicure. She only had her hair done and nails painted for prom or one of the other dances. This would be a special treat she was looking forward to enjoying.

*   *   *

As they waited in the hall to walk in for the wedding, Katie clutched Lance's arm. "You're shaking. Are you nervous?" He finally asked.

"I am."

"Why?"

"Because I know Stacey has invited all of our friends from college, which includes Seb."

"As in *the* Seb? The one from last Saturday? The one we talked about last night?"

"Yes. The other reason I'm nervous is that I haven't heard from Nick since last night when he got called out. I realize he probably got in really late, but I have been keeping an eye out and haven't seen him yet."

Hearing Katie's concerns, Melody turned around and said to Katie, "I'm sure he just got delayed. He'll be here. As far as Seb? Trust me, none of us will let him get within ten feet of you."

"Ever the protective one, huh Mel?" Brian winked at his wife.

"Well, you know me."

"Very much so," he said, and kissed her cheek so he wouldn't ruin her lipstick. "Wouldn't have you any other way."

"Y'all are really cute!" Katie smiled at them.

"Ohhh," Lance groaned, "I *so* miss that southern accent. I'm fixin' to go home here in a couple of months and I can't wait!"

"Fixin' to?" Melody questioned.

"It means 'going to,'" Katie corrected. "It's a southern term. There's fixin' to, y'all, all y'all, djeet yet, far piece…"

"Oh, please stop." Lance begged. "You're breakin' my heart!"

"Why?" Katie laughed.

"Please tell me you don't know how to play Texas Hold 'em," he begged.

She giggled. "With my eyes closed."

"You're killin' me!"

"Why?"

"Because you are about as close to perfect as I can get with my list, yet you don't want to date at the moment," he explained.

"Doesn't mean we can't have fun tonight with the dancing and joking around."

He shook his head. "You're still killin' me."

Just then, the music began to play for them to walk in. The wedding planner, Mrs. Lopez, went into her zone, getting everyone down the aisle at the appropriate times.

"We're next," Lance said quietly to Katie.

"Shhh!" Mrs. Lopez insisted. "Now. Go….go!" She shooed them down the aisle.

"Do you see them?" Lance asked through his smile. Mrs. Lopez said they could talk as long as there was a smile on their face.

Katie searched the people in the rows. When Seb waved to her, she quickly looked at Lance.

"I saw. Ignore him. Is Nick here?" he asked, hoping to distract her. "Smile, or Mrs. Lopez will have your head later."

She forced a smile on her face as she continued to scan the aisles. By the time she reached the front, she had a sick feeling in her stomach. "Nick's not here."

"Just breathe and smile. If you get stressed, look at me and I'll make a face," Lance said, and let her go to take her place beside Melody, as he took his position beside Brian.

"What's wrong?" Melody whispered, as Marissa and Alex made their way down the aisle.

"Seb is here, but Nick isn't."

"Hmmm. I'll say a prayer. Keep a smile on your face. Nothing is wrong. Don't let Stacey see you upset."

"I wouldn't dare. This is her day. I wouldn't dream of putting a damper on it."

Melody squeezed her hand as she said, "Thank you. They've waited for this day for so long."

"I know," she said, squeezing her hand back as Larissa finished her walk down the aisle.

Dressed in a white, A-line wedding dress with a plunging, yet modest neckline, the dress had a fitted bodice, dotted with beaded motifs and appliques. The pleated waist revealed her curves as the skirt cascaded down to the floor with a court train. Her veil was a tiara headpiece, which flowed down around her.

Scott grinned ear to ear as he watched his bride walk down the aisle to him. Katie couldn't help but be caught up in the scene of pure love that played out in front of her. She knew their story and understood what all they went through together. To see Stacey achieve her goal of graduating with her psychology degree while Scott waited for her made her appreciate the idea that true love really did exist in the world. She prayed that the Lord would grant her that feeling someday.

*   *   *

It was a long night. The reception did not take place in the church, because they wanted dancing and to have champagne. Katie danced most of the night with Lance, until she thought her feet would fall off. Seb kept his distance, but a couple of the girls let her know that he kept an eye on her all night. Despite Lance's attempts to distract her and keep her occupied, she couldn't help but be concerned in regards to not seeing or hearing from Nick. It was not like him to stand her up without even a phone call. It was then that she realized she never checked her answering machine…which by that point had three messages she didn't know about.

About halfway through the night, she relented and danced a couple times with Ethan, who gushed over how gorgeous she looked. She politely thanked him before giving Lance the look they already agreed on, where he would come down to save her from someone she didn't want to dance with that night. While she appreciated Lance, she wished with all her might that it was Nick who was coming to rescue her.

*   *   *

When she got home that night around two in the morning, she was exhausted. Taking her shoes off in the elevator, she knew her feet were too swollen to keep them on any longer. Dangling her shoes on her fingers as she finished the walk to her apartment, she hummed one of the last songs she danced with Lance to. When she got her door open, she tossed her shoes to the side before making a beeline for the phone when she saw the answering machine blinking.

"Six messages?" She observed with a furrowed brow. Grabbing a pen and paper, she listened to her messages, her heart rate picking up its pace as each one played. The stress in Seth's voice caused her major concern.

After the last one, she called Seth's cell phone. "Simmons," he answered.

"Seth, it's Katie."

"Katie! Oh! Thank goodness! You have to get down here right away. Are you okay to come down or do you want someone to come get you?"

"I just got back from the wedding. Do I have time to change?"

"No. Come straight here."

"Got it," she said and hung up. She grabbed her slippers with the rubber soles on them so she could wear them in the hospital and ran from her apartment, locking it behind her.

Seth didn't give her any details, but the tone of his voice told her all she needed to know. She was right to be nervous when she didn't see Nick at the wedding. Something went wrong on the raid.

Chapter 5

Spring to Life

Katie rushed into the emergency room in her slippers, green dress from the wedding, and her hair looking frazzled. Her face showed the obvious stress of the situation, as she demanded, "What happened? What's going on? Where is he?"

Emma, Claire, Dakota, Todd, Sandy, and Seth met her in the waiting room. "Nick's been shot," Seth explained.

Katie felt as if he punched her in the stomach while her entire world imploded around her as soon as the words left his mouth. *'If it was a minimal wound, Nick would have been home'*. She took a deep breath to clear her mind. "What happened?" she asked, doing her best to focus on Scott while the room spun around her.

"I'll explain my part so I can get back to work," Sandy explained as she stood there in her scrubs.

"Is he going to be okay?" Katie asked.

"He was in surgery for 3 ½ hours. He was shot in the lower right leg, and lower left chest cavity," Sandy started, and Katie gasped, covering her mouth in shock. "Katie, he's in critical, but in stable condition for now in the ICU. He also suffered a severe concussion, which meant that we had to surgically relieve the pressure from his brain,"

"This can't be happening." Katie hugged her stomach, beside herself. "This *cannot* be happening!" Panic had overtaken her usual responses as she had flashes of Jax fly through her mind.

"Katie, please listen. We have him in a medically induced coma to improve his survival chances and reduce the possibility of brain damage. He is currently on a ventilator, meaning a machine is breathing for him. Additionally, he has a chest tube to drain the blood out of his lungs. He also has a feeding tube, urinary catheter, and an IV, so it looks like he's in pretty bad shape with all of the tubes in him and the machines in the room to monitor him. However, it's just standard medical practice and precautions. We use the tubes to give him fluid, food, and monitor his input and output in order to increase his chances of survival. The good news is that he has many things going for him. He's extremely fit and is a strong-willed person. He's being closely monitored and I suspect he'll make a full recovery. Knowing him as well as I do, I'll bet he'll be walking out of here in about two weeks."

"I don't…What happened on scene?" Katie asked Seth.

"That's my cue. Katie, here's my card with my cell number." Sandy gave her the card. "Keep it with you and call me if you need me…day or night."

"Thank you." She accepted the card. Sandy gave her a hug before she left the waiting room. "Seth. I want to see him, but I need to know what happened first."

"We had been tracking down a shipment of guns by the Rodchenko's and finally got a tip on a possible place where they were being stored," he explained. "I know he was supposed to go with you to the rehearsal dinner and I should have let him go," he sighed, beside himself.

"Please. I need to know what happened. Please focus?" Katie asked

*   *   *

"They had it hidden under our noses?" Nick asked, stunned as they pulled up to a six-story apartment building. It was the older style brick, with fire escapes along the backside of the building, which was not in a good neighborhood.

"We were concentrating on warehouses, thinking they were bringing it in all at once. Instead they brought it in a little at a time," Seth explained, putting his gear on.

"Sneaky buggars."

"Ready?"

"Let's do this," Nick said, and the teams exited their vehicles. Four black Jeep Cherokees crowded the front doors of the apartment building. "Nice place," Nick commented as a rat ran by his feet when he started up the staircase.

They quickly, but quietly made their way up to the top floor while the other agents cleared the building, and guarded the entrances of the building. "Of course. They couldn't live on the bottom floor," Dakota sighed.

"Consider it your exercise for the day," Todd quipped.

"Will you guys quiet down?" Seth snapped.

There were a few kids in the hallway, so Nick told them to be quiet as he sent them the other direction. There was another team on the floor with them to back them up.

When they arrived to the apartment in question, Seth knocked and shouted, "Rod Danshov! Open up! FBI!" When he didn't hear an immediate response, he instructed Nick, "Kick it in."

"With pleasure." Nick obliged.

When the door flew open, Dakota was the first to see the window wide open to the fire escape. "We got a runner!" he shouted, seeing the man head down to the next level.

"Momma always said there'd be days like this," Nick sighed. "I got him. You guys check it out in here," he said and ran for the window. "These times do try me," he growled, climbing out the window before heading down the fire escape.

Seth followed Nick out the fire escape from the window as soon as Todd and Dakota gave the all clear in the apartment. He decided with it clear in the apartment, he would give Nick back up. By that point, Nick was halfway down the fire escape.

Rod Danshov reached the bottom level and slid down the ladder to the safety of the alley below. When Danshov got to solid ground, he spun around and fired two shots up at the agents.

"Locke! Look out!" Seth shouted, but it was too late.

Searing pain penetrated Nick's lower right leg and he fell forward. A second bullet bit into his left side, on the edge of his bulletproof vest, taking his breath away. He fell forward onto one of the stairs. The last thing he saw in his mind before his head crashed into the iron stair was Katie's face.

* * *

"Wow." Katie felt like she was going to throw up. "You saw him shot in the leg and chest before he hit his head?"

"There was blood everywhere. The chaos that ensued afterward was yelling and shouting of orders, closely followed by sirens blaring. All the commotion made my head spin. All I could see was my friend practically dying in my arms. I actually prayed and I don't pray." He sighed. "I know you're a Christian. You need to pray. I know that God of yours listens to you."

"He would listen to you too, if you were one of His. And, when I say listen to, I don't mean I tell Him what to do and He does it. It's actually the other way around. What I don't understand is, doesn't he wear a bullet proof vest?" Katie asked confused. "How did he get hit in his chest?"

"Rod Danshov fired off a 9 mil. that penetrated his vest on the side where the coverage isn't so thick. It clearly slowed the bullet down or he would be dead instead of in the ICU. As you know, most of the stopping power is in the front and back of the vest. It was a lucky shot…or in this case, an unlucky shot that hit Nick."

"Why did *he* go out the window?" she asked in a slight daze.

"I don't know. I should have gone. I should be the one in ICU, not him."

"I need to see him."

"Are you up for it?"

"Yes."

"Look, I know you have had a lot swirling around you over the last several years, one thing after another. I also know this is the last thing you needed after your last week, but you both are really close."

"We are, but we're keeping it on a friend level."

"I understand that." Seth took her hand into his as he explained, "I know you two are more than that at heart. I know my friend better than he knows himself. You're a perfect match. You both are aware of the rules, but your integrity will not allow either one of you to cross that line. Having said that, he needs to hear your voice. Sandy won't tell you, but the next forty-eight hours will be critical. He needs you."

Katie nodded in understanding. She looped her arm through his as they walked down toward ICU.

*   *   *

"Please remember that this looks worse than it is," the nurse said, taking Katie to Nick's room. "It is bad, but it looks worse."

As soon as Katie saw him, she gulped. Tubes were hooked up to Nick from several points, while the machines monitored him, and another machine breathed for him. Placing her hand on the glass, she rested her forehead on it and took a deep breath to keep her emotions under control. Nick was the strong one. He was the one others looked to in order to keep them safe. He kept *her* safe.

"You want to go in and talk to him?" Seth asked.

Katie stared at Nick, in shock. *Would God take away another friend?* Resting her forehead on the glass, she took a staggering breath of air, her emotions spiraling out of control. *Was God really that cruel? No! He loved her! God loved her! He doesn't want her to hurt. He wants to show her love. He wouldn't have brought her through everything He brought her through to do it again. No one was that mean!*

"No!" She pounded her fist on the window as tears stung her eyes. "No! He wouldn't do this to me! He can't take another one!"

"Katie, are you okay?" Seth rested his hand on the small of her back.

When Katie turned her head toward Seth, he gasped. Pale and shaking, her voice was barely a whisper, "John 15:13, 'There is no greater love than to lay down one's life for one's friends.' Jesus did that. Nick went down the fire escape so you wouldn't. He went down so you guys could stay safe in the apartment."

"Katie, you don't look so good. What if I get you a chair?"

As he turned to go get a chair, Katie whispered, "Please don't take him too." Her knees buckled, and the world spun around her as she dropped to the ground and the dark cloud took over her mind.

*　　*　　*

"I don't know what to do here," Seth said to Sandy, as they stood, talking quietly near the bed Katie was laying on.

"You need to give her time. She'll come to in her own time and then we'll give it another shot. We pushed her. I should have known better. Her week was bad enough, and now this?"

"What happened?" Katie groaned, grabbing her pounding head.

"Katie, I need you sit up, but take it slow," Sandy coaxed, with her arm behind Katie to steady her.

Katie cradled her head in her hands as she sat up in bed. Taking a couple deep breaths as she sat cross-legged on the bed for a few moments, she weakly asked, "Please tell me this is a nightmare?"

"It's not. Now, I need you to be strong for Nick. *He* needs you."

"'I can do all things through Christ who strengthens me,'" Katie quoted Philippians 4:13. "I can do this. God will carry me through. Jesus will walk with me. And, the Spirit will guide my steps. I can do this. Nick needs me."

"Yes, he does. Now, are you ready?"

"I don't know," she admitted as her bottom lip quivered. "I've never been in this position before."

Sandy sat down on the side of the bed and tucked a piece of Katie's hair behind her ear as she said, "You're stronger than you realize. Others have been strong for you. Now it's your turn."

Katie nodded in understanding.

With that, Sandy led her back down the hall to Nick's room. Katie caught her breath when she saw him. Shaking, she slowly let out a breath of air in an attempt to gather her strength. Turning the knob for his door, she said a prayer, "I need you, Lord. Please give me strength?"

Sitting down in the chair next to the bed, she took his hand into hers. Felling the warmth of his hand, she longed to see his smile and hear his laughter. Sighing, she shook her head. "You really need to open those beautiful blue eyes of yours, please?" Resting her chin on her hand, she propped her elbow on the bed.

"They say you can hear me and that you should respond to me. Sandy told me to just talk to you and you'll hear me."

Noticing a Bible on the nightstand, she picked it up. "What do I have to lose?" She closed her eyes and opened the Bible, pointing to the passage before she opened her eyes again. "Isaiah 40:31, 'but those who hope in the LORD will renew their strength. They will soar on wings like eagles; they will run and not grow weary, they will walk and not be faint.' Okay, what else you got?" she asked, and followed the same formula. "Joshua 1:9, 'Have I not commanded you? Be strong and courageous. Do not be terrified; do not be discouraged, for the LORD your God will be with you wherever you go.' Good one. Okay, I'm finding some encouragement here. Let's see what else you got," she said with a smile, and followed the same sequence of closing her eyes. "2 Samuel 7:28, 'O Sovereign LORD, you are God! Your words are trustworthy, and you have promised these good things to your servant.' That's a *really* good one. That one can be used for both of us. Did ya hear that one, Nick?" she asked, and looked up at him. There was no response, so she took his hand into hers and prayed, "Father, Your words have brought encouragement to my heart. It calmed my spirit and soul. I ask You to be here in this hospital with us. I ask You to wrap Your hands of protection around Your servant. He has been a witness for You. You have made him strong. You have surrounded him with people of equal strength of spirit and encouragement. Please give Sandy and the other doctors wisdom regarding his case. Please bring healing to his body and mind. Father, You say in Your word that wherever two or more are gathered that You will be there. We're here. You also say to knock and the door will be opened up to you, seek and you will find. We're seeking. We're begging. Please heal him and let him come back to us. He is in Your hands, Lord. In Jesus' name I pray, Amen."

Wiping the tears from her eyes so she could see, she picked up the Bible again. "Might as well read longer passages. You just sit there and look pretty…" She smiled, remembering when he told her that. "I mean, you just relax while I read. Open your eyes when you're ready. I'm not going anywhere." She opened the Bible to Romans and read, "Paul, a servant of Christ Jesus, called to be an apostle and set apart for the gospel of God…'"

*   *   *

Seth finally kicked her out of the hospital late Sunday night. Knowing she had to begin the police academy the next morning, he wanted her to have a solid night's sleep.

When she got in, she took a shower and went right to bed. Seth was right, it would be a long day, and she wanted to get through it to get to Nick. Her homework would be done in the room, and she could eat at the cafeteria. Nick didn't abandon her at the hospital, she wasn't about to abandon him. Unfortunately, life couldn't come to a complete halt in order for her to be there as much as she wanted to, but she could still be there when she wasn't at the academy.

*   *   *

The police academy was much more difficult than she anticipated. She was grateful to Nick for all of the practical work he did with her, which in turn, allowed her to focus on the details instead of everything being 'fresh and new.' Nick created an excellent foundation for her to build on in regards to training.

Paired with Martin Phillips on day one, only time would tell if they would make it all the way through. At the close of each segment, they would be given a final test. Some of those were critical, which meant that they *had* to pass or they couldn't continue. At which point, if their partner didn't pass, and they did, they would have a new partner.

Instructor Brock began class with, "Welcome to the first day of your worst nightmare."

"That's encouraging," Katie's partner, Martin Phillips, said under his breath.

Katie hid her smile as Instructor Brock continued, "Take a good look around the room. I promise you that half of the people here will not be here at graduation. Chances are, whoever your partner is today, will not be your partner at the end of this…provided *your* still here. This will be the toughest twenty weeks of your life. We do that to make sure you know what you're doing when you go out into the real world. We do it to make sure you can handle the stress of what goes on in the field. What you learn in these twenty weeks could very well save your life."

Katie figured she would take things one day at a time. Knowing what all she had already gone through in life, she didn't think the police academy could be any worse.

*   *   *

Her first week was brutal. With Nick on her mind when she was at the academy, and the academy on her mind when she was at Nick's bedside, she thought for sure she would lose her mind before it was over.

"Nothing personal, but you look like you've got a lot going on…besides the obvious," Martin said, sitting down with her to eat lunch. His light brown hair hung over his face, so he brushed it to the side, showing his dark brown eyes. Standing at around six foot three, he carried his two hundred pounds well.

"Yeah, you're too pretty a young thing to have so much weight on your shoulders," Terry Baldwin, another cadet pointed out as he and his partner, Lee McDaniel, sat down with them.

Katie narrowed her eyes at him. "You don't know a thing about me."

"I know you're a nice, tall drink of water," he said, looking her up and down. "Gotta appreciate that."

"And, I'll bet you think every girl should fall at your feet," she countered, slightly amused.

"Not fall at my feet, but at least shine my shoes."

Martin called him a nasty name under his breath.

"What was that, Phillips?"

"You don't want to know," Lee said with a smirk. He appreciated Katie and Martin's candidness that he had the opportunity to witness over the week, and he didn't appreciate his partner. He couldn't *wait* for Terry to not pass one of the critical areas so he could be rid of him.

"Eh, no matter. Point is," Terry looked back to Katie, "I have a feeling you and I will be going out before the end of these twenty weeks."

"Amazing." Katie sat back in her seat and crossed her arms. "Egotistical *and* conceded. How do you manage to tear yourself away from the mirror each morning?"

He sighed. "It's not easy, but I know things have to get done."

"I'll bet you spend more time on your appearance than I do."

"That's because you're a natural beauty."

"And, your heart is naturally hideous," Katie said, and got up from the table. She took her lunch out into the courtyard to eat it instead of staying to eat with Terry.

Martin, carrying his lunch, met her out in the courtyard. "That was awesome! I knew I liked you!" He chuckled as he settled on the ground next to her.

"Sorry I left. He seemed to be enjoying himself so much, I didn't want to infringe on his territory."

"You're funny. My wife would love you."

"Well, we get through this and maybe we can all get together. I would love to meet her."

"Sounds good. Now, wanna tell me what's on your mind?"

"Honestly?"

"If we don't trust each other, we won't make it through all twenty weeks, so might as well start now."

"I have a friend who is in the hospital in a medically induced coma. That's where I go to straight from here. I'm having a hard time staying focused on where I'm supposed to be. I know I can do this with my eyes closed. Not that it will be easy, mind you, it's that I was already trained by an FBI agent."

"Really? That's cool!"

"They want to fast-track me into Quantico, but I have to get through the academy, then two years as a cop before I can head out there."

"Well, it sounds like they have a lot of faith in you. How well do you shoot?"

"See that sign in front of the building?"

"The little 'stay off the grass' sign?"

"Yeah."

"That's, what, fifty feet from here?"

"Yep. I can hit that without a problem all day."

"Nice! How's your driving?"

"Oh, that was a fun lesson," she laughed in remembrance. "Nick was terrified on the first day, but I'm a quick learner and…" she sighed.

"What is it?"

"Nick's the one in the hospital."

"Ohhhh," he said in understanding, "You and Nick are really close, huh?"

She nodded in response.

"Are you more than friends?"

She shook her head.

"What happened to him?"

"He was shot."

"Wow. Sorry."

"We won't even know anything until they take him out of the coma."

"When will that be?"

"Well, it's been a week. His chest tube is getting pulled today. They will probably start to bring him around next Monday, but I'm hoping they do it on Sunday so I can be there."

"Wow. That *is* heavy."

"He'll make it, though," she said, lost in her own thoughts. "He has to."

*   *   *

Saturday was almost torture as it dragged by slowly. Sandy wanted to give Nick one more day before she began to bring him out of the coma. Slowly weaning him off the ventilator starting on Saturday morning, Sandy was confident she would be able to pull it Sunday morning with no problem. Her bigger concern was when he would wake up. Nature, God, and Nick would have to work together on that one. She wasn't sure how long Katie would be able to handle it, though. She looked rough, but she needed to stay focused on her work in order to pass the academy. There was a lot riding on her passing the police academy, but she knew where Katie's heart was…it was with Nick.

*   *   *

Katie ran into the hospital on Monday night after class hoping to see him wide-awake and telling jokes. When she ran onto the unit, the nurse stopped her. "Katie, there's been no change."

She stopped short, almost dropping her books. "But, Sandy said –"

"It may take days," the nurse said, hoping to give her some form of comfort.

Katie gulped. Her lip quivered as she said, "But, he's doing well. That's why they took him off the ventilator. He'll be fine. You'll see."

"I hope you're right, but I wanted to warn you."

Katie walked into the room, looking as if she were carrying the weight of the world on her shoulders."Hey, dude, we need to talk," she said, sitting down on the chair. "See, you're supposed to be awake already. You're strong. You're supposed to be around forever. Did you know that? Did you know that if something happens to you, that it may be the last straw for me?" she asked, as a single tear slid down her cheek. "Don't you know what you actually mean to me? My life was changed the instant you walked into it. I know I should have told you all of this before, but I feel if something happens to you and I didn't tell you, that I would regret it forever. I only wish I could see your beautiful blue eyes and gorgeous smile. I want see those dimples and quirky grin. I want to hear that Aussie accent say something that will require you to put your foot in your mouth again. I want…" her voice trailed off. She sighed before she admitted, "I don't know why we're dancing around this issue. I'm in love with you just as much as you're in love with me."

*   *   *

"Any news yet?" Martin asked when she walked into the room the next morning.

She shook her head. "None."

Instructor Brock entered the room with his arms full of manuals. "Situation: A husband is in a local convenient store late at night due to his pregnant wife's craving for butter pecan ice cream." He set the books down and went to the front of the table, leaning on it with his arms crossed. "He picks up the precious cargo and only gets two steps toward the counter to pay for his ice cream, so close to completing his mission of mercy. The mercy was on him, by the way. Anyway, another man enters the convenient store and pulls a gun on the young man behind the counter." There were a few whispers as he continued, "Now, knowing how women are when they are pregnant, of absolutely no offense to Cadets MacKenna, Thompson, or Sullivan, of course, women tend to get testy when their cravings are not met. This poor man has a decision to make. He has to get out of the convenient store with or without the ice cream. With the ice cream comes with rewards beyond measure…without it could mean certain death," he said, and snickers were heard throughout the room. "If the man kills the person holding up the convenient store, would that be justified use of deadly force?"

The room burst out in laughter.

"Depends," one of the cadets spoke up.

"Depends on what, Cadet Barker?" Instructor Brock asked. Cadet Baker had a way of bringing the comedic diversion to the classroom.

"Depends on how far along in her pregnancy she is."

The laughter filled the room once again as class began. Katie enjoyed the little comical scenarios the instructors came up with to lighten the mood of the otherwise heavy topics they broached each day.

*   *   *

"Under what situations would you surrender your firearm?" Instructor Williams asked as they were studying Tuesday afternoon after lunch.

"Never," Katie piped up, but quickly covered her mouth because she spoke out of turn.

"Didn't see a hand, but you're right. Good answer," he acknowledged. "Please come forward, Cadet MacKenna."

Katie nervously left her seat for the front, her heart racing. When she got there, he whipped her around with his arm around her neck and his gun was suddenly to her head. There were gasps in the room as the instructor asked, "What do you do? If you come on scene and this is in front of you? These are real situations, folks."

Katie tapped his arm to get his attention.

"Yes?" he asked, surprised she could still think straight. In past classes, the cadet was scared stiff, and looked to the other cadets for help.

"Two options."

"Really?" Now he was intrigued. "What would they be?"

"Shooting the hostage taker could prove deadly for the hostage if he fires his gun on the way down. So I would say to shoot the hostage, preferably in the leg. If you shoot them in the leg, they go down, and you are taking the hostage out of the equation."

"While I would not condone that, I gotta ask what your second option is?"

Katie grabbed his arm, bent in half, and used the inertia to flip him over her shoulder. She then stepped on the wrist that contained the gun before she pulled the gun from the instructor's hand and pointed it at the ceiling, making sure the safety was on. "The hostage gets themselves out of the situation. Under normal circumstances, I would point it at your head to dissolve the situation. However, since I know this is loaded," she said and dropped the magazine before popping the bullet from its chamber, "I wouldn't point a loaded weapon at anyone without the intent to shoot."

The instructor, while impressed, was in shock. He got off the ground and accepted his disarmed weapon, the bullet, and the magazine before Katie took her seat. "Okay, well," he cleared his throat as he looked just as stunned as the cadets and the two instructors who were seated in the room with them, "seems Cadet MacKenna has some interesting theories. Any other input?" When no one spoke, he continued his class on Active Shooter.

Just as class let out, Katie grabbed her books, hoping to get to the hospital as soon as possible…to Nick.

"Cadet MacKenna, can you stay after for a minute?" Instructor Williams asked as people dispersed.

Martin looked at Katie in concern. He knew she wanted to get to Nick as soon as possible. "I'll, uh, catch ya out in the hall when you're done," he said, making it clear to her that he wanted to know what happened.

Nodding in response, she headed to the front of the room where the three instructors, Williams, Brock, and Hancock, were waiting. "Um," she nervously cleared her throat, "What, uh, did I do something wrong?"

"Wrong? Oh! Heavens no!" Instructor Hancock exclaimed. "Quite the contrary. We are curious, though."

"About what?" Katie couldn't help the nerves that were screaming at her from the inside.

Instructor Williams crossed his arms, making him look more bulky than he was already. "Where did you learn to do that?"

"Yeah. That's not the first time you've surprised us since we started last week," Instructor Hancock pointed out.

Katie nervously rubbed the back of her neck. She shrugged, understanding the truth would come out eventually. "I have been trained by an FBI agent. Chief Anderson is working with Director Shultz of the FBI Cleveland Office in order to get me through the academy, through my two years as an officer, and then their intention is to get me sent to Quantico."

"I see," Instructor Williams said, deep in thought.

"Thank you for your honesty. Our concern was that you could possibly be a ringer or someone sent in to check us out," Instructor Hancock explained. "Exactly how long have you been working with this FBI agent?"

"A little over two years," she responded, still unsure if she were in trouble.

"So, you've never been through the police academy before?" Instructor Hancock asked.

"No, sir."

"And, it is your intention to complete the training, only to be an officer for two years?" Instructor Williams asked.

"My intention and God's plans may differ. Only He knows what my future truly holds."

"Ohhhh, you're one of *those*," Instructor Williams said snidely.

"One of what?"

"A Christian."

"Whether or not I'm a Christian does not determine whether or not I am a good officer," Katie said, feeling on edge. "My instincts and your training determine that."

"Well, from what I've seen, you shouldn't have any problems," Instructor Hancock pointed out. "You took down Williams without even breaking a nail."

Katie bit her tongue. Ohhhhh! How she wanted to respond to that comment. If it were anyone but one of her instructors, she would have floored them with her words. However, she needed them for the next nineteen weeks, so she would keep her tongue in check.

"Enough said," Instructor Williams snapped.

"Thank you for your time, Cadet," Instructor Brock said, in effect dismissing her. "We'll be curious to see how you fair in our training."

"I could respond in such a way that would sound like I was buttering you up. So, instead, I'll just say 'so am I' and leave it at that."

"Wise too," Instructor Brock observed. "That will serve you well. Have a good evening, Cadet."

"Thank you, sirs," she said and left the room.

She no sooner stepped out of the room, when Marin grabbed her arm and escorted her down the hall. "You look pale as all get out. What happened?" he demanded.

"They know an agent trained me."

"Well, of course they know. All of the cadets also know you set the bar way higher than they anticipated. What you did was amazing!"

"Thank you. I didn't think, though. I just did it."

"That's what makes it amazing. Look, you're going to have to show me some of those moves."

"I'm sure they'll show you when we get to self-defense. I have to get to Nick."

"I know. Look, don't worry about them. This should be a breeze. I'm just thankful you ended up as my partner."

"Thanks, but…"

"I know. Go. Maybe he'll be awake this time."

"From your lips to God's ears."

*   *   *

Katie's feet couldn't get her to Nick's room quick enough. "Katie, I'm sorry, but there's still no change," the nurse explained as she got near their desk.

"I see. And, what does Dr. Simmons say?"

"She said any day now."

"What *else* did she say?" Katie asked, sensing there was more.

The nurse looked both ways down the hall to make sure no one saw her. She quietly said, "Between you and me?"

"Definitely," Katie agreed, leaning on the counter.

"She said she's surprised he hasn't woken up yet. She said he's stronger than this and she doesn't know why he didn't wake this morning at the latest."

"I see," Katie squeaked out. She glanced over her shoulder toward his room, where he still lay motionless. Her heart skipped a beat as she asked, "What happens if he doesn't wake soon?"

The nurse gave her a sympathetic look and rested her hand on Katie's shoulder. "He'll wake. I know he will."

"But, what happens?"

"You just have to have faith."

Irritated, Katie went into Nick's room. Setting her books and jacket on the chair, she walked over to Nick's bedside and took his hand into hers. "Okay, enough of this," Katie reprimanded him. "I have been here every day for over a week now. All I want is to see those beautiful eyes and that gorgeous smile of yours. So, you need to open your eyes now," she demanded, with no response. "Seriously, Nick," she sat down, with his hand still in hers, "We've read the Bible. We've talked for hours. They took the ventilator off on Sunday. They've taken you off the medicine keeping you in that coma. It's your turn." She growled in frustration. "Do you understand what all you're missing? You've been training me for over two years. You're missing the actual classes. I need you to wake up. I need you to open your eyes. I need you to…I need you, Nick," she admitted. "Look, I know I am in love with you. I know it may not be reciprocated, but I also don't want to lose you. If I can only have you as a friend, I'm okay with that. However, the key is to have you in my life. Will you please wake up?"

After the conversation with her instructors, this was *not* what she wanted. "Why won't you wake up?" she asked as she got out of her seat and paced the room. "I've done everything I was supposed to do." She looked toward Heaven, realizing this conversation should be between her and God, not her and Nick. "I know You can hear me, Lord. I have a ton of admiration, honor, and respect for You, but a girl can only take so much. Why is it that when I get close to someone, You pull them away? I swear! There are times where I don't understand Your methods at all."

The Spirit brought Isaiah 55:8&9 to her mind. *'"For my thoughts are not your thoughts, neither are your ways my ways," declares the LORD. "As the heavens are higher than the earth, so are my ways higher than your ways and my thoughts than your thoughts.'"*

"I understand that," Katie acknowledged. "What I don't understand is why you let it happen in the first place."

"Hey, Katie." Seth walked into the room. "Am I interrupting?"

"Nope. C'mon in," she said, upset, as she sat down on the chair beside the bed.

Seth rested his hand on her shoulder. "Sandy said it could be a while."

"There's something I'm missing," Katie said, doing her best to connect the dots. "This doesn't make sense. Why would doing his job as well as he does, cautious as he is, land him in here?"

"Katie, not everything in this world makes sense. Nick's my best friend. In doing what we do each day, we frequently see things that make us wonder."

"If there's a reason, I'm not seeing it. I don't understand. In John 15:13, it says, 'There is no greater love than to lay down one's life for one's friends.' He does that. He lays down his life every day for his country, without a care about his own life. He does it when he runs into a problem situation in order to protect those on his team. He does it when –" she stopped, her thoughts interrupted by memories of Nick. She took a deep breath as she dropped her head in her hands. "I just don't understand."

Seth crouched beside her. "There are people who lay their lives on the line every day, but people don't think twice about them. Whether it's the soldier fighting to keep the battles away from his homeland and family, or the agent, doing their best to stop the next terror attack, it happens around you every day. Officers lay their lives on the line every day as well. That's why your instructors are so hard on you in training. They don't want you to become a statistic. They don't want to have to wear a black band on their shield to mourn for you. They don't want to have to listen to the heart wrenching 'last call' over the radio, hearing the radio controller calling your badge number, searching for you…and not finding you. They want to make sure you are all safe. Every military member, firefighter, police officer, and agent runs into the horrible situations this world throws, doing their best to keep those they love safe. But, people badmouth them. They yell at them. They even punch, shoot, and at moments, succeed in killing people who are only trying to keep them safe."

Seth let out a slow breath of air as he looked toward the ceiling to control his emotions. "I have buried my share of friends. I have seen things that you see in your nightmares. That's real life for me. All that stuff you see in the news? That's our daily life. And it infuriates me beyond words when someone disrespects a military, EMS, police, FBI, or CIA member. Not everything we do will make sense to everyone, but with our integrity intact, and our focus on keeping this country safe, I can promise you that my team sleeps well at night…and Nick is currently resting comfortably."

"I don't want him to permanently rest in peace, though. Not yet," Katie said, wiping the tears off her cheeks.

"He knows that. He's a fighter, and you can bet that he's fighting this with everything he has in him."

Katie took Nick's hand into hers as she explained, "I want to be on your unit. I know your unit is full of people with integrity, who look out for each other." She looked Seth in the eyes as she said, "Your unit is a family…one that I have never had. I want that, but…" she looked back to Nick.

Seth swore as he stood and paced the room. "I know. I also know the rules. There has to be a way –"

"There won't be a way if he doesn't wake up!" Katie yelled. "I am in love with this man, but if he doesn't wake up, I won't be able to tell him!"

"I heard you," Nick's voice suddenly penetrated the heaviness of the room, sending pure joy into Katie's heart.

"Nick?" she caught her breath.

His eyes fluttered open, as his baby blue eyes locked onto hers. "I heard you."

Seth took in the scene in shock. He was at a loss as to what to do next.

"What happened?" Nick groaned. "Did someone get the license plate of the mac truck that took me out?"

Seth went to the other side of his best friend's bed. "No, man."

"Please tell me that drongo didn't get away?"

"Oh, he did at that moment, but we got him on Monday. Dakota and Todd were like a dog with a bone. They were not letting him get away when we had all that evidence he left behind."

"I don't...ohhhh," he groaned in pain.

"I'll, uh, go get the nurse," Katie excused herself.

"She's a looker." Nick smiled when she left the room. "Who is she? My nurse, maybe?"

Seth gasped, feeling the wind taken from the elation he felt only moments before. *Sandy said his memory might be spotty, but how could he remember the gunrunner and not Katie?* "You, um," he gulped, "you don't know who that was?"

"She's hot. Do you know her?"

"Oh no," he groaned, dropping his head into his hand, shaking it. If Nick lost his memory, it could jeopardize his position as an agent.

"So, I hear you're bright-eyed in here and alert," the nurse walked into the room, closely followed by Katie.

"I don't know that I would go that far." Nick suggested, "Maybe we should just stick with awake for now."

"Um, we have a bit of a problem," Seth told the nurse.

"What's that?" she asked, taking his vital signs.

"He doesn't remember who she is," he said, nodding toward Katie.

Katie gasped, covering her mouth in shock. Tears stung her eyes.

"I know who Katie is, you moron. How could I forget her?"

"But you…you said…"

Nick slapped him on the arm. "You're too easy."

"You have *no idea* how terrified you just made me! Do you realize that could have cost you your job?" Seth shook his head, not sure if he should be angry with him. He sighed. "There are some days I want to smack you!"

He grinned. "Yeah, but you love me just the same."

"I need some fresh air," Seth excused himself. "Be nice to her while I'm gone or I'll sick Sandy on you. She's had one doozy of a week, and that didn't help. I'm surprised she didn't just pass out again," he said and left the room.

"Again?" Nick asked in concern.

Katie didn't move from where she stood, still in shock, so the nurse explained, "She passed out when she saw you in here for the first time. At that point it was around two-thirty in the morning, and as I understand it, she had an interesting couple weeks before that happened. You need to be nice to her, or I agree. I'll sick Dr. Simmons on you," she said, and wrote something down on his chart. "Do you want something to eat?"

"Not at the moment. I think Katie and I need to talk," he said, not taking his eyes off her.

"How about some broth? That way I can tell the good doctor that you're being a wise and cooperative patient," she coaxed.

"Fine. Just let me talk to this young lady before she passes out again."

"Will do," she said, and left.

"Come and sit." Nick gestured toward the empty chair beside the bed. "You look like you need it."

Katie shook her head, otherwise not moving a muscle.

"Please?"

"You said you didn't remember me."

"How could I forget you? Please, come and sit?"

She slowly sat in the chair with her arms crossed, hugging herself. "Why did you do that?"

"Because I figured it would break the tension I woke up to in the room." Before she could answer, he explained, "I heard you. I know you've been with me every day as well."

"I have," Katie said, cautiously. *Did he hear what she said?*

He reached for her hand, and was relieved when she took his hand into hers. "There, that's better."

"Nick, I'm just glad you're awake. How do you feel?"

"There's more than that bothering you," he observed.

"My instructors figured out that I know a lot more than the average cadet."

"Really? What did you do?"

She chuckled. "Ohhhh, I'll tell you that later."

"You're smile," he said, brushing his hand on her cheek.

"Nick, we can't." She shook her head. "I don't want to work at the FBI and not be on your unit. If we're on the same unit, we can't have a relationship."

"What's more important?"

Katie shook her head. "We have so much going on. I don't want to muck everything up. I have enough on my mind as it is. Ya see, my best friend –"

"Best friend? Is that all I am?"

She hesitated before she responded, "You know you're more than that."

"Then…" He gestured for her to continue.

"We can't," she said, dropping her head. "We both have worked too long and hard to get to where we are."

"How can we live life to the fullest like God wants us to, if we're focused on only our careers? Do you love me?"

"Of course I do."

"Are you *in love* with me?"

"Of course I –" she stopped, realizing what she was about to say. "I don't think I should answer that."

"Why not?"

"Because I don't want Him to take you too."

"Who?"

"God."

"*What*?"

"When I get that close to someone, He takes them away."

"Katie, you have to trust Him more than that."

"I do."

"John 10:10, says, 'The thief cometh not but to steal and to kill and to destroy. I am come that they might have life, and that they might have it more abundantly.' Don't let him steal and destroy us. Jesus wants us to live life to the fullest. What if His plan includes us being together?"

"What if it doesn't?"

"Oh my word! Katie! I'll say it first. I'm in love with you. Do you hear me?"

"I…I can't," she said, shaking her head. Grabbing her stuff from the other chair, she ran out of the room without another word.

"Oh, this shouldn't be so complicated." Nick groaned, covering his eyes with his hands. "It shouldn't be!"

*   *   *

Over the next few days, Katie avoided going back to the hospital. She loved Nick, but now was not the time. She needed to focus on her training or all the work they'd done over the last two years would have been in vain.

"Okay, break up in teams of two with your partners and spread around the room," Instructor Hancock ordered. "We're going to venture into self-defense today."

"Sir," Martin raised his hand. Before the instructor could call on him, he said, "May I change partners with Cadet Baldwin?" he asked, referring to Terry.

Snickers came from around the room while the instructor asked, "Why?"

"Well, I know who trained her," he started. "I also know that given the right circumstance, she could very well slap me into next Tuesday. However, I love my wife and want to make sure to see her after this is over…without the use of crutches," he said, as laughter came from around the room again.

"So, how does you switching with Baldwin make any sense?"

"Well, since he seems to think that women should fall all over him and are created to do his bidding, I think it only appropriate that Cadet MacKenna have the opportunity to either confirm that or show him the error of his ways. And, I do believe that this is the opportune time to do such a thing."

Instructor Hancock considered his words for a moment before he asked Katie, "Are you okay with this?"

"I don't have a problem with it, as long as he's aware that I've had an extremely difficult week."

"I'll take it easy on you," Terry said with a wink.

"That was warning to you, not a plea for mercy," Katie clarified.

His eyes just about popped out of his head when Instructor Hancock agreed. "Go ahead and switch."

Katie took mercy on him in the beginning until Katie had him in a headlock, and he said, "MacKenna, while I appreciate having your arm around me, feeling your sweet breath on my face, I –"

Katie cut him off by wrapping her leg around his ankle and kicking it out from under him. As soon as he hit the ground, Katie grabbed his wrist and flipped it behind his back. She pulled up on it as she got down near his ear, and explained, "I would never give you the time of day, let alone give the slightest inclination of adoration in your direction. You are a worthless scumbag who needs to be taught that the world does not revolve around you. You need to understand that women need to be cherished. They are not here to do your bidding. Now, either I, or another woman down the road will have the pleasure of teaching you that lesson. Take this as a warning," she said, and pulled up on his arm a little higher. He let out a yelp, and since her intention was to teach him a lesson, not dislocate his shoulder, she let him go.

He scrambled to get off the ground. When he did, he balled his fist and pulled his arm back. "You little –"

Katie grabbed his fist and kicked him in the knee. Seeing him drop to the ground while she still had a hold of his wrist, she twisted it and explained. "Do *not* mess with me. Do we have an understanding?"

"Yes, ma'am," Terry said with tears in his eyes. "Just let me go."

"You make my skin crawl," she said, disgusted.

As cheers and whoops of celebration rung from around the room, Instructor Hancock leaned over to Katie and asked, "Would you please release Cadet Baldwin now?" Terry Baldwin was not a small guy, and as angry as Katie was, she could still see the pleased look on the instructor's face. "I believe he learned his lesson. On a side note?" Instructor Hancock continued as he knelt in front of Terry, "It's better that your fellow cadet taught you this lesson rather than you learning it out on the streets. Criminals are not anywhere as nice as she has been."

"Yes, sir," he said, and his arm dropped to the side as Katie released him. "I'm sorry, Katie."

"That's Cadet MacKenna to you," Katie corrected and walked off to the side to get her water. "And don't you forget it."

*   *   *

Katie was so relieved to walk out of there on Friday she couldn't stand it. With the admiration of her classmates, she felt the need to celebrate. She wanted to tell…she stopped the thought in her mind. She couldn't go to Nick. With the question still in

138

the air, and the way she left things, she felt embarrassed and mortified at the same time.

By the time she arrived at her apartment, and saw Nick's across the hall, any feeling of celebration was diminished. All she wanted to do was take a long, hot bath, and start the week over again.

She got a knock on her door around eight that night. Being in a secure building, she knew only someone with a key card would have access. She looked out the peephole to see Seth. "What in the world?" she asked, opening the door in her pajamas. "Seth, what are you doing here?"

Surprised to see her in flannel pants, a tank top, and slippers, he brushed that aside as he went into the apartment and paced the living room. "I need to talk to you."

Crossing her arms as she watched him wear a spot in her new carpet, she sighed. "I was wondering when this was coming."

He stopped and looked toward her. "He loves you, ya know?"

"I do. And, I love him, but it can't happen."

"Why not?"

"Because if we do, then all of the work we did would have been for nothing."

"Why?"

"If we can't be on the same unit, I don't want to be an agent. If I'm not an agent, all the work we did would have been in vain. I want to be an officer, and then an agent."

He thought for a moment before he asked, "What's more important to you?"

"Meaning?"

"Do you want to be an agent or do you want to be with him."

"I don't know."

"Oh!" He threw his hands in the air, exasperated. "Why can't you both just be in love and work together?"

"Ask the FBI." Katie rolled her eyes. "According to their rules, we can't be on the same unit if we're in a relationship. That is a hardened fact we cannot get around."

He took a moment and locked eyes with her. "Not if they don't know."

"I won't get y'all in trouble."

"What if you two just have a relationship for now, and we'll breach the subject in a couple of years if it's still intact."

"Meaning?"

He rested his hands on the sides of her arms, and explained, "You have a little over two years with the police department before we even have to think about it being a problem. If you two continue, there are other areas where you could work and still be on the same unit."

She cocked her head to the side. "How is that possible?"

"Time has a way of working things out. Look, he's been a mess since you left on Tuesday. Whatever progress he has made has been slow at best. He has no motivation. He needs you. Whatever the dumb lug said, he needs you."

She sighed. "Okay, let me change and we'll go down to the hospital."

"Thank you. I think you will make a world of difference!"

*　*　*

Katie's stomach was in knots the entire ride to the hospital. *Would they be able to have a relationship? Would he want a relationship with her anymore after the way she behaved?*

"I know you're nervous, but please don't be. You two were made for each other," Seth said, escorting her down the hall to Nick's room.

Nervously nibbling on her nails, she only nodded in response.

"Trust me. I know he loves you."

"I know," she said, taking a deep breath when she saw him through the window of his new room that they moved him into the day before. He looked despondent while he played with his food. Claire and Emma were in there doing their best to convince him to eat.

"What is *she* doing here?" Claire leapt to her feet, upset, when they walked into the room. "Get her out of here!"

"No. She needs to be here," Seth said. "Nick needs her."

"He does *not*," she growled. "He doesn't *need* anyone…especially a spoiled Irish princess. This is ridiculous!" She threw her hands in the air.

"Katie?" Nick asked, not taking his eyes off her as soon as she walked into the room.

"Emma, would you and Claire please excuse us?" Seth asked.

"With pleasure. Maybe her presence will be a good thing," Emma said, looping her arm around Claire's. When Claire pulled away, Emma grabbed her arm and roughly escorted her from the room.

"She's going to be his ruin! Mark my words! She will rip his heart out and feed it to him!" Claire yelled as they went down the hall until she was no longer in earshot.

"Well, that was fun." Seth smirked. "Now." He rested his hands on Katie's shoulders. He nudged her toward the bed, as he said, "you two need to talk. I have a feeling it may take a while, so I'll stand outside until you guys need me."

As soon as the door closed behind him, Nick tapped the bed at his side. "C'mon over here, please?" he asked.

Katie reluctantly maneuvered over to the side of his bed and quietly sat down, wrapping her arms around herself in protection.

When he touched her, Katie jumped. "Katie, I would never hurt you," he pleaded. "Please look at me?"

When she turned to him, he saw the puffiness of her eyes.

"I would never purposely hurt you," he corrected himself. "I thought you would laugh."

"What would happen if you didn't remember me?"

"How could I ever do that? You're never far from my thoughts, Katie. I look forward to seeing your face every day. When you didn't come in these last few days, it broke my heart."

"I have to admit that I had to take my frustration out on another cadet," she admitted.

"What did you do?" he asked, as a smile formed on his face.

"I taught this insignificant, childish, arrogant –"

"Never mind," he cut her off. "I have an idea. Knowing you, I would imagine you had to teach him a lesson or two anyway."

"Yep."

"And," he took her hand into his, "knowing you the way I do, I would imagine you didn't get in any trouble either."

She grinned. "Nope."

"I love your smile," he brushed her cheek with his fingers.

"Seth said to go for it, and we would figure it out when the time comes."

"Katie, I love you, and would do anything for you. This includes giving up my career to be with you."

"But, don't you understand that I don't want you to? I love who you are. I love who God created you to be. I love –"

He stopped her from talking as he pulled her toward him. She glanced from his eyes to his lips and back again while they neared each other.

"I am in love with you, Katie Marie MacKenna. You know that, right?"

"I do. And, you know I am in love with you too, Nicolas Scott Locke?"

"I do." He smiled. He finished pulling her to him, and they embraced in a passionate kiss, taking Katie's breath away. At first, it was gentle and tender, like he was, before it escalated quickly into the undeniable love they had for each other.

"Yes!" They heard Seth cheer in the hallway and burst out in laughter.

As they rested their foreheads on each other's and looked into the eyes of the other, Nick promised, "I promise to never hurt you on purpose."

"And I promise to never hurt you on purpose. I love you too much for that."

"I agree. Are you sure you're ready to take this step?"

"I'm sure that I'm not ready to have any regrets…which I would have if we didn't at least try it."

"I agree. Life is too short for regrets."

"God said we are to live life, and live it to the fullest. I intend to do so."

"With you."

"With you," she said and gently ran her fingers through his hair as they both carried a smile that would never fade.

*   *   *

The day Nick finally got released from the hospital was a Saturday morning. Katie was grateful, because she knew she would be able to take care of him for that weekend before having to go back to class.

"Here we are. Home sweet home. You stay right here for a minute," Katie said, propping him against the wall next to the door. Grabbing a set of sheets from the linen closet, she opened the sofa bed and made it for him.

"Easy now," Nick said, wrapping his right arm over her shoulder to lean on her while they made their way across the living room to the sofa bed.

Holding his side, he gingerly sat down on the sofa bed and Katie covered him, making sure he was comfortable. "Okay, what do you want to eat?"

"Anything but hospital food," he grumbled, settling in, exhausted. It took all he had just to get up to the apartment.

"You may regret that statement," Katie commented, scanning the contents of his refrigerator. "My cookbook is limited at best."

"I need to teach you how to cook. What about something simple, like an omelet."

"Think I can try that. I've never made or even had an omelet before."

"Really?" he asked, stunned.

"Really. My breakfast generally consists of peanut butter toast and orange juice."

"Still?"

Katie laughed. "Yes."

"Have you made scrambled eggs before?"

"Yeah."

"It's kind of like that. You basically scramble everything and then flip it in half when you put it on the plate."

"Cool. I think I can do that," she said, pulling the eggs, green peppers, red peppers, and onion out of the refrigerator.

After breaking the eggs into a bowl, she added the cut up peppers and onion to the mix and dumped it into a pan. She let it cook for only so long before she flipped it onto a plate. She crinkled her nose when it flopped a little too much before it splatted. "Not sure if this is good or not, but here ya go," she said, handing it to Nick.

Nick poked at it with the fork for a moment, examining it. "Maybe I need to teach you a little more how to cook. I don't think this is cooked enough."

Katie sighed. "Okay, what about chicken and dumplings? I have that stuff in my apartment."

"Chicken and dumplings it is. Gonna have to see if maybe Emma can help you over the next couple of weeks in cooking, because I think we may need a more versatile food variety in the future," he said with a smile. "Can't see only eating chicken and dumplings for the rest of our lives."

Chapter 6

Hope Springs

For once, Katie finally felt like her life was on the right path. There was a hope and spring in her step as she sailed through the various parts of the academy. Whether it was the EVO (Emergency Vehicle Operation) class, Firearms, Active Shooter class, First Aide, Search and Seizure, Mechanics of Arrest, or the other myriad of classes she had during the academy, she went after them with everything within her. She wasn't about to let anyone or anything stand in her way. Graduating in the top of her class, closely followed by a grateful Martin Phillips to have been her partner, they were one of the few pairs who stayed intact through the entire program, with the exception of Lee McDaniel and Terry Baldwin. Katie didn't mind that Lee made it through, but she really didn't like Terry, and was not happy when she found out he was in her precinct as well.

"I'm really proud of you," Nick said in mid-October, just after her graduation. They went out to eat with the rest of the group to celebrate.

Katie grinned. "Thank you!"

"Phase two is now completed," Seth said as he raised his glass in a toast, while they sat at a table at MacGreggor's. "Here's to the next two years. May they be as swift and safe as the academy, allowing you to head to Quantico with no more problems."

"Here! Here!" Emma said as everyone toasted. Claire refused to attend, but the others from the unit were there.

"So, when do you officially start?" Dakota asked.

"I have about two weeks before I have my first day."

"I see. And, what are you going to do in the meantime?"

"Well, I actually asked for the two weeks," Katie admitted. "We don't normally get that, but I knew I still had to go to Oklahoma to retrieve my stuff."

"Are you going with her?" Todd asked Nick.

"Actually, no," Nick grumbled. "Unfortunately, the Rodchenko's have vetoed that and dictated that a vacation at this particular point in time is not possible."

"Meaning?"

"Meaning, the little buggars are up to something, and I have to figure it out."

"I see."

"Officer MacKenna?" the host asked, as he approached the table.

"Yes, sir," she acknowledged, feeling a little self-conscious about the title, even though she earned it.

"I was asked to give this to you," he said, handing her an envelope before he disappeared.

"What is it?" Nick asked, while she tore open the envelope.

"Interesting." She scanned the note before flagging the waiter as she replaced her hand with a napkin to hold the note.

"What is it?" Seth got out of his seat from the other side of the table and looked over her shoulder. With a furrowed brow, he added, "Odd."

"What does it say?" Dakota asked, concern evident on everyone's face.

"It says," Katie cleared her throat, "'Congratulations, Katie. I had faith that you would be able to complete the academy without any problems. Of course, that now places us on opposite sides of the law. So, let's play a little game. Are you the hunter…or the prey?'"

"Yes, ma'am?" the waiter asked, appearing to Katie's side.

"Would you mind getting me a plastic bag?"

"Would plastic wrap work?"

"Yep. That'll do," she agreed.

"Where's the host?" Nick asked, scanning the restaurant. He got out of his seat with Seth on his heels. "Who gave you that note?" Nick demanded.

"I don't know."

Nick showed him his badge and ID. "I'm going to ask again. Who gave you that note?"

"I honestly don't know," the host exclaimed, fear laced through his voice. "The young man gave me a twenty dollar bill and asked me to give it to her."

"If we have you look at photos, would you be able to identify him?"

"No. It happened too fast."

"What about the twenty?" Nick asked. "Where is it?"

When the young man pulled it from his pocket, Nick snatched it, wrapping it in a napkin.

"Sir! I must object! That's mine!"

"It may be, but it could contain fingerprints. Sorry, mate, it's evidence," he said, leaving the host stunned.

"Nice. But, you know there could be a ton of fingerprints on that thing."

"Hey, if we even remotely get a hit, it will give us a place to start."

"There's always hope," Seth sighed.

*   *   *

Katie and Nick had a rather strong discussion about her upcoming trip to Oklahoma after she received that letter. She refused to let whoever gave her that note dictate her schedule, and decided to continue with her trip. She needed to clean out her storage shed, talk with her father, and finally visit the graves of her mother, Jax, and Anna. She felt she needed to say good-bye to them. She also felt she needed settle things between her and her father, so there were no more loose ends in her life. Only then could she feel free to move forward without regrets or shadows of her past haunting her.

"Are you sure you're ready?" Nick asked, while he stood with her beside the gate at the airport.

"I am. We're in a wonderful place. I don't want my past hanging around my neck anymore. I need to deal with it all and get it over with."

"You're very brave."

"I don't think so, but thank you."

"You are not only facing your past, but you're finally dealing with your dad one-on-one. You've graduated at the top of your class in the academy, and are headed into a very courageous position when you get back."

"Yeah, a rookie. Like *that's* going to be easy."

"Just watch your p's and q's, and pay attention to your training officer, and you should be okay."

"That's what they tell me. Of course, not quite sure how I made it in the top of my class with Instructor Williams gunning for me."

"Why was he gunning for you?"

"Because I'm a Christian. He didn't care for that."

"That's nothing other Christians in their professions haven't faced. Just stay focused on Jesus and He'll get you through."

"How do you think I've made it this long?" she pointed out.

"Oh, I thought it was my brilliant teaching," he teased. She laughed as she jokingly shoved him. He took the moment and grabbed her in a hug. "I don't want to let you go," he admitted.

"I'll be fine. Trust me and trust the Lord. He'll keep me safe. If He's not done with me, then I'm not going anywhere."

"I know. I only wish you weren't so flippant about it."

She looked up at him. "Really? I'm not flippant. I'm trusting. I've fought to trust Him for years. Why would it surprise you when I finally do?"

"It doesn't."

"You know how much I love you, right?"

"I do. Not sure why you do, but I do. I got an idea," he said, with a mischievous grin.

"What? Do I want to know?"

"As soon as I get a break during these two weeks, I'll fly down there, and we can fly to Las Vegas and get married."

"You're a mess!" Katie laughed. "We can't do that."

"Why not?"

"For one, Seth would kill you. He would want to be there. Besides, if we do that, then we *will* have an issue working on the same unit."

"Not if we figure out another way to do it."

"What do you mean?"

"Well, we're still flipping receptionists. What if you bypass being a police officer, and work as our receptionist?"

She shook her head. "I don't think so."

"Just think about it."

"I will. In the meantime, please be in prayer for me these next two weeks?"

"Always. I know you have a lot you're going to face. Try to keep your cool and bathe in the Lord to work through things on your own time. You have a week and a half before you have to start your drive home. Are you sure I can't come down and drive home with you?"

"That may be a possibility."

"Really? That would be great!" He grinned. "I'll do my best to see if I can swing it."

"Keep in touch, of course," she said, waving her phone before she tucked it back into her pocket.

"Every night?"

"Every night," she agreed.

He gave her a sweet, passionate kiss, temporarily forgetting they were in the airport. "Have a safe trip. Call me as soon as you land," he whispered when he pulled away.

"You'll be my first call," she said, wavering a bit after the kiss. As he steadied her, her mind came back into focus, and she looked toward the security gate. "I gotta go," she groaned. "Now I don't want to."

"I promise you, if the Rodchenko's weren't being buggars, I would be with you in a heartbeat."

"I know."

"Stay safe."

"I will. I love you," she said and adjusted the backpack on her back.

"I love you, too," he said and gave her another quick kiss before she headed toward security, which would allow her to enter the terminal.

"Please keep her safe," Nick whispered a prayer to the Lord. "We finally connected and are doing great. Please protect her heart, mind, soul, and body, and bring her back safely to me?"

*   *   *

Katie texted Nick as the plane taxied to its gate to let him know she arrived safely. Knowing she and her friends had already set up to meet for dinner, Katie rented a car and headed toward her hotel to breathe before heading out again.

As she drove, she felt older, more secure in her walk and in her life. When she drove out of there the first time four and a half years ago, she was determined, but running. God placed people in her life that helped guide and direct her along the way…and for that, she was grateful. Without Stacey to talk to, without Nick's guidance and love, without the strong support of her friends, and most importantly without the love and protection of the Lord, she knew she wouldn't be where she was on that day.

*   *   *

After unpacking her belongings in the hotel, she still had over two hours before she was to meet with her friends for dinner. She used that time to get over the goal she struggled the hardest to face. Picking up three bouquets of flowers at the store, she then drove over to the graveyard. It took her quite a while, but she finally found her mother's grave. It was the first time since her funeral that Katie had gone to her grave. She flipped the stone vase over, and poured part of the gallon of water into the vase before placing the flower food and flowers into the vase.

"There," she said, satisfied. Then she sat down on the ground, and sighed. "I, uh, I'm not sure where to start. There has been so much. I know you've been following me from up there." She adjusted her position by wrapping her arms around her legs. Propping her head on her knees, she continued, "I know I haven't been here. At first, it was because I was too young." She sighed. "Then it was a matter of survival." Taking a moment to arrange the thoughts that flooded her mind, she said, "I guess, to be honest with myself, I have to admit a few things. I'm mad at you," she explained, as a tear slowly crawled down her cheek. "You left me with him. I had to battle a lot growing up without you. You weren't supposed to leave me. Abby did her best to be there for me, but you were the one who was supposed to talk to me about my first date. You were supposed to be the one who did my hair, and fussed about with the camera. Why did you leave?" She sniffed. Wiping her face, she sat up on her knees. "Look, in order for me to move forward, I have to get this out. I'm sorry if it hurts you, but it's hurt me for years. You are my mother, but you weren't there. You could have saved me from being beaten, but you weren't there." She continued, getting louder with each statement, "You weren't there when Jax and I had our first date. You weren't there when I got my driver's license. You weren't there when I lost Jax and Anna. You weren't there when I left for college. You weren't there when Jillian and Aaron were killed or when I was kidnapped. You weren't there when I graduated college and the academy. And, you won't be there one day when I get engaged or married. You won't be there to hold our newborn child…your grandchild. This isn't fair!" Looking toward Heaven, she shouted, "Do You hear me, Lord? This isn't fair! You cheated me out of my mother!"

As she sat, a calm feeling did its best to penetrate and heal her shattered heart, while John 16:33 drifted through her mind, *"I have said these things to you, that in Me you may have peace. In the world you will have tribulation. But take heart; I have overcome the world."*

She struggled with the connection. "I don't understand, Lord."

The Spirit whispered John 14:27 in response, *"Peace I leave with you; My peace I give to you. Not as the world gives do I give to you. Let not your hearts be troubled, neither let them be afraid."*

"In other words, 'For your thoughts are not My thoughts, neither are your ways My ways,'" declares the Lord,'" she said, quoting Isaiah 55:8.

Sitting back down on the ground, she wrapped her arms around her knees. Dwelling in the Spirit, It brought James 1:2-4 to mind, *"Count it all joy, my brothers, when you meet trials of various kinds, for you know that the testing of your faith produces steadfastness. And let steadfastness have its full effect, that you may be perfect and complete, lacking in nothing."*

"Because those trials are what made me stronger," she said in understanding.

"The Lord is near to the brokenhearted and saves the crushed in spirit," Psalm 34:18 was the answer.

"I know You were there. You have shown me many times that I am Yours and that You will never leave me." She looked toward Heaven and explained, "But I don't understand why. I get that all things work together for good, but there has been so much pain and loss."

The Spirit reminded her of Isaiah 43:2, *"When you pass through the waters, I will be with you; and when you pass through the rivers, they will not sweep over you. When you walk through the fire, you will not be burned; the flames will not set you ablaze."*

"So, You're saying what I've been saying all along? Basically, whatever happens, if You're not done with me, You won't let anything happen to me. Thank You for those words of encouragement, Lord." She stood and walked to Jax and Anna's graves as she continued, "You have walked this path with me and have never left me. I see that. In Psalm 46:1-2, You tell me that, 'God is our refuge and strength, an ever-present help in trouble. Therefore we will not fear, though the earth give way and the mountains fall into the heart of the sea.' Even though people close to me have been taken home, You have never left me. Nick even says that while people will let us down, You never will. You are the constant and I can have confidence in You." Remembering Psalm 18:2 from her devotions, she quoted, "The Lord is my rock, my fortress and my deliverer; My God is my rock, in whom I take refuge, my shield and the horn of my salvation, my stronghold.'"

Feeling His peace surrounding her, she placed the flowers on Anna's grave the same way she did her mother's grave before heading over to Jax's. She couldn't fight the pit in her stomach that formed at the thought of going to his grave. Anna's was the easiest of the three to go to, knowing she was a friend, she also knew Anna would forgive her for not coming sooner. She knew her mother understood her reluctance for not coming. But Jax, that was a different story. Jax was her love. There was no forgiveness or excuse for not coming, as far as she was concerned. It was just plain avoidance of pain…a pain she knew needed to be dealt with if her and Nick were to succeed.

As she placed the flowers on Jax's grave, she read the verse on the bottom of his gravestone a loud. "Matthew 5:4, 'Blessed are those who mourn, for they will be comforted.' I have not mourned for you, so how could I be comforted," she said in understanding. She looked toward Heaven, where she knew Jax, Anna, and her mother to be, and said, "I forgive you for leaving, Mom. I know it was not what you wanted." Wiping the tears from her eyes, she said, "I know you are safe and enjoying God's presence, Anna. Your spirit of love and compassion will be missed in this world. Jax, your strength of heart and kindness have left a dark spot in my world that I need to fill again. All three of you, along with Jillian and Aaron hold a piece of my broken heart. I know none of it was your doing, though."

Psalm 18:28 crawled through her mind, and crept down to the dark parts of her heart, bringing light into those dark places. "'You, Lord, keep my lamp burning; my God turns my darkness into light.'" As she said those words aloud, she felt the burdens of loss she had been carrying with her all this time finally lift away. She then quoted Psalm 55:22 as the Spirit guided her thoughts, "'Cast your cares on the Lord and He will sustain you; He will never let the righteous be shaken.' I know. My strength lays solely in You, Lord. You are a strong tower and will protect me. I am giving these burdens to You. Please take care of my mom, Anna, Jax, Jillian, and Aaron. I ask You to allow their sacrifices to continue to make an impact, whether I see them or not. I ask You to forgive me for holding this portion of my heart back from You and ask that Your light and life fill those dark spaces. You are the light of the world. Please allow me to be a portion of that light that brings others to You. Thank You Jesus, for Your sacrifice of love and mercy. Thank You Father, for your gift of grace and justice. And, thank You Spirit, for Your guidance and direction in this chaotic world. In Jesus' name I pray, Amen."

For the first time in her life that she could remember, she felt light. Walking out of the graveyard, she couldn't figure out what took her so long. Finally feeling the desire to celebrate life and not just survive it, she understood at that moment what John 8:32 meant, *"Then you will know the truth, and the truth will set you free."*

Chapter 7

Spring Cleaning

Arriving at the dinner with a spring in her step, grinning ear-to-ear, she surprised her friends. Ryan, Eden, Emily, and Ty were already seated and waiting for her.

"Why do you look like the cat that swallowed the canary?" Ty smirked, glad to see her happy.

"Yeah. Are you coming to tell us you're engaged or something?" Emily asked, hopeful.

She plopped down in her seat. "Nope."

"Then, spill it, Katie," Ryan encouraged. He couldn't help the smile that appeared on his face when he saw hers.

"I was just at the graveyard for the last two hours," she explained.

"Really?" Ty asked, stunned by her answer. "Why would that make you happy and not sad?"

"Because I know where they are, and the Lord finally helped set me free from all the weight I've been carrying all these years."

"I see. There's one more weight you need to release, though," he reminded her about her father.

"I know. And, I'll get there. Right now, I want to enjoy my friends," she said, taking Ryan's hand, who was to her right, and Ty's hand, who was to her left. "To me, life is finally starting. I finally feel free to enjoy what the Lord has given me."

Ty squeezed her hand. "Nice!"

"Thanks!"

Celebration was the theme for the evening. With graduation behind them, they discussed what their futures held.

"Well," Ryan started, "I've secured a position with the weather station as a storm chaser. My life will be chaotic at best, but I know I get to see the beauty and power of nature that God has created around us."

"But, how can you see beauty where others see death and destruction?" Eden asked.

"Simple. Imagining all that power, knowing it's only a portion of what God can reach, I know that with Him, how can I lose? He created this world around us. I do have to see the horrible side effects, but I also get to see the celebrations of life. Ya see, when that F5 hit our town back in high school, it changed me. It was then that I had just a tiny inkling of how strong God actually was. He saved Katie and my life that day, along with each of yours. Yes, there were lives lost, but I choose to look at my job in the positive. The more I work, the more the meteorologists can study the footage, and possibly learn more about them. The more they learn, the quicker they can get warnings out. If people would be more prepared and listen to the warnings, more lives could be saved."

"That goes with Christianity as well," Ty pointed out. "We can only warn people so much. They have to make the choice to follow Him. We make choices every day. While some of these choices aren't so life-altering, some are life-ending."

"I know it wasn't completely the driver's fault that his tire blew, but I can't help wondering if he had actually been given some training before driving, would it have helped on prom night? If that were the case, would Anna and Jax still be with us?" Emily asked. "I think about that a little too often. Don't get me wrong. I love that we're here, but I wonder what kind of impact Jax and Anna could have had if they were still here."

"Their job was done…whatever it was," Katie confidently pointed out. "If their job wasn't, they would still be here."

"If the accident didn't happen, I wouldn't have been in AA. I also wouldn't have been in a position to help Brent," Ty explained. "What Satan uses for evil, God can, has, and will use for good. While we may not see it, God does."

"Speaking of which, how is that going?" Eden asked.

"Good, all the way around. And, now that I've graduated, I am able to work on *real life* and go forward as an Art teacher at the High School here." He grinned. "I just got the news the other day. The Art teacher is retiring at the end of the semester, and they want me to take over."

"Nice!" Katie said, giving him a high-five.

"Congrats, bro!" Ryan gave him one as well, while the others congratulated him.

"Well, we're moving forward as well," Emily said, holding up her left hand, which had an engagement ring on it.

"What? When?" Ryan asked, stunned.

"A couple weeks ago, but we wanted to tell everyone at once," Eden explained.

"Eden, man, you dog!" Ty patted his back, since he sat next to him. "That's awesome! When's the big day?"

"We're thinking of two summers from now," Emily said. "With me teaching elementary school, that allow us to save up some money, and it would also be a good time to take off for the honeymoon."

"Yeah, I can take off anytime at the garage, so it's no big deal," Eden added.

"That's great! I'm so happy for you!" Katie got up and gave Emily a hug before returning to her seat. "Well, I guess that leaves me. I start the force in about two weeks. I have to work there for two years before I can go to Quantico for the academy."

"And, your police chief is aware?" Emily asked.

"Yep. He and Director Shaw have already worked it out. They've known since the beginning."

"And, is Nick okay with this?" she pressed.

"Yes. He's the one who's been training me."

"He's been training you, but is he okay with it?"

"I'm sure he is." She explained, "He knows what I can handle, because he's the one who trained me. Trust me, he *did not* give me any mercy either. He said the criminals wouldn't give me any, so neither was he. He wanted me prepared."

"And for that, I'm grateful," Ryan pointed out. "I'm just glad we're all connected online as well. We seem to all be headed in different directions, and I don't want to lose touch."

"You could never lose us, bro," Ty assured him. "We're all in this together."

"Yeah. Until death do us part," Emily added.

*   *   *

Katie enjoyed the next few days, spending time with her friends. She knew she was avoiding her final hurdles, but wanted to relish in the freedom she felt. Finally, about four days after her arrival, she got the guts to go knock on the door.

"Katie!" Jax's mom squealed when she answered the door. She threw her arms around her in a hug that Katie didn't think she was ever going to let go. "We have been worried about you for so long. Please tell me you have come to talk?"

"Yes, ma'am," Katie responded.

Jax's mom, Sandy, led her to the kitchen, where his dad, Matt, was at the table drinking a cup of coffee while reading the newspaper. Looking up in shock, he slowly put the cup down, afraid he would spill the coffee. "Katie?" he asked, rubbing his eyes to make sure he saw her clearly. "Are you really here?"

"Yes, sir," she said, taking a seat at the table while Sandy anxiously buzzed around the kitchen. "There is something I should have said and done a long time ago, but it hurt too much," she said, feeling her stomach lurch.

"I see. Sandy, please come have a seat so she doesn't lose her momentum. After that, I'm sure we can relax."

"Thank you, sir," Katie said, grateful. Opening her sketchpad, she pulled out several sketches of Jax. One was from the first dance. There was another of him playing in the band, while the

165

others were various moments of different people in the group. She debated for a moment before she pulled the final one out. It was from the accident. She had actually redrawn that one a couple of times, because there was more than one person that picture was for and she wanted them to be perfect.

Setting aside the accident one, face down, she handed the other pictures to Sandy and Matt. Tears instantly came to their eyes as they lovingly looked at each one. "He had a beautiful soul," Sandy exclaimed, running her fingers over his lifelike face in the drawing. "I know the good Lord is all-knowing, but there are some days I wonder why he took him so early."

Matt rested his hand on Sandy's and explained, "Ours is not to question. Ours is to trust."

"I often wondered that myself," Katie admitted. "You see, I just went to his grave for the first time the other day. I know it has taken me forever to get there, but I also know it was finally time. I wasn't able to handle it before then. Jax was my first love. I will never forget him. I adored his smile and laughter. His love for life was evident, and he lived it to the fullest. I half wonder if he knew his life would be short by his comments about life being short and his urgency in talking to people about the Lord. There's, um," she nervously cleared her throat. "There's one more picture I have for you. I wanted you to remember him laughing and enjoying life before you saw this one. Please know this is a picture to comfort you, not to hurt you," she pleaded, as she passed them the picture of the accident.

They were taken aback, and for several moments neither said a word. The tears that poured down their cheeks spoke for their hearts.

"He, um, was never and will never be alone," Matt barely got out as he held the picture. "God was with y'all that night. He will be with you to the end as well."

"I know," Katie said, wiping the tears off her face. "It took me about two and a half years before I drew that one. That is the one that has made the biggest impact, yet has given me the most comfort."

"I love it," Sandy whispered.

"It's confirmation of what we knew to be true," Matt added. Resting his hand on Katie's shoulder, he said, "Thank you for bringing us peace. We needed this."

"I've, um, been struggling. It usually hits around graduation, but has held on longer the more time passes," Sandy admitted. "With our youngest graduated and off in college, I can't help but dwell on the 'what if's.' I know quite a bit that has come of this, but some days it hurts worse than others."

Katie abruptly stood. She couldn't handle any more. "I, uh, need to go, but know that I will stay connected with y'all. You guys were an important part of my life. Without your grace in letting Jax stay with me, and without your patience in letting him talk with me, I wouldn't have been exposed to the Lord."

Sandy jumped up from the table and ran out of the room, returning momentarily with a tiny box. "I think you need to have this. I'm sure he would have wanted you to have it."

With her hands shaking, she opened the box. Unrelenting tears poured shamelessly down her cheeks as she looked at his class ring. "I-I can't."

"He loved you, Katie. We know you're in love once again, and we appreciate that. Sandy and I both feel that the ring should have been, and probably would have been yours if Jax were still alive. It's a part of Jax that you can have with you. It's to remind you that life is short and love is rare. Grab and hold onto both when you find it."

She gave them each a hug before she retook her seat. They shared stories of Jax for over three hours, reminiscing on the cherished memories he left behind. Afterward, Katie excused herself and walked over to her father's house.

"Okay, Lord, you've done another miracle. Time for miracle number three, please?" she begged and knocked on her father's door.

"Katie!" Brent hugged her.

She felt a chill run down her spine as she looked past his shoulder into the house. Flashes of her past flew through her mind. Taking a step back, she rested her hands on his arms. "I, uh, think I need to talk to you," she said, getting a grip on her memories.

"I'm so glad you've come. I knew you were here, but I wanted you to come on your own time. I've wanted to talk to you for so long."

"I know. Ty talked to me about it at graduation," Katie explained, as he ushered her to the table.

Brent was having a difficult time containing his excitement. He saw the hesitation written all over her, but knew the Lord provided this moment for them to potentially repair the damage he created a long time ago through his actions.

He got them each a glass of sweet tea before he sat down. "If you would let me talk first, I would appreciate it. There's something I have needed to say to you that I haven't had the guts to tell you before now."

She nodded for him to continue, while inside, she braced for what she knew was coming her way.

"You know that when Meg died, she took a part of me with her," he started. When she only nodded again, he nervously cleared his throat before he continued, "She was my true love. She was my soul mate. When God took her, it knocked me for a loop I couldn't get out of, and I progressively spiraled out of control." He put his hand up to stop her when she went to open her mouth. "Now," he continued, "that is in *no way* an excuse for the nightmare I put you through. I am very sorry, and there is no excuse in the world that I would even attempt to put past you, because you would see it a mile away. I can only ask for your forgiveness."

"Why should I?" she asked, crossing her arms.

Not quite the answer he was expecting, it took him a moment to recover before he responded. "I love you. What I did was so beyond wrong, it's not even funny. I used alcohol to drown out my feelings. I wanted to scream, cry, and shout at God in anger. Deep down, I knew that was wrong, so I bottled my feelings. That's not the best way to deal with feelings, by the way."

"I'm aware of that," Katie acknowledged. "Unfortunately, bottling my feelings was one of the few things I picked up from you."

"I know, and I'm sorry. I was a sorry father and a sorry excuse for a man. You have every right to be furious with me and to never speak to me again. I know I more than deserve it."

"Yes, you do," she said. Leaned forward, she looked at him intensely. "You don't deserve forgiveness. Neither do I. Fortunately for both of us, God gave us a bigger and better example to follow." As she continued, tears formed in Brent's eyes until they overflowed. He did his best to keep his eyes clear, while she continued, "We, as humans, are a sorry excuse for followers of the Lord God Almighty. He could very easily speak us out of existence, but He, in His mercy and grace, chooses to pick us up, dust us off, and set us back on the path again. We all fail miserably at this life. As a matter of fact, we screwed it up so bad that He had to send His one and only Son to fix it. Can you imagine sending your child to die for someone else?"

"No," he shook his head, feeling beaten up inside. "There is no way I could give you up for someone else."

"Jesus came to this world to take on our sins. We were *so* bad, that it was the only choice. He loves us *that much*. He *knowingly* came down to stay with us. He showed us how to live this life. He even provided us a guide to walk with us as well after He left. We only need to pay attention. We need to ask Him for forgiveness of every one of those sins that He physically carried on the cross. He was beaten and then displayed without mercy for the entire world to see. But, the story doesn't end there. He beat death, giving us a living Savior to worship, love, and adore. *He* is the One you need to ask for forgiveness. *He* is the One who carried each of those sins on His body."

"I have, but I also know I need to ask you as well. You are my daughter. You are my only family. Please tell me it's not too late for us to repair this relationship. Is there even a slight glimmer of hope for me to hold onto in repairing us?"

"There is." She nodded. "The Lord forgives me, even when I continuously stumble. We all have our problems, Dad," she said, reaching for his hand. It felt foreign, but she knew she needed this as much as he did. "I'm willing to do a restart. We both have grown a lot over the last several years. We're both adults. I believe we can do this if we work together at it. Now," she held her hand up to stop him from speaking, "there is some distance between us physically, but I believe that may be a help, not a hindrance. I'm sorry, but being in here has me on edge. I think we can work on our relationship a lot easier if memories weren't in the way."

"I agree. And, thank you so much. You have made me the happiest dad on this planet."

When she hugged him, and they both burst out in tears as they held each other. She could feel the brokenness in her father. She understood what it felt like to face her past and her mistakes. She was grateful to the Lord to be able to work through her past issues, allowing her to face her future with a clean slate. Forgiveness and grace was restored on all fronts, and the relief allowed her to feel that feeling of freedom once again.

*　　*　　*

There was one more person Katie knew she had to visit before she, Eden, and Ryan loaded the truck the next morning for her to take to Cleveland. Stopping by the police station on the way to the hotel, she asked the officer behind the desk, "Is Officer Herman Williams working?"

"Actually, he is," he confirmed. "He just brought a frequent flyer for DWI in, and has taken him down to holding. He'll be up in just a couple minutes if you want to have a seat on that bench," he said, gesturing toward the bench on the side.

Sitting on the bench, she rested her sketchpad on her lap, watching what was going on in the bullpen. Some officers were writing reports, while others were joking around or talking with each other regarding a case, and others were on phones or packing up to head out to their vehicles. It gave her a feeling of pride to know she would be among them. Even if it was halfway across the country, there was a bond between her brothers and sisters in blue that was understood when they ran into each other.

"Katie MacKenna?" Officer Herman Williams asked, surprised when he saw her sitting in the lobby. "What are you doing here?"

Katie stood and nervously tucked a portion of her hair behind her ear. "I, uh, have something for you."

"Oh my word! I'm so glad to see you…and see you healthy! You've been through a lot. What are you up to now?"

"I actually just graduated from the police academy last week. I start next week on the Cleveland Police Force."

"Nice!" he said, giving her a high-five. "Great job! Welcome to the family."

She nervously cleared her throat, while she shifted her feet. "Thank you, but I have to talk to you for a minute."

"Sure. C'mon over to my desk," he said, and lead her through the maze of desks and people over to the back corner. "Have a seat." He gestured to a chair next to his desk.

When she sat down, she slipped a piece of paper from the sketchpad and placed it on top, face down. "These last several years have been rough. I'm not gonna lie. However," she held her hand up to stop him when he went to speak. "However, there were a few things that helped me get through it sane. God, along with the graciousness of my friends to work with me were among them. I also had my drawings. One in particular helped me in regards to the accident. I've re-drawn this one three times, and have marked them as such. This one makes me nervous to give to you, but I hope it brings you peace for when you come to work each day. I kept one for me, gave Jax's parents one, and the third I'm giving to you," she said, and placed the picture on the desk in front of him.

"Wow," he breathed out while he studied it for several moments. Picking it up, he shook his head and said, "The detail in this is amazing. It's like a photograph."

"What it basically means –"

"Let me try." He smiled. When she nodded for him to go on, he continued, "I'm assuming this bald guy here is me." He chuckled when she nodded. "Is this Jesus with His hand on my shoulder, and angels among you guys in the vehicle?"

"Yes," she said, relieved he understood. "It took me drawing this to understand Isaiah 43:2, which says, 'When you pass through the waters, I will be with you; and when you pass through the rivers, they will not sweep over you. When you walk through the fire, you will not be burned; the flames will not set you ablaze.' When you're one of His, you will not be left alone, no matter how alone at times you feel."

"Well said." He nodded in appreciation. "Are you sure this is for me?"

"As an officer, there are days where I'm sure you feel like it's a thankless career, but rest assured, there are people who appreciate the fact that you put that uniform on each day. I, for one, am grateful you were there behind us on that night. I don't think it was a coincidence you were there. If you weren't, we may have lost Ty as well. Anna and Jax didn't have a chance, but because of your actions, Ty and I made it out. I know God had a hand in that, and I'm grateful. I also have a greater appreciation after going through the police academy of what you guys go through."

He chuckled. "They put you through the ringer, huh?"

"Yep. I had a good trainer before I went in," she admitted. "My instructors were thorough. As tough as they were, I'm still nervous to start my first week."

"As a rookie, just keep an eye around you at all times, even in the precinct, and listen to your FTO."

"FTO?"

"Field Training Officer. He or she will be your lifeline. Field experience outweighs book knowledge any day. Your FTO has been in the field for quite some time, and they know how to do their job well, or they wouldn't be in that position."

"Right."

"You have had a lot go on around you. I'm curious to see what God has in store for your future."

"What do you mean?"

"These trials you've gone through are only preparing you for things to come. It's a gradual growth of strength each time."

"I see. So, you're saying that since I've already been through so much, that God has something big for me?"

"Oh yeah." He chuckled, pushing his glasses up on his nose. He sat back in his seat and rested his intertwined fingers on his stomach as he continued, "Life throws a lot at us each day. Some people have a harder path than others. Those are the people I tend to keep an eye on, because those are the people who tend to do great things. You see," he sat forward, "God only gives His strongest warriors the biggest tasks. He created you to be strong. You are a formidable opponent for His Kingdom. Keep in mind, though, that God's not the only one keeping an eye on you."

"What do you mean?"

"The devil is sent to steal, kill, and destroy. He's watching the Lord's people just as much as God is. He's picked up a few tricks over his time here on earth. He knows the same thing that most strong Christians do. He knows that when God puts one of His children through the wringer, that He's preparing that person for what is to come."

"But, why is it when we're going through something really rough, that it feels like we're alone?"

"Because the teacher is always quiet during the test."

"Wow." She sat back in her seat, stunned by the depth of that statement.

"You see, each test is ultimately a trial of faith. Do you trust that He will get you through? Do you trust that He won't give you any more than you can handle? Ultimately, where do you place your faith and trust? Is it in Him, or in someone…or some*thing* else?"

"Good question."

"It's only when you can fully answer that question, that you will be ready."

"I can answer it now. You see, even when I was being held, I felt His peace. I knew He was with me. Now, I don't think I'm ready for His big plan yet, but I know I am on the right path."

"Stay on that path, and stay focused on Him, and in time He'll reveal what it is He has in store for you."

"Thank you."

"Thank *you*," he said, gesturing to the drawing. "I'm going to frame this. During those rough days, I know this'll be a comfort to me."

Katie stood and gave him a hug before she left the police station. It was at that moment, that she understood why she needed to take this trip by herself. She needed to come to terms with the deaths of her mom, Anna, and Jax. She needed to bless Jax's parents and Officer Williams with the drawings, and in turn, it blessed her in knowing it brought a sense of peace to them. She needed to face and finally forgive her father for all that had happened in her teen years.

As she drove back to the hotel, she dwelt on those moments. She found herself amazed by the amount of grace God showered on her, her friends, and her father. His grace is what brought her dad back around to Him, restoring him to the path he was initially set on with Meg's help. The Lord's mercy brought comfort to Katie's heart and mind in regards to the passing of her friends. His allowance of the gift of drawing that He gave her, allowed others to have their peace restored in their hearts. Her only regret was that she didn't do it sooner. She fought Him in the timing, but ultimately, it was His timing that allowed it all to work together for the good of the Kingdom and her brothers and sisters in Christ. She had to agree with Officer Williams. She was curious to see what God had in store for her. Where the journey would land, only He knew, but she understood it would all be revealed in His timing.

As she walked up to her room, the same verse that brought her comfort many times, went through her mind again…

Jeremiah 29:11, *"For I know the plans I have for you,"* declares the Lord, *"plans to prosper you and not to harm you, plans to give you a hope and a future."*

Chapter 8

Spring to Mind

Katie rented the smallest moving truck in order to clear her storage shed the next morning. Ryan and Eden helped her return her rental car and load her truck for the trip.

"I can't believe you're leaving so soon," Ryan complained as they loaded.

"I need to be able to sort through this in my new apartment before I start work. I feel anxious about starting. I want to make sure I've cleared this hurdle as well."

Eden smirked. "Gettin' 'em all done at once, eh?"

"Well, it's taken me a while to get the guts to face them," she admitted.

"I can't see you struggling to face anything. You're so strong," Ryan said, carrying a heavy box into the truck.

"I appreciate that, but there were some things I was running from. This stuff, for example." She gestured toward the almost empty storage shed. "This is mostly mine and Mom's stuff. I loved her, but I have boxed her up long enough. I'm not even sure what all Dad put in here. The only thing I know for sure was her dishes."

"He gave you her dishes?" Ryan asked, shocked. "Those were his favorite dishes."

"But not Cami's," Katie pointed out.

"Ohhhh, I see," Ryan said in understanding. "The ugly green monster reared its head in regards to your mother's stuff?"

"Exactly. I *do* know there are a bunch of photos in here that I need to wade through as well."

"Are you going to scrapbook them?" Eden asked. "Emily loves that stuff."

"Thinking about it, but that will take quite a while. I have enough trouble making sure I have time for drawing lately."

"I'm sure! So, you start as a rookie cop in a week, huh?" Ryan rested his arm over her shoulder. "I can't imagine you as a cop."

"Yep. I carry a gun and everything. And, if you are having trouble imagining me a cop, try imagining me an FBI agent," she reminded them. "That's the next step."

When a car pulled up to the storage gate, Katie shaded her eyes to see who it was, but they were too far.

"Who is that?" Eden asked.

"Dunno. Maybe another storage shed owner." Ryan shrugged. "C'mon, only a couple more boxes and we're done. Lookin' forward t' that steak dinner ya promised us."

Eden grinned. "Oh yeah!"

The person returned to the vehicle, and the gate opened. As the car came closer to them, Ryan and Eden flanked Katie, making sure whoever it was knew they were with her. When he stepped from the vehicle, Katie shoved Ryan and Eden out of the way and jumped into Nick's arms. "NICK!" she screamed in excitement.

"Seth said he would cover the Rodchenko's for a bit. He said he was tired of seeing me so frumpy," Nick explained.

"Frumpy?" Katie furrowed her brow. "Why would you be frumpy?"

"Because I have been away from my love for way too long," he said, and gave her a kiss.

After a few moments, Eden cleared his throat. "Glad y'all reconnected, but there's a steak dinner callin' our names."

Katie giggled as she took a step back.

Nick blushed. "Sorry, mate. It's been too long."

"Don't apologize, just grab a box and let's finish up," Ryan said. "We only have a few more."

After they loaded the truck, Nick followed Katie to the hotel so she could change and leave the truck, while Eden and Ryan took off in the other direction. Eden would pick up Emily for the dinner, while Ryan would pick up Ty. They set to meet at the restaurant in an hour.

"So, how long have you been here?" Katie asked, walking out from the bathroom, dressed, after her shower.

Nick sat on the bed with a sly grin on his face. "I've been here for a while."

Katie narrowed her eyes. "How *long* a while?"

"Long enough."

"Long enough for what?"

"Long enough to run a few errands before looking for you."

"That sounds suspicious at best."

"Oh, it's for a good cause. Do you trust me?"

She sighed. "If you can't trust the FBI, who can you trust? Hey, can we make one stop before we head over to dinner?"

"Of course. We're on your time table here," Nick said, putting his coat on. "Where are we going?"

"It's a surprise."

*　　*　　*

"Not quite my idea of the perfect date," Nick remarked as they pulled into the cemetery.

"Do you trust me?"

"If you can't trust the police, who can you trust?" he quipped.

"You're quick, I give you that." Katie smiled. Then she pointed over toward the left. "Pull over right there."

"Will do," he said, pulling into the area she requested.

When they got out of the car, Katie felt nervous about what she was about to do. Clasping Nick's hand, she led him over to a grave that she visited earlier in the week. "Nick, I'd like to introduce you to my mother. Now, I know she's not really here, but this is the best I can do."

"Wow," Nick said, choked up.

"Mom," she said, placing her other hand on the gravestone, "I'd like you to meet Nick Locke. I'm sure you've seen him over the last few years with me, but I wanted to formally introduce you."

"Goodness, you really do look like her," he said, crouching down to look at the picture on the gravestone. He ran his fingers over the photo before he looked up at her. "I can't believe how much you look like her."

"Yeah, neither could Dad," she pointed out.

"I'm honored that you brought me here. What made you do that?"

"Well, I thought it was only right to introduce my mother to my love. She means the world to me, and so do you. It may seem a bit morbid, but –"

"Not at all. It's very touching and very sweet. Thank you so much for introducing me to her. I'm honored."

Shoving her hands in her pockets, she let out a slow breath of air before she explained, "I really wish I could introduce you to her, and allow you to feel her hugs. They were true and genuine, just like she was."

"From what I've read about her in the reports, she seemed like a sweet and caring woman. There was nothing negative in our findings of her. Her friends only had great things to say about her."

"Ryan's mom was her best friend. When she passed, I lived with them for about a week before I begged Dad to let me move back home."

"Why?"

Sitting down on the ground next to the grave, she admitted, "Because I had just lost my mom, I didn't want to lose my dad too. He's right. We're the only family we have. If it wasn't for God and the miraculous way He transformed Dad, I would consider myself an orphan."

"God can take the coldest heart, and melt it," Nick said, sitting beside her, with his arm around her to keep her warm.

"There are times that I really wish, with every fiber of my being, that she was still here. If she was, though, I might not be where I am today. I may have never gone to Cleveland and found you."

"And that, my dear, would break *my* heart."

*   *   *

Dinner with the group was fun. Nick enjoyed getting to know her friends a little better and they seemed to be more accepting of him, despite the age difference between them. Stories were shared and laughter rang almost the entire night.

When Katie excused herself to go to the restroom about halfway through the night, there was a sudden shift in disposition of those left at the table. "What are your intentions with Katie?" Ty asked.

"Don't know what ya mean," Nick said, stunned by the abrupt shift of the conversation.

"Knowing Katie's past, you have to understand that we're protective of her," Eden pointed out. "We're also aware of your age difference."

"Our age difference has nothin' to do with how I feel about her. She is a mature twenty-two year old, and you know it."

"How do you feel toward Katie?" Emily asked.

"I love her. I have been in love with her for quite some time, but she wasn't ready for a relationship. I don't think she was ready when Seb asked either."

"I agree." Ty explained, "We've seen how you are with her here, but you have to know that our concerns are not unfounded."

"I agree," Nick conceded. "But what you don't know is that I am very much a gentleman and will not hurt her. I would sooner hurt myself."

"Is she another notch in your belt?" Ryan bluntly asked.

"Definitely not. She is a young lady that is to be treasured."

"What are your intentions?" Ty asked again.

"I intend to marry her," Nick said, and then added, "I've already asked her father…and he said I have his blessing."

"Admirable," Emily said, impressed. "When did you ask him?"

"When I came in this afternoon. That's how I knew she was at the storage shed."

"I see." Ryan shifted in his seat, agitated. "So, when are you planning on asking her?"

"When the time is right. That, with all due respect to you as her friend, is between me and Katie."

"All right, y'all, he passes my inspection. Ease off the Spanish Inquisition a bit," Emily said. "It's getting tense, and she will definitely pick up on that."

"She has a way of picking up on the way people are feeling," Nick agreed. "So, are there any more questions?"

"Do you approve of her wanting to be an FBI agent?" Ryan asked.

"Whether I approve or not, it's her dream and desire, and if it is in my power I will make all her dreams come true."

"But, do you approve of it?"

"Again, that's not my call."

"Do you like the idea?" Ty asked.

"I like the idea of her achieving her dream," Nick explained, getting irritated. "I feel that she is more than prepared to do this. Whether she chooses to follow through or not, is completely up to her. I will not squelch her dreams. God gave her that desire for a reason. Whatever path He leads her down, I feel it's my job to support her to the best of my ability."

"What if it gets her killed?" Ty asked.

Nick took a moment before he asked, "Ty, you're a Christian, right?"

"Yes."

"Where does your faith rest?"

"What do you mean?"

"Where do you place your faith? Is it the world, your job, or yourself?"

"I have faith in the Lord."

"So, why is it you have faith in the Lord when it comes to your eternal security, but not to keep your friends safe?"

"That's not fair!"

"It's totally fair. She has even said as much herself, that if God's not done with her she's going nowhere," Nick pointed out. "You need to trust her and God…as I do."

Ty put his hands in the air in surrender. "I give."

"That's two," Nick said, looking at Ryan and Eden.

Eden gave up as well. "I'm good. I trust Katie's judgment, and you have answered any concerns I had."

"Ryan?" Nick asked.

Ryan crossed his arms, deep in thought. "Will you protect her?"

"With everything I have, but I'm not super-human. I can't do as good a job as God can either," he added. "He created this world. I'm certain He can protect Katie. He has a plan for her, or she wouldn't still be here. That goes for each one of us at this table. You guys should be more aware of that than most people your age, due to losing Jax and Anna so early in life."

"You have no right to bring them into this."

"I have every right. They're not to be used to hold Katie hostage. Jax, Anna, Aaron, Jillian, and her mother are not here, that I will concede, but you are not to use those against her. She's her own person. She's independent and strong. Trust her. Trust God."

"Thank you," Katie said, sitting down in her chair. "I only caught the end of that, but I assume by the feeling at the table that you were just questioned regarding us?" Katie asked Nick.

Ryan shook his head in amazement. "How do you do that?"

"I know y'all. I'm fixin' to get upset though, if y'all don't stop protecting me. I'm a big girl."

"We know you are. We're only concerned when it comes to your heart," Ty explained. "Please don't take it as control or protection. We love you and only want the best for you."

"And, I'm good too," Ryan added.

"Good for what?" Katie asked.

"That's between us."

"Oh, don't even go there!" Katie snapped as anger flashed across her face. "If y'all are going to have a conversation, don't talk over me like I'm a two-year-old. You know I hate that."

"I wanted to make sure he knows, whether he's looking for it or not, that he has my support of the two of you," Ryan admitted.

"Thank you," Nick said, appreciatively.

With that, while the others continued the conversation, Katie was on edge. She was not one who liked to be talked about. Knowing her friends, she knew it was coming, but she felt bad for Nick.

*   *   *

With Eden's help, they returned Nick's rental car and then dropped Katie and Nick off at the hotel. Nick's room was down the hall from Katie's but they were talking in Katie's room before going to bed. "It's all good," Nick dismissed her concerns when they got back to the hotel that night.

"I don't think it's right, though."

"Are you telling me that you haven't been questioned by Seth, Emma, Dakota, or Todd yet?"

"Not really."

"Probably because they already have a feel for you. They're an observant bunch. Meanwhile, your friends haven't had much exposure to me."

"I agree, but I would imagine it was more of an interrogation."

"Of a mild form, but yes," he agreed. "Nothing I couldn't handle, and nothing I wouldn't do for someone I loved or cared for either."

She rested her arms around his waist as they stood by the door. "Well, I appreciate you fielding their questions. I assume you got approval from all of them?"

"Yep."

"Good. Now that I've cleared all lose ends from here, I can continue going forward."

"Good to know. Now, we have a very long drive starting tomorrow, so we need to get some rest. What time do you want to take off?"

"Since it's about a seventeen hour drive, how does three or four sound?"

He chuckled. "Like I'm going to need a lot of caffeine."

*   *   *

After a long drive, Seth, Emma, Todd, and Dakota met them the morning after they got back and helped them unload the truck. It took less than two hours to empty the truck and return it to the company. When that was done, the group stopped at MacGreggor's before Seth dropped them off at the apartment complex that night.

"That was fun," Nick said, pushing the button for their floor, as Katie flipped through her mail for the last week and a half.

"Yeah," she said, absentmindedly. Pulling a five-by-seven envelope from the stack, she noticed no return address. "Hmmm."

"What's that?"

"Good question. Here, can you hold these?" she asked, handing him the stack of mail. Looking through its contents, she could feel the color draining from her face. "I...uhhh...."

"What is it?"

"They're, uh, wow," she said, taken aback. "This isn't interesting anymore. It's more along the lines of scary," she said, taking the mail from him, and passing the photos from the packet to him.

Nick shook his head. "How did…wow."

The photos contained various places that Katie was at, down in Oklahoma. There were pictures of her at a restaurant with her friends, walking across the road from Jax's parents to her father's house, of them loading the truck, even of her in the graveyard where she thought she was alone. She shuddered. "There's a note."

"What's it say?"

"It says, *'You may think you are alone, but I see it all. When hunting a prey, the hunter must study the habits of its prey in order to decide where to lay the trap.'*" Looking up at Nick, she admitted, "Okay, now I'm officially scared. Who is this?"

"I'll take it with me to the lab tomorrow and see if there are any prints. However, this person seems to be cautious and knows what we look for when tracking people."

As they walked out of the elevator, Katie could see a package at her door. "I don't want to know," she groaned.

"Just breathe. Let me check it out. You stay here," he told her as he left her several apartments down the hall. He picked the lock of her door and took the package inside with him. When he poked his head out the door a minute later, he said, "It's clear. Come on in."

Katie cautiously entered her home, feeling sick to her stomach. The vase of black roses that was in the package occupied a spot on the counter, where Nick held up a card. "It's a local florist, so I can track this tomorrow."

"What does the note say?" Katie asked, her heart pounding out of control.

"It's a congratulations on your graduation, signed by your admirer. He calls himself 'The Hunter.'"

"You don't think it's Dom, do you?"

"Don't know. I'll know more tomorrow. It's too late to track anything down tonight. When I show these to Seth tomorrow," he held up the photos and card, "he'll want me to figure this out. He's not going to let this go."

"Good, but, uh, what, um, am I safe here?"

"Yes," he said, confidently. "Just keep the phone by your bed."

"I will," she said, nervously tucking her hair behind her ear.

Resting his hands on her shoulders, he promised, "I will do everything I can to protect you."

"I know you will." Taking a deep breath, she slowly let it out in order to keep herself under control. "It's just unnerving, and brings back memories of the whole Dom thing."

"You're a cop now. Keep your gun handy. This is now a requirement. Do you understand?"

"I do."

"No exceptions. I don't care if it's permanently in your ankle holster. It's to be on your body at all times or within your reach. Am I clear?"

"Yes."

"This is your safety. I understand that God will protect you, but you need to make sure you carry that with you."

She nodded. "I understand."

"I love you. I don't intend to lose you just yet. I will use what I have available to me to track whoever this is down. On that, you have my word."

*   *   *

While Katie sorted through her mother's belongings, incorporating them into the decorations that already adorned her apartment, she was grateful to have them. Making a conscious decision, she planned that this upcoming St. Patrick's Day to celebrate her mother's life instead of it being a dark spot on the calendar.

Working through all of her feelings toward losing her friends and her mother, she was ready to move forward. Spring, this year, would be a new beginning. December would no longer be dark. March would no longer bring pain and agony. And May would no longer be a time of mourning.

*   *   *

The following Monday, Katie reported for duty at her precinct. "Chief said you can go in now," his secretary mentioned, as she continued to work on the report she started when Katie arrived.

"Officer MacKenna?" the Chief stood when Katie walked into the office.

"Yes, sir. Thank you for the time off. It was much needed and appreciated," she said, shaking his hand.

"Of course, of course," he said, sitting on the edge of his desk. "Please, have a seat," he gestured. Then he called out to his secretary, "Nancy, please have Officer D'Antonio come in here when he arrives?"

"Yes, sir. He should be here any minute."

"Thank you," he said, and shut the door. Taking his seat behind the desk, he commented, "Director Shaw thinks highly of you."

"Thank you. I think highly of him as well."

"I wanted to let you know that I agreed to keep you for two years before you head out to Quantico, because you intrigue me."

She gulped. "I…what?"

"Director Shaw doesn't think too highly of too many people," Chief Anderson pointed out. "We've been friends for years, and you are only the second one he has sent to me with the fast-track purpose. When he does this, it makes me take notice."

"I see."

"I don't think you do. I've spoken to your instructors from the academy. Not sure what you did to tick off Williams, but the other two sung your praises up and down. Keeping that in mind, I have paired you with Officer D'Antonio. He's one of my best training officers. I only give him to certain officers, and those officers have gone on to do great things. He's good and he's wise, but very serious about his work. You need to listen to him."

"Yes, sir."

"Now that you understand this, you will also understand how much it pains me that you are only going to be here for two years. I know you will do well. And while I know Director Shaw will be upset at me for suggesting this, I would like you to consider staying here after the two years. You see, I'm betting you would make a terrific detective if you stay. I would be willing to bet that you could blast through the detective test and pass it with flying colors."

"Thank you. Your confidence in me is flattering, but I still feel the need to exceed those expectations."

He nodded in approval, as there was a knock on the door. "I would expect no less." Then he raised his voice, "Come in."

A young man, that Katie would peg around twenty-eight, walked into the office. His stature told of the confidence he had in himself, yet he was also respectful in his manners. "Morning, sir. Nancy asked me to come here." Keeping his short, blond hair in a military style, his blue eyes seemed to notice everything around him. She imagined that his stocky build intimidated many, but hoped he had a heart under that tough exterior.

Chief gestured to the other chair. "Have a seat, Andy." When he did, Chief continued, "Andy, this is Officer Katie MacKenna."

Andy groaned. "Oh no."

"What?"

"Sir, there may be an issue you need to be aware of."

"What is that?"

"With all due respect to you," he said to Katie before he turned back to Chief, "Parker's new partner, Terry Baldwin, has not said single nice thing about her."

Katie chuckled, but immediately covered her mouth. "Sorry, sir."

"What did Baldwin say?" Chief asked, curious.

"He wasn't very nice at all, and warned us to look out for her."

"Meaning?" Chief pressed.

"Meaning that she will plow over anyone to get to her goal."

"Not true!" Katie objected. "Terry's a condescending jerk!" She covered her mouth again, crouching in her seat. "Sorry!"

"Officer MacKenna, what happened between you two?" Chief asked.

"Off the record?" she asked, shifting to sit up straight.

"Yes, if you wish it will remain between the three of us."

Tucking a portion of her hair behind her ear, she nervously cleared her throat before she explained, "He thinks that women need to fall at his feet. He also thinks that women should not be on the force. My partner, Marty Phillips, decided to let me teach him a lesson on the day we started hand-to-hand."

"I see. And, how did that go over?"

"I was already upset, so…" her voice faded.

Chief and Andy both chuckled in understanding. "So, he didn't have a prayer?" Chief asked.

"Correct," Katie agreed. "I don't think he appreciated the lesson either."

Chief sat back in his chair, resting his hands on his stomach. "Andy, do you think you can work with that?"

"Oh yeah." He smiled. "It's not going to be easy, though," he warned her. "With Baldwin already here spreading the stories, and you being a female, you're going to have to prove yourself."

"I've never stopped," Katie pointed out.

"According to Director Shaw, she's got a lot of tenacity," Chief explained. "If anything, you may have to rein her in. Are ya up for the challenge?"

"I am most certainly not a challenge, sir. While I do stand up for myself, and know how to handle myself, I also know when to pull back and when to listen," Katie said. "I know who trained me, and with what my instructors added to it in the academy, while I am confident, I know I still have much to learn. What's taught in the classroom and training, will not compare to what is taught in the field."

"Well said." Andy nodded. "I can work with that."

"Then, off you go." Chief gestured to the door. "If there is any trouble, let me know."

They stood. "Yes, sir."

"I won't have drama in my precinct."

*   *   *

When Katie put her seat belt on, the nerves got the better of her. "I have to admit that I'm nervous."

"If you didn't admit that, I would wonder," he said, starting the car.

As they went through the day, Andy taught her the 'dos and don'ts' of the precinct. He told her about the Chief, and filled her in on the other officers they worked with. While Katie understood he could only tell her so much, she also knew it would take experience to teach her how things worked.

That night, she changed at the station before meeting Nick down at a local diner for dinner.

"Katie!" Damian looked up, surprised when she walked in.

"It's Officer MacKenna now," Nick corrected. "First day, how did it go?" he asked, pulling her chair out for her. When she sat, he bent down and kissed her cheek before taking his seat.

"Nice! Congrats!" Damian congratulated her.

"Thank you." Katie blushed. Then she answered Nick, "It was good. I have a great Field Training Officer."

"What's his name?"

"Officer Andrew D'Antonio."

"I'll check him out."

"Chief said he was one of his best."

"I'll be the judge of that. Anyway, while I know we were supposed to meet for dinner, I got a call about a half-hour ago from Damian, here."

"Yes," Damian cleared his throat, "you see, I have a problem."

"What's that?"

"Someone bought my home."

"What?" Katie asked, confused.

"The warehouse I'm living in has been bought."

"By whom?" Nick asked.

"While that's important, that's not why I called you."

"Okay," Nick said, hesitantly. "Why did you call me?"

"It got me thinking. I'm over eighteen now, so I need to do something with myself, but I don't know where to start."

"Do you have your birth certificate?" Nick asked.

"No."

"Okay. Well, I can get that for you."

"Are you going to get your GED?" Katie asked.

"I think that's a good place to start," Damian agreed.

"Tell ya what," Nick thought through his proposal. "I've known you for years now, and I know you are a good person. I'm gonna trust you with something."

"What?"

"If you go for your GED, you can stay on the couch in my apartment, giving you food and a chance to get a good start in life. Now that your building is sold –"

"No, I can't do that. I don't want to be a burden. I will accept the help and guidance, though."

"I respect that. Where are you going to stay?"

"Oh," he waved him off, "I'll stay in the warehouse. What they don't know won't hurt them."

"How will you live there and them not know?" Katie asked.

"I've been a shadow for years. I only wanted to get a hold of Nick, because I knew he would know where to start for a GED."

"Well then, let's celebrate your future along with Katie's first day." Nick smiled, raising his glass.

"A toast to the future," Katie raised the glass of water that was already in her place. "May the good Lord keep us focused and safe as we begin anew. As the Irish blessing goes, 'May love and laughter light your days, and warm your heart and home. May good and faithful friends be yours, wherever you may roam. May peace and plenty bless your world with joy that long endures. May all your life's passing seasons bring the best to you and yours.'"

"Here! Here!" Nick said and they toasted their glasses.

*　　*　　*

About a month into her first year as an Officer, Katie and Andy were doing a night shift, when they came up on a vehicle swerving over the yellow line at around one o'clock in the morning. "Why do they get behind the wheel when they're drunk?" Andy shook his head, turning on his lights and sirens, as Katie called it in.

It took a couple of minutes before the vehicle pulled over. When it did, Andy and Katie both got out of their vehicle. "Be careful," Andy warned as they walked toward the other car.

Noting only one person in the vehicle, Andy waved her behind him. She hung back, resting her hand on her gun in case of trouble. As the window was lowered, Andy showed his flashlight into the car. Katie was surprised to hear him burst out in laughter. He waved her forward as he asked, "Have you been drinking, sir?"

"No."

"Why were you swerving?"

"Honestly?" he asked, as Katie got a good look at him.

She covered her mouth in laughter at what she saw. There was a young man in pink spandex pants and a leopard print tank top sitting in the driver's seat. His hair was a disaster and he looked disheveled at best.

"Honesty would be a good thing," Andy pointed out.

"Well, sir, ya see, when I got home from work, I stopped off at my girlfriend's apartment. She threw my clothes into the wash, while I took a shower. Afterward, I went to ask her something and we got into a fight and she stormed out of the house in a rage. She's a bit of a spit-fire and I was worried, so I grabbed the first thing I could to put on." He gestured toward his outfit. "While I was driving, I needed a cig, so I lit up. I saw you turn onto the road behind me, and in my nervousness, I dropped the cigarette onto my lap."

"So, you're telling me that you were all over the road because I pulled out behind you?"

"Yes, sir. And, because I burnt a couple of holes in these pants with my cig."

"Sir, please exit the vehicle. I do believe we may need to do a sobriety test on you."

Katie watched in amusement while Andy did the sobriety test. Sure enough, the young man was also drunk. Katie had to stifle her laughter the entire ride back to the station. While she felt bad for the young man, his attire, along with the few holes burnt into probably the worst possible places on his spandex pants, were not going help him when they got him to holding.

As a matter of fact, once word passed around about the scene down in holding, some officers went down to see for themselves. It was not often that something of that caliber of humor passed through their holding cell, and they wanted to see it.

Later, when she tried to explain it to Nick, she almost didn't get it out through the laughter. She enjoyed sharing her stories with him, and he, in return, would share some funny stories of his own…of course leaving out the confidential details.

*   *   *

To Katie, her job seemed tedious at times, and sometimes boring, there were those days where excitement was the call for the day. For example, about a week after the drunk driving incident, she and Andy pulled up to a red light. A car blasted through the light, going at least seventy miles per hour.

Andy and Katie looked at each other in shock for only a moment before Andy floored the gas pedal, while Katie called it in. "Unbelievable!" Katie said, stunned, when she finished.

"They had better have an *extremely* good reason, or they're in for a *very* long night," Andy growled. "They could have killed someone!"

"They still may," Katie pointed out, while three other cars joined in the chase.

Finally, one of the patrol cars had gotten next to the car and attempted to bump it off the road before it took out another vehicle. When it did, the car pulled over to the side of the road. Andy and Katie pulled behind them, while the other vehicles blocked it from the front and side, so they wouldn't get away.

While Andy approached the vehicle from the side, the other officers had their guns aimed at the vehicle. Katie heard a scream, followed by shouting and yelling. From what she could tell, there was a man and woman in the car. The man was in the driver's seat, while the woman was in the backseat.

"Keep your hands on the steering wheel where I can see them!" Andy ordered.

"My wife! I need to get her to the hospital!" the man pleaded.

Katie inched closer to the back seat window, looking in to see the woman writhing in pain as she screamed. "What's going on?" Katie asked.

"Her water broke! I was at work when it broke. We don't have money to call the ambulance, so I put her in the car to take her," the man explained, with tears in his eyes. "Please help me!"

"Get an ambulance out here," Andy told one of the officers, and then he went around to the driver's side and asked the man to get out. When the man complied, Andy patted him down before he talked to him to get more information.

In the meantime, Katie opened the back door. "Ma'am, can you tell me how far apart your contractions are?"

The woman only screamed in response.

"Ma'am? I want to help you, but –"

"Then get this baby out of me!" the woman growled.

Katie looked at her, wide-eyed. "What's your name?"

"Andrea," she got out before she screamed again.

"Are you trying to scream the baby out?" Katie asked.

"No....I....help!" she shouted in between her heavy breathing.

"How far apart are they?" Katie asked again, placing her gun back in the holster.

Another female officer from one of the other cars came around to Katie's side. "How far apart?"

"They look close," Katie said over her shoulder. Then she turned back to the woman and asked, "Do you feel the need to push?"

"Get....it....out!" the woman snarled before a string of swear words followed.

Katie looked to the other officer for help. "I got this. I've done this before," the other female officer said. "Why don't you watch for the ambulance?"

Katie gladly let her take over. The woman was giving Katie a migraine. She was happy for them that they would get the help they needed, but the poor woman desperately needed medicine!

Just as the ambulance pulled up, another scream was heard, shortly followed by the bellowing cry of a baby. Katie, who was standing beside the car, looked in to see a baby, covered in blood and goo, and he was bright red from crying so hard.

The female officer placed the baby in the woman's arms as the paramedics rushed to the side of the car with a bag over their shoulder and blankets under their arms.

To Katie, that was a loud, but beautiful moment. For the first time in her life, she saw an actual miracle take place. The bellowing cry of a new life being brought into the world was nothing to take lightly, and she knew she would never forget it.

*   *   *

Later that night, when she told Nick about the experience, she exclaimed, "I have never seen a baby being born! It was an amazing miracle! I've never seen an actual miracle."

"Yes, you have," Nick said. "You see them every day, but you don't count them as miracles."

"Such as?"

"You're here for one. It was a miracle that you and Ty survived the crash. It was a miracle that we found you before you froze to death when Dom kidnapped you. It's a miracle that you even woke up this morning. Every breath you take is a miracle. You may not think about it, but we are surrounded by miracles every day. The fact that I'm even standing here is a miracle."

"I see your point," Katie agreed. "So, tell me where y'all are in regards to finding out who the guy is who's leaving me messages."

"I'm afraid we're not. Whoever it is, isn't leaving too many clues. Trust me, though, we're not giving up easily."

"I would hope not!"

"You're important to me. As a matter of fact," he said, resting his forehead on hers, "you're *my* miracle. When I see your smile, it brightens my day."

"You're very sweet," she said, and lightly kissed his lips.

"And, you are my love," he countered.

"And, you're mine as well. I love you with all my heart, Nick."

"Someday I hope you will be my wife, so I don't have to say good night to you and have you leave me each night."

"In time."

"When the time is right," Nick agreed.

*   *   *

Things over the next several weeks were quiet in regards to her 'admirer,' until Christmas. When she arrived to work, there was a package on her desk waiting for her.

"Okay," she said, setting her coat on the back of the chair.

"What's that?" Andy asked. "I would think Nick would celebrate it with you in private."

"Me too." She looked around, nervously. "Does anyone know where this came from?"

"It was dropped off yesterday morning while you were off work," another officer mentioned as he was writing a report.

"Do you know who dropped it off?"

He looked up, noting the tone of her voice. "Some guy dropped it off at the front desk and the desk officer asked me to put it on your desk."

"I see."

"Is there something you want to tell me, MacKenna?" Andy crossed his arms. "Why are you so on edge?"

"I've gotten some scary 'gifts' from someone calling himself 'The Hunter' over the last couple of months."

Sitting up in his chair in shock, Andy asked, "And you didn't tell me?"

"I knew Nick and his crew were looking into it. Kind of thought they would tell Chief."

"Want to open it?"

"Not sure."

"Open it. We're right here," he said, grabbing the officer who placed it on her desk by the arm, so he stood beside him.

Katie took the card off the top and read it aloud, "'My dearest Katie, I do hope you have a peaceful Christmas. I know I have many exciting plans for the upcoming New Year, so you'd better enjoy life while you can. Love, The Hunter.'" She looked up at Andy. With her hands shaking and her face pale, she admitted, "I'm sorry, but this scares me."

"Open the package," Andy encouraged. He turned to the other officer and said, "Go get Chief. He needs to know. We're probably going to have to call her friends at the FBI as well."

When the other officer left for Chief's office, Terry Baldwin walked into the office area. "Well, looks like someone got an early Christmas present. I thought we were exchanging gifts later."

"First off, I wouldn't give you a present, except maybe a white elephant gift. As far as this," Katie gestured toward the box, "I don't want to open it."

"Why not?"

"Go ahead, MacKenna," Chief said, walking into the office area with the other officer. "Director Shaw's sending Simmons and Locke over here as soon as they get in."

"Thank you, sir," Katie acknowledged, still not wanting to open the box. After putting on a pair of gloves, she took a deep breath before she slipped the ribbon off and then gently unwrapped it, doing her best not to trigger anything in case it was a bomb. Placing the wrapping to the side, she listened to the box, but heard nothing.

"Would you just open it already?" Terry snapped.

"Shut it, Baldwin!" Chief growled. "She's being prudent." He turned back to Katie and said, "Go ahead."

"Are you sure we shouldn't x-ray it or something?" Katie nervously asked.

"No. Go ahead. It's been in here since yesterday."

Katie used a letter opener to cut the tape, and opened the box. As soon as the box flaps were opened, a flash of light went off, along with a puff of powder that covered Katie and anyone standing near her. She froze as she looked up at Chief.

Terry laughed, shaking his head. "Nice gift. Now ya got a mess to clean up."

"Freeze, Baldwin!" Chief snapped. "Katie, is there anything else in there?"

"Another note," she admitted. "It's bouncing on a spring. It says, 'This time it's only baking powder. Next time, it could be something more deadly. You may want to be careful and watch your back, Officer MacKenna. Your time may be up sooner than you think.' This is only baking powder. What would have happened if it were something more deadly?"

Chief crossed his arms, deep in thought. "Go clean yourself up. Leave that mess for now. I want our people to look over the desk with the FBI when they get here. I need to compare notes with Shaw. If someone has been threatening you, I should have known about it. I won't let someone take out one of my officers...temporary or not," he said, and left for his office, slamming the door behind him.

"I'll, uh, go take a shower and be back in a few," Katie excused herself.

When she was gone, Andy turned to Terry, and said, "If you know anything about this, spill it now!"

"I…no way! Why would I do that? I know *exactly* what she can dish out. This is not me."

"It better not be. You'd better clean up your attitude regarding her as well. I'm getting sick and tired of hearing about your pity-party stories and knocking a fellow officer who has done nothing wrong, but to beat the crap outta you when you deserved it. Have I made myself clear?"

"Yes-yes, sir," Terry stammered. When Andy left the area to go find the recordings from the day before at the front desk, Terry turned to the other officer, "What did I do?"

"What *haven't* you done?" the other officer retorted, sitting back down to finish the report he was working on.

"Don't know what you mean?"

The officer let out a frustrated breath of air. "Ever since you've set foot in this precinct, you've done nothing but slander her name. I've observed her over the last several weeks, and nothing you've said seems to be matching in regards to who she is. She's a good officer. You, on the other hand, seem to want to sink her. I'd be careful if I were you. When one of ours gets threatened, and something like this sneaks in, the first place we look is amongst ourselves. Since you're the only one who seems to have any problem with her what-so-ever, guess where they're going to start?"

"I didn't do anything!" Terry objected.

"You need to clean your attitude. Imagine you're in a firefight. If you were MacKenna, would you want a person like you watching your back, knowing you've already stabbed her in the back? These are people who could save your life one day. Along the same lines, they have to trust that you may potentially save theirs. Have to tell you. From what I've seen? I would much rather have MacKenna on scene with me over you any day, any time."

Terry smirked. "Yeah, she's nice to look at."

The officer stood, anger evident in his body language. As he got within several inches of Terry, Terry took a step back to put a little distance between them. The officer snarled at Terry before he explained, "You had better watch your back."

"Are you threatening me?"

"Not yet. But, from what I've seen? Your actions could be construed as threatening to MacKenna."

"She's harmless."

"Wanna bet? She could take you on the firing range any day. She has more ethics and integrity in her little pinky than you have in your whole body. Consider this friendly advice, if you are to survive on this job, watch your step. You're treading on thin ice at best."

Terry didn't say another word. He only turned, leaving the office area for his partner and vehicle.

*   *   *

"Why can't you figure out who this is?" Katie demanded, as she, Andy, Chief, Seth, Nick, and Director Shaw were in the Chief's office after their examination of her package.

"He or she is good," Director Shaw pointed out. "There are no fingerprints, and they use young people to deliver. This person avoids cameras like the plague, and seems to enjoy wearing disguises to hide their identity."

Katie sighed in frustration. "I don't feel safe anywhere."

Nick crossed his arms, beside himself. "And I don't feel like I'm doing a very good job protecting you either."

"You can't be there twenty-four-seven," Katie pointed out.

"No, but I'm a bloody FBI agent!"

"Watch your mouth!" Seth snapped. "Look," he stood from where he was leaning on the table in Chief's office, with his hands on his hips, "Now that everyone is aware of what's going on, and evidence has been passed between us, we need to work together to find out who's doing this before this sick game becomes truly deadly."

"I agree, but what can we do?" Andy asked. "I'm going to lose my probie if we're not careful, and I have yet to lose anyone."

"We have some great minds in this room. We should be able to figure this out," Chief said. "Who has something against you that could potentially pull this off?"

"Against me? As in, something I've done to them?" she asked.

"Yes."

"Well, Lucca Rossi is the first to come to mind," Katie admitted. "Can't imagine splitting up his family and getting him thrown in prison went over too well. Then there's his one son, Joey. Do we know where he's at?"

"He's in school, being a good boy," Nick explained. "He was one of the first ones we looked at."

"Anyone else?" Chief asked.

"I didn't do anything to him, but wherever Dominic Cook is, I can't imagine that he's happy being separated from his brother and losing the chance to work at his business."

"Not something you could control. That was all him," Seth added. "He hunted you down. He raped and beat those women, and killed Jillian and Aaron of his own doing."

"And, trust me, we're still looking for him," Director Shaw put in.

"Anyone else?" Chief pressed.

"Um, not that I know of, but there's no telling," Katie said, shaking her head.

"What about Seb?" Nick asked. "He needs to be added to that list as well. He tried to hold you. He left you in Sandusky, and kicked your door in."

"True," Katie agreed. "I don't think he would do anything like this, but add him to the list."

"He knew your schedule, and he's a friend on your social media page," Nick pointed out.

"I'm still a friend with him. He has cleaned up his act since that weekend. I'm marking it up to a moment where he lost his mind for a couple of days," Katie said in his defense.

"Well, that'll give us a place to start," Chief said, writing them down. "Let's find out who this person is, or she won't make it to Quantico."

*   *   *

"Your 'friend' has been quiet for quite a while," Andy pointed out when they were driving, around mid-January. "Do you think we scared whoever it was off?"

"Maybe. I kind of wonder, and I don't want to think about it being him, but…" Katie's voice trailed off.

"Who?"

"You don't think Terry Baldwin had anything to do with it, do you?"

"I hope not…more for his sake. If that's true, he's in major trouble!"

"What do you mean?"

"We don't take kindly to people threatening one of our own."

"I see. Do you think he did?"

"As I said, I hope not."

Katie took a deep breath, and slowly let it out. "My prayer is that it's done and over with soon. I just want to move forward and enjoy the life God has granted me."

"Here's hoping!" he agreed. "Well, it's about that time. Where do you want to go for lunch?"

"We haven't been to Melina's in a while," Katie pointed out. Melina's was the first diner Andy took her to in her first week for lunch.

"Then, Melina's it is," he said, turning down the road in that direction.

*   *   *

Later, on February 14th, Katie got home from work and grabbed her mail on the way up to her apartment. She and Nick were to go out to dinner that night, and she was excited. She had no idea where they were going for dinner.

Placing the long package that was at her door on the counter, she set the rest of her mail on the counter beside it before putting her gun into the safe in her bedroom. Afterward, she went back out to the package. Hoping they were roses from Nick, when she opened the box, she gasped as a vapor was released, therefore inhaling the vapor. It took only a moment for her to drop to the ground, unconscious.

*   *   *

"Katie? Katie, c'mon, wake up, love," Nick tapped her cheek.

As her eyes fluttered open, she saw Nick and his unit, along with several other people she didn't recognize, buzzing around her apartment, along several police officers from her precinct. "This is dizzying. Can they stop moving for a minute?" Katie groaned.

"I'm not one hundred percent sure, but my best guess is that it is a form of Halothane," a young man announced, as he continued to inspect the box. "When she lifted the lid, it triggered this mechanism," he pointed out, setting it off with his pencil. It was empty, but still sprayed.

"Can you speak normal for a moment and translate that, Adams?" Emma snapped.

"Sorry," Matt Adams apologized. "I'm used to –"

"Right," Seth interjected, "People who know what you're saying. But, just give us the 'lab for dummies' version, huh?"

"Halothane is general anesthetic that is an inhalant. It's also known as KO gas, or knock out gas," Matt clarified.

Katie slowly sat up and rested her head on her knees, taking deep breaths. "What's in the box?"

"This mechanism is really quite brilliant," Matt said, ignoring Katie. "Whoever sent this knew what they were doing."

"She asked what was in the box, Adams?" Nick asked.

"Oh, sorry," he apologized. He tilted it for her to see the box had a single black rose, along with a box of chocolates and a note.

"What does the note say?" Katie asked.

Nick picked up the note, which was already in a plastic bag. "It says, 'Happy Valentine's Day, dear Katie. Know that I have been keeping an eye on you. You look amazing in your uniform, though I have to question whether or not you truly deserve to wear it. When the smoke clears, who will be the last one standing? With Love, The Hunter.'"

Katie groaned. "I thought he was gone."

"Obviously not," Seth said, crouching down next to her. "This is a calculating individual. We have not been able to find any prints. Even the florist is a dead end."

"Don't say dead end." Emma pointed out, "she's stressed enough."

"Right. Poor choice of words. Sorry, Katie."

"Forgiven. What are we going to do?" Katie asked.

"We're following everything we can. We're not leaving any lose ends."

"That's great, but it didn't work so well when it came to Dom," Katie pointed out.

"Katie, I promise you that we will run every lead into the ground until we find who's doing this."

"I appreciate it."

"And in the meantime, stay on your guard. It's obvious he knows where you are and seems to have access to you," Nick said, feeling frustrated and angry. Whoever this was, had proven that even the secure building they lived in was penetrable, and that he could get to Katie anywhere, and at any time.

Dakota had been silent up to that point, so when he spoke, the others listened. "Katie has been one of our own ever since she agreed to help us with the Rossi's. We're FBI agents and police officers, folks. We, of all people, should be able to figure out who this is."

"What do we know?" Seth asked, sitting on the ground next to Katie.

"We know Dominic crossed into Canada. That's where we lost him," Todd piped up. "We're pretty sure he changed his identity, but from that point, we don't know where he went."

"Okay. What else?"

"Lucca Rossi is another one who has a bone to pick with her," Emma said. "Lucca is in jail and Giovanni is elsewhere."

"What about Joey?" Claire asked. "Do we know where he landed?"

"As far as we know, he's in his senior year at Cleveland State," Emma said.

"So, you don't think this is his doing?" Claire asked. "Just because he's in school doesn't mean he's not connected. We only know where half of Rossi's men landed."

"Good point," Seth agreed. "I'll talk to Shaw and see if we can get a guy on him to keep track of him."

"Get someone on him now," Nick said. "We need to know what he's doing and when he's doing it. If this is him, I'll –"

"Don't finish that," Seth warned. "I will get someone on him in the morning."

"Stuff this for a game of soldiers!" Nick snapped, getting off the floor. As he spoke, he paced. "I'm tired of all these bloody bush rangers running around, getting away with murder. I *will not* let them get her." He stopped and looked at Seth, as he said, "I will leave this country with her if I have to."

"No!" Katie stood up. "That's not the answer. The answer is to find who's doing this and take them down."

"We need evidence to do that."

"Evidence that we don't have," Katie pointed out. "You have told me many times that we need to have the evidence." Crossing her arms, she explained, "While I appreciate the sentiment and concern, I would appreciate y'all finding this buggar and putting him or her away."

"We'll do our best," Seth promised.

"I don't want your best. I want it done."

*   *   *

"So, it's a company called Seven Seas Imports," Claire explained. "They purchased the warehouse in November."

"Who's the owner?" Nick asked, as he continued to write the report from an incident earlier in the day. He had asked Claire to look into the warehouse Damian lived in to see what she could find.

"Someone named Cristian Gombeda. Odd thing is, I can't find much on him. He's supposedly some affluent Italian. It seems that Mr. Gombeda inherited his money from his dead parents."

"What's the story?" Emma asked.

"They were killed in a plane crash while on vacation. I can only find their obituaries. As far as Cristian, he was raised by his grandparents. No siblings as far as I can tell."

"Is that all you've got?" Nick asked.

"Yeah. That's what I meant when I said it's weird. It's a sparse identity trail at best. In this day and age, I should be able to find a lot more than this. It's not even two pages worth of information."

"I see. Well, keep digging."

"I will."

"What do they import?"

"Whatever you need."

"Okay. Not a lot of help there."

"Why is this place important to you?" Claire asked.

"Because that's where one of my snitches lives, and I have never heard of them. I want to make sure he'll be safe if he stays there."

"That's not in your job description."

"Look, I've taken care of that kid since he was fourteen. I don't intend to stop until he's on firm footing. He's given us a lot of information over the years."

"All right." She shrugged. "I'll see what I can do."

"I would appreciate it. I have a bad feeling about this place."

"Well, your instincts have solved many cases, so I tend to trust it."

*　　*　　*

Damian heard voices and saw the light from the warehouse office on in the distance. He cautiously moved closer, listening for any other noise in the warehouse.

"He's supposed to have worked here on the docks. How can no one know of him?" Damian heard one of the men. He sounded quite a bit younger than the other two men in the room with him.

"Sorry, sir. We've asked around and there is no Nick Locke that has worked on these docks at any time."

Damian's heart rate picked up speed when he heard Nick's name, so he listened more intently.

"This is where he was supposed to work. Have you checked everyone?"

"Yes, sir. Locke was never even on these docks as far as they're concerned. Are you sure he wasn't at another dock?"

"Would I be here if that were a possibility?"

"No, sir."

"Just go do your job," he snapped, and the two men walked from the office.

Damian flattened himself against the wall. In the darkness of the warehouse, he was virtually invisible.

"Is he going to be able to pull this off?" one of the men asked the other.

"I know him well enough to know if he wants it to happen, it will happen."

Chapter 9

Spring Showers

"Nick, got some more information on your Seven Seas Import Company," Claire said, when he walked into the office.

"What's that?" he asked, sitting down. It had been a long weekend, and he wasn't looking forward to the workweek. With Katie working second shift for the next few months, that would put a strain on their relationship regarding their time.

"Well, Mr. Gombeda owns the import service with old money from his family."

"Yeah, we covered that already," Nick said shortly. Seeing his message light flashing, he was anxious to know if the police made any more progress than the agents did in trying to find out who was hunting Katie down.

"What you didn't know, was that he never immigrated here."

Nick's head snapped toward Claire in surprise. "What? What do you mean?"

"I mean there's no plane ticket, no visa, no passport checked for him to come in here. As a matter of fact, there's not even a driver's license on file."

"How is that possible? Is there a picture of him anywhere?"

"No."

"What do you mean no?" Nick asked, aggravated.

"I *mean* I can't find a photo of him anywhere. I suspect it's either a dummy company, or it's a false identity."

Nick furrowed his brow. "Are you telling me that Cristian Gombeda doesn't exist?"

"Sort of. I'm telling you that if he existed, he should still be in Italy, not here in the US owning and operating an import business."

"Then, how is he?"

"That, my friend, is for *you* to find out," she said, holding up a piece of paper with the information on it.

He snatched it from her hand and returned to his desk, with a feeling of irritation building up in him. Checking his messages, he wrote down the return caller information, resting on one from Damian.

"G'day, Damian, it's Nick," Nick said, returning his call.

"Dude! Where have you been?" Damian asked.

"It was the weekend. Why didn't you call my cell?"

"I tried."

Nick pulled out his cell phone. Sure enough, it was off. "What the…? I'm sorry. I always check it. It must have gone out last night."

"Right. That's when I called it. Look, I don't know who owns this place, but whoever it is, is looking for you."

"What are you going on about?"

"The owner sounded young."

"Like how young?" Nick asked, scanning the information on the paper Claire gave him. "According to our information, the owner should be around forty years old."

"Not a chance! This guy didn't sound too much older than Katie."

"That's Officer MacKenna to you," Nick corrected him.

"Right. He didn't sound any older than Officer MacKenna. Anyway, he's been asking questions, trying to find a dockworker named 'Nick Locke.' Now, the only guy I know named Nick Locke is you. It could be someone else, but –"

"No. I think I may have an idea who it is. Thanks for the information. Wanna do lunch today?"

"Sounds good. Same place?"

"Same place," Nick agreed before he got off the phone. Glancing at Claire, he asked, "Who's on Joey Rossi?"

"Edwards. Why?"

"Because the only ones who knew about my cover as a dock worker on Katie's hit list, are those from the Rossi house."

"I don't understand."

"The owner of Seven Seas Imports is *not* the person on this piece of paper."

"Unless the person running the warehouse is not the owner," Emma pointed out as she poured a cup of coffee.

"I think I may need to pay a visit to Seven Seas."

"On what grounds?" Seth asked.

"Just to have a chat. Seems we have conflicting information. And, knowing they're an import business, we need to make sure that they are on the up and up."

Seth let out a slow breath of air, running his fingers through his hair. "That's thin, but I'll tell you what. Take Todd and Dakota with you, and be careful."

"Are we the muscle?" Dakota asked, with a smile.

Nick chuckled. "Yeah."

"Get out of here and get back with me as soon as you are free of there," Seth ordered.

"What's up?" Nick asked.

"Think we may have a lead on Dominic Cook."

"Scrap Seven Seas for now. What's going on with Dominic?" Nick asked, curiosity getting the better of him.

"One of our guys found the person he got his original fake ID from."

"Original? Meaning more than one?" Nick asked.

"He's smart," Seth acknowledged. "Seems he already had a false identity on hand. He used his real identity to get into Canada, but he then used a different one for the first few months up there before he fell off grid again."

Nick sighed. "Seriously?"

"Tell ya what, we'll go to Seven Seas, while you go meet with the ID guy," Dakota offered, putting his coat on.

"Seth, you comin'?" Nick asked Seth.

"No. Take Emma with you. Think she may be able to sweet-talk more information out of him than I could."

"Yeah, just bat those pretty brown eyes at him, and he'll be putty in your hand," Todd teased her.

"Hey, I'm more than just a pair of eyes," Emma laughed.

"Yeah. You're a pair of legs, a pair of hands, and a pair of –
"

"Guns," Emma finished, showing her ankle holster, and gesturing to the gun she had on her hip.

"And a sharp shooter at that," Nick pointed out. "C'mon, let's go see what we can find out about our friend, Dom."

* * *

"As you can see, all of our documentation is in order, gentlemen. Not sure what the concern is," the manager of Seven Seas Imports asked.

Looking at the thirty-five-year-old, Ted Michaels, who sat behind the desk, Todd asked, "Where does the owner of this company live?"

"He resides in Italy."

"Have you ever met him?" Dakota questioned.

"Not personally."

"How did you get hired?"

"By his assistant."

"Who is his assistant?"

"I'm afraid I'm not at liberty to divulge that. He does a lot of work for the owner, which requires a certain amount of anonymity regarding his position. Mr. Gombeda is a very wealthy man, and he does a lot through his assistant."

"I see. And, how does one get in touch with this assistant?" Todd asked. "You see, while the paperwork here is in order, there are some questions in regards to –"

"While I appreciate your curiosity, I have to say that since there is nothing going on here against the law, I do not have to produce that information. Now, if you can convince a judge to sign a warrant for that information, I will be happy to produce it. Until then, we are a legitimate business, who happens to handle imports, with an owner who lives in another country. Thank you for your time and your service to this country. I need to continue my day before I get behind, unless, that is, you have anything else you would like to ask?"

"Not at this time. Thank you for your time." Dakota shook his hand before he and Todd left the office.

"Do you think he's telling the truth?"

"I think he's protecting the assistant and the owner," Dakota countered. "I also think Claire may need to work her magic and see what she can do about finding out who either one truly are."

"I agree."

*   *   *

"Ohhhh, Ramone. How you try my patience," Nick groaned, after the third round of questioning in the park with the fake ID provider.

"Ramone," Emma stepped in, "we're having a difficult time accepting your sudden loss of memory regarding your profession. We have evidence that you have falsified an identity for a Dominic Cook. If you refuse to answer questions here, we'll be happy to take you in and question you downtown. Now, if that's the route we go, we will also obtain a warrant to search your home and see who else you've helped."

The man looked at them, in wide-eyed terror. "If you do that, they'll kill me!"

"You're worrying about the wrong people, mate," Nick warned. "You should be talking to us. Ya see, the young lady Cook kidnapped, is one of our own. Since you gave him the means to escape by providing him a false identity, guess what?"

"What?" he asked, nervously shifting his feet while keeping an eye on every person and shadow in the park.

"That means since he's not here, that *you're* the one we're coming after. Now, be a good boy an' tell us what you know. How many identities did you give him?"

"Just the one."

"Name?" Emma demanded.

"His name was changed to 'Samuel Saxon.'"

"Good boy," Nick patted his cheek. "Now that we know you're not lying to us, did you happen to recommend anyone else to him up there in the frozen tundra?"

"No, I…no." He shook his head. "I don't knows anyone up there. Alls I knows is how to survive down here. Look, I just lives here day to day. I do the best I can to live," he stammered.

"Tell ya what," Nick said, leaning on the railing by the river at the park, "We *may* be willing to look past this little indiscretion if you do two things for us."

"What?" Ramone anxiously asked.

"Number one, if he contacts you again, you let us know immediately. I mean as soon as you hang up or read his message that you call us," he said, handing him his business card.

"Of course. Of course. And the second?"

"If you happen to run across some rather big fish that you think will be of interest to us, that you call us."

"I'm not a narc."

"No, but if you want to continue to breathe the fresh, clean air of this park, you'd better make that call," Emma advised.

"I will. Do I get your number too?"

Emma shot him a look, but relented, handing him her card. "You can call either one of us."

"But remember, girls fight dirtier than guys," Nick warned. "Either one of us can snap you in half in a heartbeat."

"Point taken."

"Good. Glad we have an understanding."

* * *

Toward the end of February, Katie and Andy were on patrol when a call for a burglary in progress came across the radio. "Time to earn your keep," Andy said, flipping on the lights and sirens, as Katie called that they were responding.

"What's the plan?"

"There are two other units responding as well," Andy pointed out. "We're going to have to wait and see who gets there first."

When they pulled on scene, they got out of their vehicle just as two masked men ran from the convenient store. "Freeze! Police!" Andy yelled.

Gunfire rang through the neighborhood as the robbers fired their guns in the direction of the officers, while they continued to run away.

Katie and Andy chased them, as another unit pulled up. "Wait," Andy said, shoving her against the wall next to him, while they were at a corner. "We go around here too fast, and we could be next."

He peeked around the corner just in time to see them get into a car and pull away. He called in the license plate as the other officers chased them in their vehicles.

"C'mon, let's cut them off. I know where that street leads," Andy said as they ran for their car.

Making a u-turn in the middle of the road, Andy headed in the opposite direction with his lights and sirens running. He pulled the car to a halt at the end of an alleyway, just as the car with the robbers turned into the same alley. "We're boxing him in," Andy told Katie.

The car stopped, and both men got out, running in two different directions. "Great!" Andy huffed, as he and Katie got out of the car, running for one of the suspects, while the other unit ran after the other one. They knew there were other units in vehicles on the way.

"Go that way and cut him off." Andy shoved Katie around the back of a house that the robber had run into.

Pulling her gun from the holster, she crouched while climbing the back porch stairs. Flattening herself against the wall next to the door, she listened intently.

Hearing Andy kick the front door in, she took a deep breath of air. In that instant, the back door flew open. As soon as the guy took one step out the back door, Katie slammed her leg into his, and he flew to the ground. She fired off a round near his head when he scrambled to get up. "You move one more inch, and the next one won't miss," she said, and he froze.

Andy ran out the back door to see Katie's gun aimed at the man on the ground. He cuffed the burglar and pulled him off the ground. "Good job, MacKenna," Andy congratulated her.

Replacing her gun in the holster, she shrugged. "All in a day's work, right?"

He chuckled. "That's what they tell me."

*   *   *

March 17th. This would be Katie's first test. She was to meet Nick, Seth, Emma, Todd, and Dakota down at MacGreggor's for dinner. She felt odd when she woke up that morning. Under normal circumstances, she would feel upset and down, but today, she almost felt happy and at ease.

"You're doing really well," Andy mentioned as they drove around.

"Thank you," Katie said, with a sense of pride.

"So, today's St. Patrick's Day. Be careful. There will be a lot of, um, we'll call them celebrations."

"I know. Thankfully, we're not in Boston."

"Yes," he chuckled. "Thank the Lord for small favors. So, where do you want to go for lunch? We're near Cook's Café," he hinted.

"Really? Why would we go there?"

"For two reasons, actually. Number one, I want to check out this Seb guy and see what I can get from him. And, number two, I think you may need to work on one more area of forgiveness. We've talked about how you've worked through everything else. Wouldn't it be good to finally be free of all your weight on St. Patrick's Day?"

Katie thought about it for a moment before she finally agreed.

When they walked into the café, Seb looked up in shock. "Katie?"

Andy cleared his throat to get Seb's attention before he corrected him, "That's Officer MacKenna. We'll just sit over here," he said, pointing to a table in the back.

Seb was at their table in seconds. "As a thank you for looking after our city, lunch is on the house."

Katie smiled. "Thank you."

"Mind if I join you guys for lunch?" Seb asked.

"Sure," Andy said, and Katie kicked him under the table. After Seb took their order, Andy moved to the same side of the table Katie was sitting on, so Seb would have to sit on the other side. "This will give us a chance to do a little investigating," Andy explained. "This is working out better than I thought it would."

Seb brought their drinks over and sat down on the other side of the table. "I feel like it's been forever since I've seen you," he said to Katie.

"It's been almost a year," she responded in a cool tone of voice.

"And, obviously you haven't forgiven me yet."

"Why would I, when you haven't asked?"

"Look, I miss you as a friend. I'm really sorry how things played out on that weekend. You have no idea how often I kick myself for my actions."

"At least you made your intentions evident early enough for me to see what kind of man you really are."

"I'm not that bad of a guy. I don't know what came over me. I'm really sorry. Can you ever forgive me?"

Katie debated for a moment before she gave him a response. "Tell ya what. We can start over as friends, but it's going to take me quite a while to trust you again. Once my trust is broken, it's not an easy thing to get back."

"I understand that completely. Thank you."

"Speaking of the 'incident,'" Andy said, making quotes with his hands, "have you made any other attempts to contact her prior to now?"

"No. Why?" he asked, obviously confused.

"There have been a few incidents that we need to investigate."

"What happened?"

The waiter brought their food over to them, and promptly left for another table.

As they ate, Andy explained, "Someone has been threatening her. Can you think of anyone who may be doing that?"

"Well, you did tick off a mafia boss. Have you guys looked into Rossi?"

"He's in jail."

"Right, and no one can operate from jail?" Seb pointed out. "Like they can't get messages out through a visitor, or don't have a code of some sort already set up. What planet are you people operating on?"

"Okay, duly noted. Anyone else stand out to you?"

"Um…" He looked up, thinking. "His son, Joey, would be another. No one knows what happened to Giovanni after the trials either. Then there's," he lowered his voice to almost a whisper before he suggested, "Dom."

"Do you know where Dom is?"

"Nope. Haven't seen or heard from him in years. His profile hasn't been active either."

"You're still friends with him?" Katie asked, confused.

"I'm hoping he'll reach out some day, and maybe give us a clue as to where he is."

"Smart." Andy agreed. "If he'll slip up anywhere, it will be there."

"That's what I was thinking."

"Anyone else?"

"Not that I can think of…unless you've ticked someone else off?"

"Well, she has, but I'm pretty sure we've gotten that one under control. He's behaved himself lately."

"Meaning?" Seb questioned.

"There was another officer giving her a hard time, but one of the other officers set him straight, and he's been a good boy since."

"Glad to hear that."

"Ya know, I'm fixin' to get up and leave here if y'all don't stop talking around me," Katie snapped. "We haven't seen each other for almost a year, and this is the conversation I get?"

"You're right," Seb agreed. "How is Nick?"

"Good."

"Are you two still dating?"

"Yeah. How did you know?"

"The pictures and your posts on your profile are very telling," he pointed out.

Andy looked over at her as a thought hit him. "We need to look at your friend list and see who's on there."

"May want to see who's on the friends of her friends as well," Seb added. "While your settings are high, any comments from us, allow our friends to see your posts as well," he said to her.

"Never thought of that." Andy made a mental note to check those too.

"Now that we've cleared away the ugly business, let's catch up," Seb suggested.

*   *   *

The dinner that night at MacGreggor's actually surprised Katie. Relaxed and enjoying herself, she couldn't figure out why she didn't clear everything she was carrying sooner. It brought about a fresh outlook to life, and she was finally looking forward to moving forward free and clear.

"Here ya go, my beautiful lady," Nick said, opening her door.

She gasped as she walked into her apartment. "I-I…oh wow," she said, stunned.

Nick grabbed her arm, stopping her from going any further into her apartment. "We need to call Seth and get a crew in here."

Strings were draped from one end of the living room to the other, with photos hanging from them of her last several months in various locations…including one from MacGreggor's that night.

"I don't understand," Katie shook her head in shock. "How did they get in here?"

"Simmons, you need to get a crew to Katie's. The Hunter has struck again."

*   *   *

"Not a single print," Matt Adams confirmed Nick's worst thoughts.

"And the camera shows someone coming in, but they were wearing gloves, hat, and glasses," Emma added to the conversation. "Afraid we don't have a lot to go on."

"And, he's wearing a wig as well," Dakota pointed out, "That covered part of his face and ears."

Nick rolled his eyes. "Lovely."

"I don't understand his end game," Katie said, pacing her apartment while others pulled the strings and photos down, bagging them as evidence. "All he's doing is showing me that he can get to me."

"Not true," Todd pointed out. "He knocked you out on Valentine's Day."

"He seems to make his point on holidays or big events," Emma added.

"Kind of like he's just keeping an eye on you," Todd agreed.

"Who is this guy?" Katie snapped in irritation. "Why can't I just enjoy a holiday? What's his problem with me?"

"Good questions," Seth pointed out. "Do you have any good answers? He seems to have targeted you."

"Not at the moment."

"Keep rolling those questions around in your mind. You're the key to this."

"Yes, sir," Katie sighed, sitting down on the couch with her arms crossed. "As soon as I know, so will you."

*   *   *

Katie's 'friend' was quiet once again until May. In the meantime, Katie did her best to stay focused on her job at hand, her walk with the Lord, and her relationship with Nick.

"Pastor was on point today!" Nick said, charged after the morning worship service.

"I know," Katie agreed, deep in thought.

"Why is it when the Spirit hits a bull's-eye, that I get excited, and you get pensive?"

"Guess it's just part of my personality. I tend to internalize and process."

"Why don't you try processing out loud, so I can follow it?"

"Okay. He talked about the Holy Spirit and His role in our lives. While I do devotions, I have to ask myself if it's a matter of habit, or is it a matter of want and need like it used to be?"

"Do you learn when you read?"

"I do. I have read the Bible cover to cover, yet when I re-read a passage, something else jumps out at me."

"Are you consistent in your reading?"

"Not always," she admitted.

"Pastor used the example of fueling a vehicle. You're not going to only fill your car once and that's it, right?"

"Right."

"You fill it when it empties. Well, let me adjust that. When *you* fill it, it's because it's only half full. I know we've talked about the 'love tank' regarding ourselves, but what about your 'love tank' regarding the Lord? How often do you fill it?"

"I should probably do that more often."

"Now, there are many variations on how to do that. I know drawing is one way for you, so is reading or listening to worship music."

"Yeah. I tend to see God in nature."

"How so?"

"He cares for each of the critters in this world. He makes sure they have food and water. Being one of His, wouldn't He take care of us even more?"

"The Bible tells us as much," Nick agreed.

"I also see Him in the rays that shoot around the clouds when a storm is near. To me, that's God saying that even though the storm is there, He is still there."

Nick smiled. "I like that."

"Me too." She ate her lunch for a few moments before she asked, "What if God has a different plan for me other than being an agent?"

"But, you've worked so hard," Nick objected.

"Right, but what if His plan is to use the training somewhere else? It's not like I'm quitting. I'm just thinking."

"Well, I reckon He'll show you sooner or later what you're supposed to be doing. In the meantime, keep going forward. I don't think He would give you that strong of a desire and passion for something to pull it from you last minute. That's almost mean."

"Not necessarily. We know that all things work together for good, and we also know that His timing is perfect."

"Right."

"What if He has a different idea? What if we were supposed to train together, to get closer to each other? What if we met each other, to help and work together *outside* of the agency?"

Nick inhaled a slow breath of air, mulling these ideas around in his head. "This all came from one sermon?"

"Well, control is an ongoing struggle for me," she admitted. "If I keep pushing the FBI, am I going because I said I would, or is it where God intended me to be? I need to know God's will for my life, not my will. He's made it abundantly clear that He has a plan for me."

"Yeah. Sometimes I wish He would plaster it across a billboard for me, so I don't have to guess."

"While *I* have a plan for my future, is it His plan as well?"

"Good question."

"One I need to think some more on. In the meantime, what's the plan for today?"

"Meeting with the others for a game of touch football."

"Sounds like fun!"

*   *   *

The following week, while on shift with Andy, they got called to a home where a former mental patient lived, who was holding his wife and daughter hostage in the home.

"Get down!" an officer yelled to Andy and Katie when they got out of their vehicles.

Katie dropped behind the car as a bullet whizzed by her head. "What's going on?"

The officer crawled over to Katie, where Andy met them as well. "His name is Marcus James. He was just released from a mental facility last week. According to the officer who spoke with the wife only briefly, he stopped taking his meds."

"What's his condition?" Andy asked.

"Depression and Schizophrenia."

"*Why* is he out?" Katie asked, confused.

"I guess he seemed to have it under control while he was on his meds."

"Which he's not on anymore," Andy said in understanding.

"Exactly."

"How old are the daughter and wife?" Katie asked.

"Wife is thirty-eight, and daughter is eight."

"Is he negotiating yet?" Andy asked.

"Norton's trying, but it's not going well."

Suddenly, people were scrambling, so they looked over the car to see the front porch on fire. "Get it out!" The police officer in charge ordered the firefighters. "You guys watch their backs!" he shouted to the other officers.

"I'm going," Andy got up and ran over, ducking behind a tree.

Katie ran for one on the other side of the yard, where she had a clear line of sight to the front door. While other officers took positions behind trees, the firemen blasted the front porch. The fire was put out easy enough. "Do we go in?" one of the firemen asked.

As soon as he asked, the wife and daughter ran from the house. Katie grabbed the wife, and Andy grabbed the daughter. When Katie grabbed the mother, she collapsed in Katie's arms.

"Ma'am?" Katie asked her.

The woman looked down, moving her hand so Katie could see the blood all over her abdomen. "He shot me. He accused me of having an affair. He-he said no man would ever want me. I-I didn't," she said, her voice and breath catching. "I swear I didn't."

"I'm sure you didn't," Katie said, placing her hand over the woman's, putting pressure on the wound. "Once they get your husband out of the way, I'll get you to the ambulance."

"You're a sweetie. I can tell." The woman smiled. "You don't need to be working as a cop."

"Ma'am, you need to rest."

"My name is Catherine."

"Pretty name. Mine's a form of your name. Mine's Katie," Katie mentioned, as she held the woman in the crick of her arm.

"Katie. What a sweet name," she said, touching the side of Katie's face with her blood-soaked hand. She coughed, pushing more blood from her stomach. "My little Abigail. Is she okay?"

"Yes. My partner has her. She's at the ambulance, waiting for you."

"Oh, honey, I'm not going to make it." She shook her head. A smile formed across her face as she looked up. "I'll be there in a moment."

"Who are you talking to?"

"The good Lord, my child. The good Lord," she said, and took her last breath.

Suddenly the garage door flew open, and Marcus James ran out of the garage, firing at the police cars. There were several more shots heard as Katie watched his body twitch and jerk with each hit, until he dropped to the ground.

She shook her head at the death that surrounded her. She could not imagine how not taking medicine triggered this incident. What she did know, was that Abigail would now have to live her life without her father or mother, and that broke her heart.

*   *   *

That night when Katie got home around eleven-thirty, she took a long, hot bath. While she soaked in the tub, she thought about the incident earlier in the day. Holding Catherine while she died in her arms tore her up on the inside.

When she finished her bath, she got into her pajamas and headed to the couch with her sketchpad and pencil in hand. She closed her eyes in order to picture in her mind what to draw. At first she wasn't sure about the scene she drew until she drew the details of her holding Catherine next to the tree. It surprised her when she drew another figure on the scene standing behind her, with His hand on her shoulder.

"The Lord is close to the brokenhearted and saves those who are crushed in spirit," the Spirit whispered Psalm 34:18 to her.

"I know. I see that," she said, continuing to draw the details on the figure. When she finished, she marked Psalm 34:18 on the bottom near her signature and the date.

Catherine was a woman she didn't know, but was a person nonetheless. This human being had a life. She had a daughter, Abigail, who would never know what it would be like to grow up with parents. She promised herself whenever she looked at that drawing to pray for Abigail.

She hoped and prayed that Abigail would someday know the loving power of the Lord. Without her parents, the Lord would have to be her Father. Just like Nick took care of Damian, she prayed an adult would come into her life and would guide Abigail to the Lord, and would then mentor her while she grew stronger each day.

Chapter 10

Spring Back

Katie and Andy were enjoying their lunch at a local diner on Memorial Day weekend, when a sharp dressed man walked into the restaurant. As Katie laughed at the story Andy just told, she glanced up to the cashier to see her glance nervously from her to the man in front of her. "Um, Andy?" Katie asked, cautiously.

"What?"

"I think the diner's being robbed," she said, not taking her eyes off the cashier, who was slowly emptying the register into a bag.

"Move slowly," he cautioned.

Katie got up from the booth and walked over to the register. "Sally," she said, reading her nametag, "lunch was great as usual."

"Thank you, Officer MacKenna," Sally acknowledged, while the man suddenly stiffened.

Katie asked, "Is everything okay here? You don't look too well."

Before Katie could react, the man whipped the pistol from his pocket and used it to slam into her face. She fell to the side, hitting the ground with a thud.

"Police! Freeze!" Andy yelled, gun aimed at the man.

Katie scrambled off the ground, leaping on top of Andy, shoving him to the ground as a round went off from the man's gun, barely missing them both.

"Get him!" Andy shouted as he got out from under Katie.

Katie called in the incident, and then warned everyone in the restaurant. "Stay in here and stay down!"

Running from the restaurant, gun in hand, she dropped to the ground when she heard the man's gun go off again, shattering the window of the patrol car.

"Ugh! I just got that fixed from three weeks ago!" Andy growled.

"Where is he?" Katie asked when she ran over to him, ducking behind the cars.

"Behind the Hummer."

"You go left, while I go right?"

"Sounds good."

Ducking behind the vehicles, Katie made her way over to the yellow Hummer. She stopped, hiding behind a tire of the Ford 250 next to the Hummer. She took a deep breath and held it as she ran around the truck and aimed at the man. "Put your hands up or I'll shoot!" she ordered.

Seeing Andy come around the other side, he knew he was caught, so he raised the pistol to his head.

"No! Look, man, just put your hands up," Andy said. "Don't pull the trigger."

"I didn't get the job done. I'm dead already."

"What job?" Katie asked.

The next few moments seemed to move in slow motion to Katie as the man pulled the trigger and his brain matter splattered on the vehicles around them. Katie screamed, covering her head as the glass in the window behind him shattered.

Standing in shock, the world around her rang in her ears. Andy ran over to the man to check for a pulse, while other police vehicles pulled into the restaurant parking lot. An ambulance also arrived, but hung back until they got the 'all clear' sign.

She turned to the restaurant to see a crowd gathering there, as she stood in shock, with her gun to her side still in her hand.

"Katie? Are you okay?" Andy asked, but she barely heard him. "MacKenna!"

"Everything clear?" another officer asked.

"Yes. He's gone," Andy explained as he went over to Katie. Placing his hands on her shoulders, he asked, "Katie, are you okay?"

Katie didn't answer. She stared at the man in shock. This was the first time she had seen someone shot right in front of her close enough to have killed her himself. While she didn't pull the trigger, the feeling of shock seemed to overwhelm her.

"MacKenna!" Andy shouted, shaking her. "Answer me!"

"Why did he do that?" she asked, blankly.

"Martinez, take over. I need to get her centered," Andy said, ushering Katie to their car by her arm.

"Thank you!" Sally ran out of the restaurant over to Katie and hugged her. "Thank you so much! You saved my life."

Feeling her brain coming out of the fog, Katie asked, "Did he give you a note or anything?"

"He demanded that I give him what was in the register," she explained. "He seemed jumpy and sniffed a lot."

"Got it," Andy said in understanding. "Have you seen him here before?"

"No. He was dressed so nicely, I didn't think anything was wrong."

"I'm going to go help the others," Katie said, leaving Andy to talk to the cashier.

That afternoon was traumatic for her as she filled out report after report and cataloged evidence. After that, she went and spoke with a counselor. The counselor determined that while Katie experienced trauma, she felt confident that Katie could handle coming back to work for her next shift, but let her go for the rest of the day.

That evening, Katie met Nick and his crew at MacGreggor's for dinner right after leaving the police station. She sat down and rested her head on her hands, taking a deep breath. "I need friends tonight. I'm glad we met here for dinner."

"What happened?" Nick asked. "I thought it was kind of odd that I didn't hear much from you via text this afternoon. I didn't expect to see you here either. I figured you would be at work until eleven."

"There was a robbery at the restaurant where Andy and I were eating. We chased him out into the parking lot where he shot himself in the head not more than three feet from me."

Emma gasped. "Good heavens!"

"Are you okay?" Nick asked.

"I am. I was just shaken up."

"Do you want to go home?"

Katie shook her head. "I'd rather spend it with friends. Today has been rough."

Claire burst into the restaurant and made a beeline for their table.

"Claire," Seth grinned, "didn't expect to see you here."

"Me neither. Look," she said, pulling a chair from another table and sitting down, "I finally figured out what's been going on with Seven Seas Imports."

"What do you have?"

She placed several sheets on the table as she explained, "Something's been bugging me. I don't like it when I can't find a digital trail. That tells me something fishy is going on. I checked into the bank accounts and any little bit of information I could find on Cristian Gombeda. When I put all of the information together, here's what I found. Cristian's parents had *two* children, Cristian, and his brother, Lucca."

"As in Rossi?" Katie asked.

"The one and only. You see, to combat their family's reputation, Lucca used his mother's maiden name, Rossi, when he came to the States."

"So, are you saying Lucca Rossi owns Seven Seas?" Nick asked.

"Not necessarily. Cristian is the one paying for Joey's continued education."

"What has young Rossi been doing while he's not in school?" Todd asked.

"Seems he's been working at the gym, but somehow ditches our trailers on various occasions, otherwise, as far as we know he's been a good boy."

"And, those missing time slots? What was he doing during those times?" Nick pressed.

"Don't know." She shrugged. "He lost his tails, so we don't know where he went."

"How often was this?" Seth asked.

"That's the interesting question. What I found out, was during those times, Katie received a mysterious package within forty-eight hours."

"Really? Does he know he's being tailed?" Dakota asked.

"I'm sure he does," Katie said. "He's been a tracker for a very long time. As a tracker, pretty sure he could spot one a mile away."

"Well, here's how I connected more than one dot in his direction. You see, I was packing up to head home when I got a notification on my computer. Remember when we flagged all of Rossi's men for any information?"

Seth nodded. "Yeah."

"Well, one of his henchmen's names came across my computer regarding an incident today."

"Who was it?"

"Donovan Evangelista." As soon as Claire said his name, Katie's head snapped toward her as she sat up in her chair.

"What is it?" Nick asked, noticing Katie's sudden shift in disposition. To him, she went from upset to alarm mode.

"He's the one who shot himself in front of me. He said he didn't get the job done, and because of that he was dead already," Katie quickly explained, as she felt her worlds collide in front of her eyes. "Was he there to kill me?"

"He's one of their hit men. They nicknamed him 'the gentleman,' because he is always dressed in a sharp suit," Claire said. "He's never missed. What happened?"

"I don't know. He gave me this," Katie pointed to the mark on her cheek, "and then Andy shouted at him. When he went to shoot Andy, I shoved Andy to the ground, and then the man ran out of the restaurant. When we caught up to him, he put a gun to his head and said he was a dead man anyway. He, um, shot himself right in front of us."

"Wow." Todd sat back in his seat, taken aback. "Who is he afraid of? Is it Cristian or Joey?"

"That's the million dollar question," Claire pointed out. "I have it narrowed down to one of the two, but I am having a hard time sorting out who is where and in charge of what."

"What's Damian been saying about the warehouse?" Seth asked.

Nick cleared his mouth of food before he responded. "He's been doing his best to stay clear of any of it, but he has said there has been some interesting stuff coming in and out. There's nothing concrete, but now that we know to center in on the warehouse, I think I'll pull him in the morning and put him up in a hotel until this is over."

"Good idea."

"Let's shift the conversation to something less heavy," Todd said, glancing at Katie. "She seems a bit thrown by all of this. We can target it in the morning."

"Sounds good. You're staying for dinner, right?" Seth asked Claire.

Glancing at Katie out of the corner of her eye before looking back at Seth, Claire felt torn. Her distain for Katie didn't seem to make any difference to anyone else. While Katie didn't seem to be out to hurt Nick, she still wasn't sure how she felt about her. Deciding to keep her friends close, and her enemies closer, Claire agreed to stay for dinner.

*   *   *

Toward the end of dinner, they pressed Katie for more information about the incident that day. In doing that, Katie felt more stress and pressure, and it was evident on her face and body. Fighting the feeling of wanting to clam up and shut down, she dropped her head into her hands. "Can we please stop?" she begged. "I was done before this dinner started. I needed friends and laughter tonight."

"Okay. This conversation's finished," Nick effectively ended the subject matter.

Katie stood from her chair. "I want to go home."

"You can't drive in the mindset you have now," Todd said. "Tell you what. Since you guys are just down the road, Dakota, why don't you follow me while I drive Katie's car home, and you can bring me back?"

"That would be great," Nick agreed.

Dakota nodded. "Sure. I can do that."

"You don't need to. We don't live too far away," Katie objected. "I can drive."

"Na. Let us be gentlemen," Todd said. "It allows us to feel chivalrous once and a while."

Katie reluctantly handed Todd her keys and got her coat on. She looped her arm through Nick's while the four of them headed out of the restaurant.

"Hold our place. We'll be right back," Dakota told Emma, Seth, and Claire. "I want the rest of my wine."

"Will do." Seth chuckled.

As they walked out, a blast of cold air cut into Katie. "Seriously?" she huffed. "I parked over –"

"Na. I got it," Todd cut her off, using the key fab to find the car. He unlocked the car, and when he relocked it to see the lights, Katie's car exploded, knocking the four of them back onto the ground. Nick grabbed Katie as she screamed, covering her head. "Make sure they're not still here!" Nick snapped at Dakota, covering Katie. "And find Todd!"

"I'm good!" Todd yelled, running out into the parking lot to see if he could find anyone watching her car.

While Dakota took off into the parking lot, the others from their group ran out of the restaurant. "Where are Todd and Dakota?" Seth asked, apprehensively.

"They're searching. Call it in while I try to calm her down," Nick explained. "They weren't hurt."

"Good," Seth breathed in relief. While he, Claire, and Emma went with Todd and Dakota to clear the area, Nick kept everyone in the restaurant, and Katie just sat in her spot, rocking in place.

*   *   *

"There's no one. We'll have to wait for the firemen's report about the vehicle," Seth said, as the fire vehicles pulled up.

"Just glad she's safe." He looked down at her and crossed his arms, unsure of what to do.

"Katie?" Emma crouched down beside her. "Katie, you're okay. You weren't in the car."

"But, Todd was supposed to be. He could have died, and it would have been my fault."

"What? No." Todd knelt beside her. "You can't let yourself think that way."

"That guy killed himself today because he didn't kill me." She looked up at him, bordering on anger and hurt at the same time. "What would propel someone to kill themselves because they didn't kill someone else?"

"Someone who doesn't want to go to jail," Claire pointed out.

"If Rossi junior's out here, and papa Rossi's in jail, if they don't do their job…" Todd started.

"Then they're done for," Dakota finished.

*   *   *

Everyone operated in a state of shock as they gave statements and watched the firefighters put the fire out. The blast was so big, it did major damage to the vehicles on either side of Katie's car.

"Who did this?" Katie asked, wrapped in a blanket while the group sat on the benches in front of the restaurant. There were people everywhere. Customers, vehicle owners, police, EMS personnel, and FBI personnel flooded the parking lot of the restaurant.

When Katie and Nick finally got home around eleven that night, they were both exhausted. "I'm tired, but I still have to go to work tomorrow," Katie said, unlocking her door.

"No, you can't. You should take tomorrow off."

"No," Katie insisted. "I'm *not* letting whoever this is define my life. He's coming after me, and in doing so, almost took out Todd. I *will* find him. I promise you that I *will* end this myself."

* * *

In the morning, Katie got ready in a daze. When she finally got sleep that night, she was awakened with a nightmare around four.

"You look horrible," Andy remarked when she walked in the next morning.

"MacKenna, D'Antonio, my office...*now*," Chief ordered, walking through the desks.

Andy watched him, stunned. "What's going on?"

"One of the FBI agents went to drive my car home last night, and my car blew up when he went to try to find it," Katie explained, heading toward the Chief's office. "He's okay, but my car? Not so much. Nick dropped me off this morning before he headed into work."

They each took a seat across from the Chief. "Why are you here this morning?" he bluntly asked Katie.

"Because I'm on duty today," she said, simply. "I don't want my co-workers to carry my load. If I am able-bodied, I'll be here."

He leaned forward in his chair and rested his hands on his desk. "While your work ethic is admirable, you were almost shot yesterday. Then the guy blew his brains out in front of you. *Then*, if that wasn't bad enough, your car blew up last night, and almost took one of your friends with it. Why are you here?" he asked again.

Katie took a deep breath, sorting through her answer before she responded. "Sir, I won't let someone dictate how I live my life. Whether it's this Gombeda guy, or Joey Rossi, I *will not* let them make me live in fear. I choose how I face each day. I won't give him control of my life. That's what he wants, but that's not what he's going to get."

"I appreciate your integrity and willingness to come to work, but in this case I think you may need to –"

"Chief?" Nancy poked her head into the office.

"Yes?" he asked, irritated by the interruption.

"Sir, I know one of Officer MacKenna's snitches lives near the Seven Seas Warehouse."

"Right," Katie said, her heart rate picking up speed at the mention of Damian.

"There's just been a 9-1-1 call to that location for suspicious activity. I heard it and flagged the operator, knowing you were in here," she explained.

"Sir?" Katie asked. "Damian is too young for something to happen to him. Please let us get this?"

"You get this, and then I am ordering you to take some time off. Am I clear?"

"Yes, sir," she gratefully acknowledged, jumping out of her chair.

Andy radioed their response as they ran for their vehicle. There was another unit in the area who said they would respond as well. "Good. I feel better with at least four of us," he said, starting the car.

As they flew through the streets, Katie couldn't help feeling responsible for Damian at that moment. She would do her best to find him and make sure to get him out of danger before she went for Joey Rossi or Cristian Gombeda.

"Relax. We'll get him out of there," Andy assured her.

"I hope so. I don't want anyone else to die because of me."

*   *   *

Katie's rapid heartbeat was all she heard pounding in her ears while she scanned the area. Shadows danced around her, playing tricks with her eyes as a few strategically placed fluorescent bulbs lit what they could of the warehouse. Crates of various sizes were strewn about in uneven stacks, making navigation difficult. The musty warehouse smell, along with the scent of the wooden crates, overpowered Katie's senses while she continuously reminded herself to breathe with each step she took. *A warehouse? How original.* She shook her head.

The scuff of a shoe to her left made her jump. Silently, she crept around the wooden crate with her gun aimed and placed it on the back of the young man's head. "Police. Place your hands on your head. Otherwise don't move."

"Officer MacKenna, it's me, Damian. You know, Nick's friend?"

Katie let out a breath of relief. "Damian! What in Sam Hill are you doing here? You scared me to death!"

"I live here. Scary people work here, though, so I'm hiding."

Katie knelt beside him and asked, "Do you think you could get out of here safely? Is there a back way out?"

"I can get out the front unseen. What are you going to do, though? You can't stay in here. I've seen some nasty stuff over the last few months. These people will kill you on sight!"

"I'm not in here alone. There are three other officers in here with me."

"They have someone tied to a chair. I already called Nick. He's on his way."

"Where?"

"That way, on the other side of the warehouse," he said, pointing to his left. "He's got some vest on him with what looks like gray clay bars."

"Got it. I need you to get out here and tell Nick what's going on. Look," she placed her hands on his shoulders, crouching down to look at him at eye level, "I don't want anything to happen to you. You're only, what, eighteen years old?"

"I'm nineteen," he corrected.

"You have your whole life ahead of you. You're straightening out your life. Your GED should be in the mail any day. I want you to continue to chase after your dream."

"You're not all that old either. You shouldn't be in here."

Glancing around the warehouse, she explained, "I'm here because they're after me. I want to end this."

"You can't do it alone."

"I'm not alone. If I'm not done with what God has planned for me, He'll protect me."

"I hope you're right."

"I know I'm right," she said, confidently. "Now, go," she said, and then shoved him in the direction of the front of the warehouse.

Running outside, almost blinded by the amount of flashing lights from the federal, along with the police and rescue vehicles, Damian spotted Nick in the distance, talking with several people. Practically running to him, Damian hugged Nick, relief evident on his body.

"Wha...?" Nick was stunned for a moment before he saw the dirty face and grungy clothes of the young man he had been taking care of for several years. "Damian, what are you doing here?"

"She's here," he said, slightly panicked.

"Who?"

"Officer MacKenna! Katie! She's here. She's in the warehouse."

Looking toward the building Nick's stomach lurched. "Are you sure it was her?"

"Yes, I talked to her. She said – " A loud 'BOOM!' cut him off.

To Nick, everything suddenly began to move in slow motion. Damian's body slammed into his before Damian flew overhead, landing like a rag doll several feet away. Seeing his other friends and co-workers near him soar through the air, along with the debris from the warehouse, Nick curled into a ball under the car next to where he landed in order to prevent further damage.

Covering his ears when glass shattered, metal twisted and turned, and screams and shouting joined the mix, creating a cannonade of thunderous disharmony. A deafening crash of vehicle that flipped and landed within feet of him sent a shockwave through his body that took his breath away. The ringing in his ears irritated him while he struggled to recover from the daze of surviving the devastation created around him. Looking toward the warehouse, he gulped when he remembered Katie was now encased in the mountainous remains. Adrenaline coursed through his body as he pushed to stand before staggering toward the warehouse – to Katie.

Seth grabbed him. "No, man, you can't go."

Dakota and Todd leapt in front of him to push him back as a secondary explosion went off toward the back of the warehouse. Hoping nothing else would explode, it took all three of them to hold Nick down.

"You can't go in there!" Seth shouted over the chaos.

"I have to get her! I can't leave her! I'm not losing her! Katie!" he shouted, struggling to get off the ground and get to the rubble that the warehouse had become. "KATIE! KATIE! NO!"

Chapter 11

Between Winter and Summer, Lies a Beautiful Spring

It was surreal to Katie as the explosion in the warehouse occurred. A roar quickly followed a blinding light when the warehouse blew. Feeling like a rag doll as her body sailed through the air, she then crashed into a stack of crates that shattered under her. The pressure in her head was immense, and the pain her body felt was only overpowered by sheer terror when the wood from the crates and their contents immediately covered her. As the second explosion occurred, she screamed, and was thrown back once again. Her own scream sounded far away to her and she could barely hear it over the ringing in her ears. She let out one more scream and covered her face as a crate headed right toward her, smashed her into what was left of the wall. The last thing she saw before passing out, was a fireball in the distance that threw another crate headed right for her.

* * *

When the dust settled outside, Dakota, Todd, and Seth got off Nick. "Katie's in there," Nick said, feeling sick to his stomach.

"Wait for the EMS to find her," Seth pleaded. "We don't want to lose anyone."

"I'm not waiting for anything. I'm going to find her," he said, getting off the ground. Yanking Damian off the ground by his collar, he demanded, "Where *exactly* was she?"

"Over in that part, but there was a guy with a vest on in the other corner that had clay bars on it. She knew about it. Pretty sure she was headed in that direction," Damian stammered.

He set Damian down and ran for the warehouse, closely followed by Dakota, Todd, and Seth. Claire and Emma yelled in their earpieces, begging them to wait.

"I told you she would get him killed!" Claire growled when they didn't listen.

"Shut it, Claire!" Emma snapped, glaring at her. "She has been nothing but good for him."

"Todd was almost killed last night because of her, and now Nick, Seth, Todd, and Dakota are running into a building that just exploded because she's in there. How can she be good for him?"

Emma got up near Claire, and with an icy tone in her voice, she warned, "If you don't stop being selfish in regards to Nick *you* will be the one losing him as a friend. He loves Katie, and she loves him. Katie is a strong, very resourceful young lady, and we will be more than happy to add her to the team if she survives this. Now, shut it about her, and get a grip. Those guys need us, not your whiney attitude!"

"Well, tell me how you really feel," Claire huffed.

"Due to my Christianity, I'm not *allowed* to tell you how I *really* feel," she sneered, "but if you don't get your behind in gear, you'll feel it."

Claire sat upright in her chair, and immediately commenced typing on her computer, pulling up the schematics of the warehouse.

*   *   *

"Where is she?" Nick growled, shoving debris out of the way.

"Over here!" one of the firefighters shouted.

When they made their way over to where he was digging, they pulled Andy from the rubble. "Stop!" Andy shouted as he cringed. "Broken leg."

"You got this?" Nick asked him.

"We got it," another firefighter said, as he and four other firemen ran over to where they were.

Seth, Dakota, Todd, and Nick returned to the section they were originally working on, searching feverishly through the rubble for Katie. When he heard the paramedic put an air splint on Andy's leg, the shout of pain and agony that he let out made Nick cringe.

"That had to hurt," Dakota commented, throwing a pile of debris to the side.

"Just keep digging. If she's under here, she'll need help," Nick said, focusing on where he felt Katie was in the pile of rubble.

"There's another over here!" another firefighter shouted after several more minutes of digging.

When they got over there, they helped uncover the officer, who passed away due to his injuries. "He was too close to the blast," another firefighter said, as they got him into the rescue basket.

Nick growled in frustration at it not being Katie, but in this instance, he was thankful. While he felt bad for the officer's family, he was grateful she wasn't there. With not finding her yet, he held onto the glimmer of hope that she was still alive.

The group of four trudged back to their search area. "Are you sure we're in the right spot?" Todd asked. "Everyone else seems to be found over there." He gestured toward where the others were found.

"Damian said he left her over here. If I were her, I would come down and go around, knowing the other three officers were heading in the same direction," Nick explained. "I trained her. I know how she thinks."

"Fair enough," Seth said, and they continued to dig.

The closer the rescue crews got to the blast point, the more bodies and body parts they found.

"If she survived this, she would *have* to be over here," Dakota pointed out, as the rescuers pulled body parts from the debris.

"She is," Nick assured them, waist deep in rubble. "I can feel it."

"Then, let's keep digging."

"You guys need some help?" a firefighter asked, as several men and a couple women came over to help. "There's plenty over on the other side."

"Please…and thank you," Nick said in appreciation. "There's an officer who's supposed to have been over here."

After another fifteen minutes, finally, one of the women from their group called out. "I found a hand."

Nick felt his heart drop into his stomach. He gulped. "Is it moving?" he asked, scrambling over the rubble as half the group converged on the area, while the other half continued their search for others in the explosion.

"No."

As they scrambled to uncover Katie, relief and fear conflicted with each other deep inside of Nick. "Please be alive. Please be alive," he repeated as they cleared the debris.

"She has a pulse," the female firefighter declared. "It's slow, but it's there. We need to get her out of here."

Pulling off the debris that did its best to bury her alive, Nick saw the blood coming from her head and legs. As it mixed with the dirt all over her, it created a dark paste. He looked toward Heaven, as he simply said, "Thank you, God!"

"She's not out of the woods yet," a firefighter reminded him. "She's not conscious."

"But, she's alive," Nick said, hopeful.

*   *   *

Seth sent Nick to the hospital with Katie. After clearing the scene, the others met at the hospital to find out what was going on.

"What's the story?" Nick asked.

"How's Katie?" Seth asked the same time Nick asked his question, with him, Todd, and Dakota arriving with Damian before Claire and Emma got there.

"You tell me yours and I'll tell you mine," Nick offered.

"Okay. Rossi junior is not among the dead," Seth said, giving Nick the main information he knew he was looking for. "Now you?"

"She has a concussion, obviously, along with some cuts and bruises. She has several stiches in her forehead from where the crate hit her, along with several in her right thigh and lower left shin. She broke two ribs on her right side. She also dislocated her left shoulder, so she'll have to wear a sling for a couple weeks. They're going to keep her for three to five days for observation and because of the broken ribs. Having said that, she actually came out of this pretty well. Her partner, Andy, ended up with a broken leg, broken arm, a concussion, and a couple broken ribs."

"Can we see her?" Damian asked.

"Yep. I've been in there, but I knew you were coming so I came down to meet you."

On the way up to Katie's room, Seth explained, "There were a couple of Rossi's men there who lost their life, along with the customs officer who had the vest on. From what we could piece together, they had him tied to a chair. There was one officer who lost their life, along with another who has a broken arm and a massive concussion as well."

"What's her mental state?" Dakota asked. "She's had a lot going on lately."

"Not great," Nick admitted. "I'm thinking of taking a vacation, and taking her with me."

"Where?" Seth asked, curious, knowing Nick hadn't taken a vacation in several years.

"Home."

"To your grandparent's home in Montana?"

"No." Nick shook his head. "I want to go home to my parents and my grandparents. I want to go home to Serenity Wells…and I want to take her with me," he clarified, leaving the trio in a stunned silence. "We're going to Australia."

"When?" Seth asked.

"Well, she's gotta get over her injuries, so I'm not sure."

"Why don't you guys wait it out, then? She'll probably be on desk duty for about four to six weeks because of her injuries anyway. That will also give her some time to work with a counselor through all of this stuff. I know you're stressed," Seth said, holding his hand up to stop Nick's interruption. "I think you need to finish this Rossi or Gombeda thing out. Otherwise, you'll be running, and it won't do anyone any good. We're working with the police department on this and we'll get it settled so you can go to Australia with a clean slate, hopefully."

"I know you're right, but I feel as if I need to protect her."

"If you go now, you'll be cutting her wings. She's strong, and at this point *highly* motivated to see this to the end," Dakota pointed out. "Do you really think she'll want to leave with this hanging in the air?"

"No," Nick admitted, feeling defeated.

"Look, I know you want to protect her, brother," Todd rested his hand on Nick's shoulder, "but we have to finish this. It won't do anyone any good to still have this hanging over anyone's head."

"I know. I just –"

"Ever the protective one, huh?" Seth huffed. "Last time I checked, there was no 'super human' or 'God' after your name. You can't protect her, that's God's job."

"Convenient of you to bring God into this," Nick snapped.

"Dude, you *really* need to calm yourself down," Todd said. "Let's go get her some food so she doesn't have to eat hospital food. Think we need to talk, man."

"You're right, but –" Nick stopped short, as Emma and Claire walked up to them in the hallway.

"Are we too late to see her?" Emma asked.

"What are *you* doing here?" Nick asked Claire, not sure how to react.

"Look, I know you two are together. I also know there's nothing I can do about it. But, I don't want to lose you as a friend," Claire explained.

"If you behave yourself, you may just find another friend in her," Nick hinted.

"Don't push it," Claire jokingly said with a smile. "I wouldn't want it to get around that I may actually like that spoiled Irish princess."

"Stop calling her that!" Nick snapped, crossing his arms, not amused. "She's a sweet girl, but you won't give her the time of day. I'm telling you that you would probably get along great if you gave her half a chance. I don't know if I even want you here."

"Give me a chance," Claire pleaded. "I'll be good I promise."

"If not, she'll be dealing with me," Emma threatened her. "She and I have an understanding."

"I'll bet you do." Seth smirked, looking from one woman to the other.

"What about Katie?" Damian asked.

"That's Officer MacKenna to you," Nick corrected him.

"Right. What about her?"

"Hey, Locke," Director Shaw called out to Nick, as he and Chief Anderson came down the hall to Katie's room. "Downstairs said Katie's room was up here."

"She is. Do you want to talk to her before we do?" Nick offered.

"That would be good. Make sure you're all on the same page," Director Shaw said, making a point to Claire.

She put her hands up in surrender. "I'm here for good reasons. I don't want to see her hurt."

"Just keep it civil, or you're dealing with me in the morning," he threatened.

"That's after I get finished with her," Emma added.

"Understood," Claire agreed.

Director Shaw grabbed Nick's arm, as he and Chief Anderson went into Katie's room, leaving the others outside.

"Who's there?" Katie asked from the closed curtain.

"It's just us, love," Nick said, bringing Director Shaw and Chief Anderson around the curtain.

"Oh! Ouch!" Director Shaw cringed when he saw her.

"Yeah," she agreed, touching her forehead. "Just keep it down, please. My body and head hurt beyond belief."

"I understand your injuries." Chief nodded in understanding. "Your doctor and I talked downstairs."

"Yeah. She said I have three days before I can get out of here, and at least four to six weeks on the desk," Katie said, upset.

"You're better off than your partner," Chief pointed out.

"This is true."

"Ohhhh, he's not happy at all," Chief chuckled. "I stopped in to see him before coming up here. They're going to keep him for a couple days as well. He's got a soft cast on his leg, and they're going to give him a regular cast in a couple of days. He's not going to like being on the desk for as long as he has to be on it."

Katie smiled. "If he weren't a Christian, I'll bet he would be cussing out the doctors and nurses."

"Oh, yeah! He's finding his own way to do it," Chief assured her. "His bigger concern when I visited him was for you, though. With the man killed right in front of you, your friend almost getting blown up in your car, and now this, he is surprised that you're still sane."

"I think I remember something about an order to take time off," Katie reminded him. "I think I may take you up on that."

"Why don't you come in for desk duty?" Chief suggested. "You have mandatory counseling anyway. And, I would be shocked if she cleared you right away to go back to work anywhere near as quickly this time. You squeaked through with the shooting incident, but with the other incidents?" He shook his head. "You're going to be on the desk for quite a while. Clear that up before you take some time off, okay? I would think you would want to be healed for your vacation, so you can rest."

"Ugh," Katie groaned. "I *hate* the idea of being on a desk!"

"Nick, since Katie doesn't have anyone at home, and she obviously won't be back to work for at least a week, why don't you take a week off as well?" Director Shaw suggested.

Nick objected. "But sir!"

"That will give us a chance to see what we can dig up on Joey Rossi," Director Shaw added.

"But –"

"I'll make it an order if I have to."

"It's not that I don't want to spend time with her or take care of her. I do. It's just –"

"You're too close to this," Director Shaw cut him off again. "If you get your hands on Rossi, I'm afraid of what will happen. Trust your team to take him down. There's another unit who is actually in charge of tracking him down, but your unit is involved as well. They're starting with the MO of the bomb builder and going from there. Trust me," Director Shaw said, anger visible on his face, "he almost took out two of ours. Wherever he is, he cannot hide deep enough."

*　　*　　*

The day after Katie was released from the hospital, the funeral for the fallen officer from the explosion took place. Operating in a daze, Katie went in full uniform and stood by her brothers and sisters in blue for the funeral. This was something she would carry with her for a long time.

In doing the work she was doing, she was painfully aware as they did the 'last call', that this wouldn't be the last funeral she would attend for a fellow agent or officer. The price for the work they did could potentially be a heavy one, but to her it was worth it.

While they folded the flag and Chief Anderson gave the flag to his widow, Katie couldn't help but think about the fact that Todd was almost the one in the casket. It hurt her beyond belief to know that a fellow officer *did* lose his life because of her. Her counselor called it 'survivor guilt.' She called it just plain wrong.

After the funeral, Katie found Nick in the crowd. "Please, take me home. I don't know if I can handle much more of this," she said, feeling her head spinning. "This is getting to be too much."

Wrapping his arms around her, he kissed her head. "I know. I'm sorry. A lot of people are spinning. Dakota and Todd are running every lead into the ground, while Seth is doing his best to keep Emma and Claire focused without losing his own mind. He's actually bringing in a couple more agents into the squad."

"I know. I just..." she sniffed, wiping her eyes. "I feel responsible for his death. I feel the death of him and almost of Todd in every portion of my body. It aches."

"That's because you have such a tender heart. Are you sure you want to do this for the rest of your life?"

"I don't know," she admitted.

*   *   *

As Katie and Nick hugged, off in the distance, a young man stood by his vehicle. "Are you finished, sir?" the chauffer asked, opening his door for him.

"I am for now," he responded, leaning against the car with his arms crossed. "Today is a day of mourning for her. I have used others to no avail. It looks like I'm going to have to take care of her by myself in order to get the job done." When the driver got in his seat from holding the young man's door, the young man ordered, "Take me home now."

"Yes, sir," the chauffer said, and pulled out of the cemetery.

*   *   *

The next morning, there was a knock on Katie's door around eleven o'clock. "Yes?" Nick answered the door.

"I'm looking for a 'Katie MacKenna,'" the girl asked, looking at the delivery slip.

"I can take it."

"Um, I'm supposed to give this directly to her."

Nick showed her his badge and ID. "I can take it."

"Okay," she shrugged. She handed over the package and left.

"Who was it?" Katie called from the kitchen, where she was watching Nick make pancakes.

"Special delivery," Nick said, placing the package on the counter. "This delivery person was a girl, so I'm positive it's not Joey Rossi or Cristian Gombeda."

"Funny. Do we open it?"

"I don't want to. What if it's another friendly package from The Hunter…and I use the term *friendly* loosely."

"Isn't it my package?" Katie asked, shuffling over to where Nick stood on the other side of the breakfast bar, in her slippers, robe, pajama pants, and a t-shirt. "Can't I open it?"

"You look cute, even when you're a mess," Nick said, giving her a hug before he kissed her on her head.

"The package?" Katie questioned.

"Why don't we wait for Dakota and Todd? They're coming over any minute now. That way if something happens, they're here too," he pointed out, just as the doorbell rang. "Speak of the devils," he said, heading over to the door, while he kept an eye on Katie.

"Mmmmm! Are those pancakes I smell?" Dakota came in with a grin on his face.

"And bacon," Nick added.

"*You* are a good man," Todd said, patting his shoulder.

"Hey, I take care of my friends."

"That you do."

"We got a delivery this morning, but were waiting for the two of you before we opened it."

"I see," Dakota said, eyeing the package on the counter.

Nick went into the kitchen, wrapped his arms around Katie, and then said to Dakota and Todd, "Go ahead."

Katie wriggled in his arms. "Wait a minute! That's mine!"

Dakota and Todd ran into the bedroom with the package and locked the door so she couldn't follow.

"This could end really badly!" Katie yelled. "I don't want to…" she stopped, panic setting in. "Guys! Please don't!"

They walked out with the open package in Dakota's hands. "For once, he's not trying to kill you. He sent you a card of condolence, along with his standard dozen black roses and a warning," he said, throwing the roses into the trash. "Unfortunately, this is obviously a girl's handwriting, so it's not his."

"What does it say?" Nick asked.

"It says, '*Katie, so sorry for your loss. I thought sure I had won our little game, but you seem to have nine lives. By the way, after my friend missed his mark, your friend almost blowing up in your car, and just when I thought I had you, one of your fellow brothers in blue took your place there as well, you only have a few left. It seems that you have many who would give their life for you. Does that make you feel good, knowing people died in your place? Don't worry. I will rectify that. Consider this your one and only warning. Love you, my darling, The Hunter.*'"

"Interesting. Obviously he made his intentions known," Nick said, anger swirling through every bone in his body.

"He's right," Katie said, still in Nick's arms. "It should have been me. Jillian, Aaron, and Officer Kendrick all died because of me."

Nick held her in place when she went to leave the kitchen. "You're not going anywhere."

"Don't you understand? It's true! It's all true!" she shouted, as her body trembled in fear and anger.

"No. You couldn't be more wrong. You're the one who tells me that if you're job's not done, you're not going anywhere. You were left here for a reason."

Katie shook her head, unable to form a thought.

"Katie," Todd stood in front of her, resting his hands on her shoulders, "you are a special young lady. There have been people looking out for you all your life. While you may not have a lot of family by blood, you have a lot of family by heart."

"Ya know, God tells us that we are family," Nick continued, as he sat down with her on his lap, "In Ephesians 1:5, it says,

'God decided in advance to adopt us into His own family by bringing us to Himself through Jesus Christ. This is what He wanted to do, and it gave Him great pleasure.' In 1 Corinthians 12:26, it says, 'If one member suffers, all suffer together; if one member is honored, all rejoice together.' We're all a family. Over the last year, we have celebrated your graduation from college and the academy, along with your emotional celebrations from Oklahoma. We have all been terrified for you over the last several months and we watched helplessly as some twisted psychopath hunted you down. Officer Kendrick lost his life. We won't let him take you too. Our unit is suffering with you. You are and have been a part of our unit since the December that you said 'yes' to helping a friend. Don't you see? You're a part of a much bigger family than you realize!"

"I just don't know what to do." She sniffed. "I feel like giving myself up to protect you guys."

"Don't you *ever* give up! Do you hear me? I want you to fight him with everything that's in you, knowing we will do our best to hunt him down."

"Trust me," Todd added, "he can't hide deep enough."

*   *   *

By the middle of June, Katie's body had healed enough for her and Nick to go on vacation. She was looking forward to some time of rest and relaxation. At the rate she was going, she knew she wouldn't make it out of her police officer phase unless she could get a grip on her life.

"I want you to meet the new guys before we go," Nick said, as they were driving around doing last minute errands for their

281

trip. "We're keeping Diane's slot open for you, but we did add two more guys. They are quite a pair." He chuckled.

"Sounds good," Katie said, watching out the window.

He reached over with one of his hands and held hers. "What's wrong?"

"Why can't you guys find Joey?"

"Since the day of the explosion, he went under. His dad had this city wired. Pretty sure there are a ton of places he could hide until things smooth over. In the meantime, we're getting outta Dodge and heading to Australia. The further we are away from Cleveland, at this point, the better I'll feel."

"I don't want to run."

"It's not running. It's getting off this running freight train for a short break. You can take a break. You don't *have* to finish everything right away."

Sighing, she looked out toward the window again, as they pulled into the office garage.

"We're here. C'mon up with me, please? I'm really hoping maybe some good news will help pull you out of this funk."

"Funk? Is that what you call this?" she asked, taken aback. "It's not a *funk*, Nick. It's 'I'm about done' mode. I don't really know if I can do this job anymore. I don't know if I have the heart for this job." Nick couldn't believe his ears as she continued, "I want to experience life. I don't want to be surrounded by death and destruction anymore. Doesn't it wear on you?"

"Yes."

"Then, why do you keep doing it?"

"If I don't, who will? If evil goes unchecked, chaos will reign. You're really looking at this the wrong way."

"Nick, I don't think you understand. After everything I've experienced, the counselor told me yesterday that I have PTSD. She said there's *a lot* we're going to have to wade through before I can come off the desk...*if* I come off the desk at all. If I don't, I'm finished. If I'm finished, I don't know what I'm going to do."

"What do you mean?"

"It was my dream to work as an FBI agent. I knew it would take going through phases before I could get there. What I didn't count on, though, was what I would experience as a police officer. This is more difficult a job than even I imagined. If this is that bad, what's it going to be like as an agent?"

"It's not easy. I can promise you that." Caressing the hand he held, he said, "Look, you and I both need a break. I feel this vacation may be just what we both need. Please do me a favor and don't make any decisions regarding your future employment until we return?"

"Why not?"

"Because I want you to enjoy what Australia and Serenity Wells has to offer. I don't feel that will be possible if you're trying to make a decision on your future. I've talked to Chief Anderson and Director Shaw, and have gotten us both six weeks off. Now, this is my time that's been accrued over the years, so mine's paid. If you agree, you'll have to attach it onto the other end, extending your two years by a couple months."

"I'm not worried about that. I'm more worried about Gombeda, Rossi, and whether or not I'm cut out for this."

"Let me ask you this…when was the last time you actually just did something to relax and enjoy yourself? When have you taken time, not focused on a goal?"

She looked at him, dumbfounded.

"That's what I thought. You don't truly know how to relax. Consider this your spring break of sorts. Your winter and most of your spring has been horrendous. I'm praying that your summer will be a lot more focused. However, to reach that goal, you're going to have to enjoy a beautiful springtime of renewal and refreshment. Join me in this vacation. Let me show you how to enjoy life, so when stuff hits the fan, you can handle it better. You've given your life to the Lord, but you still do your best to keep yourself under control. Cut loose! Enjoy this trip with me?"

Looking into his eyes, she saw the sincerity with which he spoke, and knew instantly he was right. Control was a common problem for her. Yes, she gave control of her life to the Lord, but she seemed to have taken it back again. Her words needed to match her actions. "So, what you're saying is that between winter and summer lies a beautiful spring?"

"Yes! And, you *can* enjoy life without grabbing control of it all the time."

"Okay," she agreed. "I'll give you this vacation with no expectations, no control. It will be a challenge for me, so I'll ask for patience, but I'll do it."

"Great!" He said, and hugged her. "That's all I ask."

"Patience?"

"Consider it done. Now, let's go meet our two new guys. I think you'll like them. Well, you will like at least *one* of them. Knowing you, you'll have fun with the other one," he said, with a smirk.

C.J. Peterson

Chapter 12

Spring Break

"Mornin', y'all!" Katie said with a smile on her face. Both she and Nick were the only two who knew it was a forced smile. After the conversation they had in the car about her frustrations in wanting to quit, she didn't want anyone's pity.

"Hey, Katie!" Emma got up from her desk and gave her a hug, closely followed by everyone else in the office that she knew. "You're looking *much* better these days."

"Thanks." Katie blushed. "Still working on the recovery portion, but this vacation should do us both some good," she said, giving Nick's hand a squeeze.

"The full six weeks?" Seth asked. Nick nodded in response. "Good. We'll miss you, but this is a much deserved vacation."

"Are you saying we will be without your slaughtered vernacular for a whole six weeks?" a guy sitting at one of the new desks in a three-piece suit asked. To Katie, he seemed haughty from the start, and she instantly didn't care for him.

"Katie, I would like to introduce you to one of our latest acquisitions. He's still on a trial basis, though you wouldn't know it by his bold arrogance. Katie MacKenna, this is Eugene Kennedy," Nick introduced them.

As Katie shook his hand, Eugene explained, "Yes, I am Eugene Kennedy of the Kennedy family. This is only a brief stopping point before achieving my aspirations to attain a position in the real office."

Katie looked to Nick for an explanation. "The DC office," Nick clarified.

"And, he only *thinks* he's a Kennedy, but he's actually a distant relative, four times removed. I, however, *am* a relative of Lyndon B. Johnson. Chad Johnson, at your service," Chad introduced himself, taking the shot at Eugene, as he bent in half to kiss Katie's hand.

"A southern boy?" Katie asked.

"Texas. Born and bred." Chad nodded. Chad seemed more relaxed and laid back. He stood around six foot, with light brown hair, and dark brown eyes. His southern charm definitely endeared him more to her than Eugene's arrogance.

"How are you related to LBJ?"

"My great-great-grandmother was his sister."

"Oh! So you really *are* related to him?"

"Oh yeah."

"That has helped him to get to where he's going," Seth explained. "He's getting fast-tracked through here on his way to potentially the Secret Service or CIA."

"Yeah. I haven't decided which one yet," Chad added.

"Kennedy, on the other hand – "

"I *am* a Kennedy," Eugene cut Nick off. "I only need to narrow the exact route through the family tree."

"He's been too busy chasing other goals," Seth jumped back into the conversation. "Agent Kennedy *is* cocky, but he has a right to be. You see, he's a Harvard graduate, who went into the Air Force Special Operations group after graduation. His background includes sniper."

"Yes, unfortunately he *does* have a right to brag there. He's a great shot," Nick agreed. "Unfortunately, his vision deteriorated due to being in the desert so long, and they pulled him from his position."

"Much to my dismay," Eugene added. The six-foot-two, twenty-nine-year-old, had short, dark-brown hair and blue eyes. "So, I joined the FBI."

"Only because the CIA wouldn't take him," Todd said from his desk where he was doing research on his computer.

"Ya know, ya keep that up and it may discourage me from goin' to the CIA," Chad pointed out.

"Here's hoping," Todd commented. "We'd like to keep you. However, if you go to the Secret Service, at least we'll know you're moving up, instead of moving down."

"Ouch!" Katie chuckled. "Don't like the CIA much. Do you?"

Todd shook his head. "Not so much."

"They think they're better than us," Nick explained.

"Then in that case, Agent Kennedy *is* in the wrong agency," Katie quipped.

"Your first impression has much to be desired," Eugene pointed out. "I have achieved much success in my exploits. I am aware of your adventures, and am surprised that your intellect is still intact and balanced. Any accolades you receive, seem to be at the expense of others, yet your fortitude to continue intrigues me. Does it not concern you that you pose a danger to those around you?"

Katie narrowed her eyes at him as she crossed her arms. Feeling that Katie was a volcano about to blow, Nick wrapped his arm around her shoulders to hold her in place, while he covered her mouth with his other hand.

Seth finagled his way between Katie and Eugene. Getting into Eugene's face, he demanded, "Where do you get off talking to her like that?"

"I've read the reports. I'm aware of the continuous endangerment that seems to surround her. I'm not comfortable in the least at the idea of having her be a colleague of mine."

When Katie went to jump at him, Nick had to wrap both of his arms around her to hold her back. Standing her ground, she responded to Eugene with an icy tone, "Your irrational judgment of me is offensive and absurd. My past and current status is none of your concern. I am a formidable opponent on any field, despite being a target on several occasions. I know who I am and my limitations. I know *where* I came from and know *Who* has my future. You, however, shame your pseudo family supposedly routed in the Kennedy clan! Your only attribute seems to be that you can fire a weapon with extreme accuracy. However, if you cannot gain the favor of your fellow compatriots, then you, sir, are a lost cause and a liability. Get off your high horse, and come down to the real world, or you're in trouble!"

His eyes momentarily popped wide-open before he listened with intrigue. "The phraseology in which you form your argument intrigues me."

"You use big words, thinking no one else knows them. Hate to break it to you, Sparky, but this bunch is bright. You may think you're talking over them, but in reality, knowing them, they're talking circles around you."

"My, my! Your temperament has much to be desired as well." He then asked Nick, "Has she always been this bellicose?"

"Don't know what ya mean?"

"He means to say that I'm disagreeable and have a temper," Katie translated.

"Her hostility is gauged by those around her," Seth pointed out. "It's justified ninety-nine point nine percent of the time. If you want to fit in here, you'd better do a much better job of appreciating the skills and assets of those around you."

"Some are a little easier than others," he said under his breath.

"She's a feisty little filly, but I like her," Chad said, going back over to his desk. "Seems to be able to hold her own with even a pompous, arrogant, mule."

"Are you calling me a donkey?" Eugene asked, appalled.

"No." Chad glared at him, as he clarified, "Due to the ladies present, I'm not going to use the term I would like. I'm too much of a gentleman to offend them. When they're gone, I'll let you know *exactly* how I feel about your display."

"I'm not afraid of you," Eugene said, crossing his arms in a huff.

"You should be." Chad got up from his desk and stood toe-to-toe with Eugene. Looking him in the eyes, he said, "I've wrestled pigs with more manners and better breeding than you. Taking you down will be a pleasure and a treat."

"You wouldn't dare!"

"Try me," he said, and left for the printer.

"Well, that was fun," Dakota huffed. "A word of advice, friend?" he offered to Eugene, as he crossed his ankles on his desk and rested his hands behind his head.

"Do I *want* to know?"

"I would heed the advice and take notes," Todd advised. "He's been around for quite a while."

"What is it?" Eugene asked, impatiently.

"I know who trained her. There's a reason the big guy's holding her back."

"What do you mean?"

"You think her tongue is sharp? I, personally, wouldn't want to go into a hand-to-hand match with that young lady you just insulted. The one holding her back is the one who trained her. He's about the only one in here who can beat her."

Eugene slowly turned toward Katie in shock. "Her? She's lanky at best."

"It's not how many muscles ya have, mate," Nick reminded him. "It's how you use them."

"I see."

"I hope you do. We're going to be gone for six blessed weeks. I suggest you take that time to decide whether or not you're going to be able to work with this bunch…Katie included," Nick said, keeping his voice steady, as much as he wanted to punch him out. "You may want to have a conversation with Claire while you're at it. That is, if *she's* still talking to you. It seems over the course of the last couple of days, you've offended everyone in here."

"I agree," Seth jumped back in. "The temperament of this room has risen drastically over the last couple of days, and I don't like it. Then, Nick brings Katie in here, and you insult her from the get-go. You may want to re-think your strategy if you intend on sticking around here."

"Yes, sir," he said, and quietly made his way back over to his desk.

Katie took a deep breath to get herself under control. "He is the most infuriating man I have met to date, and there have been some doozies in my life! My word!" she said, shaking off the feelings of anger. "If you *are* a Kennedy, you just shamed their name!"

Eugene's face red with anger, went to respond, but just shook his head in response.

"Good choice," Nick acknowledged his restraint.

"Anyway," Seth took the cue, "you guys have a plane to catch tomorrow. Are you ready?"

Katie nodded. "Beyond ready."

"I'll bet!" Emma smiled. "You both need a vacation. Let's hope and pray it goes smoothly."

"Hopefully more smoothly than this introduction went," Nick said under his breath.

*   *   *

"I cannot believe it's taken so long for us to get here," Katie said as they began their decent into Cairns, Australia, after their stopover in Sydney.

"It's worth the trip. I promise you."

"I'm sure. I'm excited, yet nervous to meet your family."

"Wanna know the interesting part of this trip?"

"What?"

"My mum and dad don't know."

"What do you mean they don't know?" Katie asked, horrified. "Aren't we going to their house?"

"Yep. Nana and Pop know, but not Mum or Dad."

"You can't be serious!" Katie said, panic setting in.

"It's been ten years. Trust me. They'll just be happy we're here."

"You're just going to have us drop in after ten years without warning?"

"It's a good secret. There is such a thing as good secrets."

*   *   *

They pulled up to what Katie would consider a cottage type home, situated on the beach. "Nice."

"It's small, but it's all they need," he said, getting out of the vehicle.

The tiny, beachfront cottage was wrapped with white wood siding and light blue shutters. Located on an acre of land, the three-bedroom, two-bathroom home had a nautical feel to it, and she couldn't wait to see what the inside looked like. Taking a deep breath of the air, she exclaimed, "Love the smell of the ocean."

Nick pulled their suitcases from the trunk. "Mum and Dad do too, but I would much rather be on the station." He paid their taxi driver before they headed toward the front door.

When he knocked on the door, it flew open in a matter of seconds. Squealing in excitement, his mom threw her arms around his neck and screamed, "Nicky!"

"G'day, Mum," he said with a grin ear to ear. Then he gestured to Katie, as he said, "Mum, I'd like ya t' meet my girlfriend, Katie MacKenna."

"Ohhhh!" she gushed as she hugged Katie. "She's a looker! Good onya, Nicky!" At first, Katie froze, not expecting the hug, but quickly recovered and returned the hug. "Let me take a good look at ya both." She stood back and crossed her arms as she shook her head. "Yer lookin' a bit on the slim side." She turned Nick to the side, examining him. "Tsk! Tsk! Tsk! Nana's gonna fill ya till yer full ten times over!"

"We're goin' to the station?" he asked, pleasantly surprised.

"Actually, Nana told us you were comin'," she said with a grin. "She wanted us t' come out to the station, but I objected until she fessed up. Yer a sneaky lil' buggar. Ya almost got away with it. We have a barbie t'night t' welcome ya back, and then head out t' the station on Monday, givin' us Sunday t' rest."

"Great!" He grinned.

"C'mon in. Yer ol' man is in the kitchen."

He raised an eyebrow. "Too lazy t' answer the door?"

"Na. He thought maybe you were Nate. He's not happy with that ocker lately."

"Nate?" Katie questioned.

"My brother. He's a drongo of the worst kind."

"He's the reason Nicky went to the States to begin with. I'm just so glad yer here," she said with tears in her eyes. She hugged him again, not wanting to let him go.

"It's okay, Mum. I get it. It put me in a better position in life."

"But, we haven't seen ya in forever."

He hugged her back as he kissed her head. "I'm here now. Please enjoy this time we have."

"How long are ya here for?"

"About five and a half weeks."

"Nice!" she said, wiping the tears off her face. "Let's go."

"Is, uh, Nate comin' over?" Nick asked, glancing at Katie.

"If he does, she'll be shark bait," they heard a voice from the dining room.

"Hey, ol' man!" Nick smiled, happy to see his dad.

"Wait. What do you mean, shark bait?" Katie asked.

"The bush ranger likes the sheilas. Yer a looker, an' don't think it's gonna escape his eyes. And, the fact that she's with you?" His dad shook his head and sighed. "Yeah, that just sweetens the pot."

"I don't understand."

"Whenever the boys got together, there has always been trouble. Now, Nicky's always been a good boy."

"Yes, the golden haired son of the two of us," Nate said, leaning on the wall next to the kitchen from where he entered the front of the house.

Nick's head snapped up at the sound of his brother's voice. "Nate."

Katie looked from Nate, to Nick, wide-eyed. The only difference Katie could see was that Nick was about two inches taller than Nate. "Oh, dear heaven!" Katie said, stunned.

"Well, she's a beauty, brother. Did ya bring me a treat from the good ol' U.S. of A.?" he asked, resting his arm over Katie's shoulder.

Katie pushed his arm off and moved closer to Nick. She felt violated, even though he barely touched her. Still in shock by their appearance, she struggled to find something to tell them apart. If he was as dangerous as he seemed, she would need to be able to tell which one was which, or she could be in trouble!

Matthew 10:26-28

[26] "So have no fear of them, for nothing is covered that will not be revealed, or hidden that will not be known. [27] What I tell you in the dark, say in the light, and what you hear whispered, proclaim on the housetops. [28] And do not fear those who kill the body but cannot kill the soul. Rather fear him who can destroy both soul and body in hell.

Sneak Peek of Summer Secrets –

Grace Restored Series, Book 4

Summer in Paradise?

"Keep yer hands off, mate," Nick snapped, wrapping his arm protectively around Katie as he glared at his identical twin brother, Nate. "She's not for you. She wouldn't even pee on you if you were on fire. She's very intuitive when it comes to reading people."

"Nicky!" His mom smacked his arm. "Such language!"

"Oh, no. You've gone an' upset Mum. Now who's the bad son?" Nate chuckled. "You've been here all of five minutes an' you've already buggared up? That must be a record for you."

"Shove off!" Nick shot, taking a step toward his brother.

"Boys, boys, don't get yer brumbies in a bunch. Have a seat. Let's talk it out. Paige, wanna get us somethin' t' drink? Take Katie with ya," his dad, Zack, said. "She doesn't need t' hear this. Come t' think of it, we'll go t' the backyard so she doesn't have to. Way t' make a first impression, Nate."

"Nothin' I did," he objected while Zack shoved them out the door.

When they were out of earshot, Paige mentioned, "There's a set of twins in each generation. In his father's case, the boys are fraternal, but they're a lot alike. In the case of Nicky and Nate, they're identical, but couldn't be more opposite if they tried."

"I can't believe how much they look alike. I'm really struggling to find something different about them."

"It's in the eyes, love. The anger got a hold of Nate early. We sent Nicky away so it wouldn't get him too. That's my only regret in life," she said as they went to the kitchen. "Would ya mind gettin' the glasses from that cupboard t' yer left?" Paige asked, pulling the lemonade and beer from the fridge. "I assume yer gonna want the lemonade?"

"Oh, yes please. I don't drink."

"I knew ya looked like a good girl." Paige smiled. "Just two glasses. The boys are gonna want these." She lifted the beer to the counter.

"Um, Nick doesn't drink anymore either."

"Oh! Didn't know that. Okay." She shrugged. "Then pull out a glass for him too. He's gonna need it," she said, nodding toward the window where they could see Nate and Nick yelling at each other, while Zack leaned against a tree with his arms crossed, keeping a close eye on them. "He doesn't know what t' do with 'em. This is not how we wanted Nicky's homecoming t' be. Maybe at the barbie he'll relax."

"Bar-b-que?" Katie asked.

"Yes. We're gonna have t' teach you some new terms, or yer gonna miss half the conversations…especially when we get t' the station. Nana doesn't take mercy on anyone. She's a tough ol' bird. Tough as they come."

Katie watched her pouring the drinks before she asked, "Please don't take this the wrong way, but you look tired. Would you like me to take these outside?"

"Oh, sweetie, I couldn't take it wrong. I *am* tired. But, no worries, I'll take them out." She patted Katie's hand.

Katie cocked her head to the side, watching her. "With all due respect, is there something Nick doesn't know about you?"

Paige froze at her words. Gently setting the pitcher of lemonade on the counter, she slowly looked up at Katie. "How do you know?"

"My mother died of leukemia when I was seven. I know what someone looks like who has gone through chemo. Is that the reason Nana had to tell you Nick was coming? Was it because you were too tired from chemo to go to the station?"

"Amazing." Paige shook her head. "Yes, that's why. And, no, Nicky doesn't know."

"Does Nate?"

"No one in the family knows except Zack. We've been keeping it from them in hopes of remission."

"What is it?"

"Breast cancer."

"How bad?"

"Not too bad for the moment. Please don't tell Nicky."

"I won't, but please don't wait until the last minute. That wouldn't be fair to him."

"I'll tell him if it gets really bad," she promised. "He really likes ya, ya know? He's never brought a girl here."

"Thank you." Katie smiled. "I like him too. He's such a sweetheart."

"Very protective, though. However, using my powers of observation, I'm thinkin' you don't need protectin'."

"What do you mean?"

"Ya look strong. What do ya do for a livin'?"

"I'm a police officer."

"Yeah. He doesn't like wimpy girls. Well, he used to, but now he's lookin' for substance over looks…not that ya don't have both by the look a' ya," she said with a wink and a smile. "C'mon, looks like Zack may need that beer already. Nicky may even reconsider an' want one when he's finished with that conversation."

See the rest in Summer Secrets!

Books in the Grace Restored Series

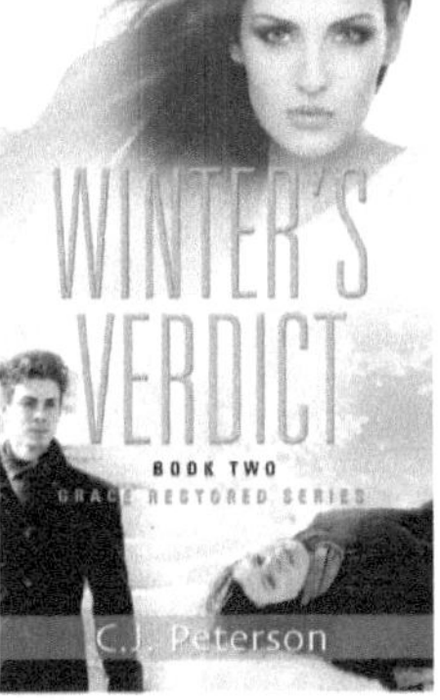

Book 1   Book 2   Book 3

Book 4   Book 5

Also check out C.J. Peterson's other series –

The Holy Flame Trilogy

Divine Legacy Series

Connect with C.J. – <u>CJPetersonWrites.com</u>